Eugene McEldowney is an Assistant Editor with the *Irish Times* in Dublin. He was born in Belfast, educated at Queens University and now lives in Howth, County Dublin.

THE FALOORIE MAN

Martin McBride is a young Catholic boy growing up on the streets of post-war Belfast. As he emerges from the cocoon of his parents' love, Martin faces a world of unpredictability and surprise: the shocking discovery of the crucial difference between boys and girls, the scrapes of street and schoolyard, the rigours of education, Teddy boy mania, and the dubious pleasures of illicit sex. But the accidental discovery of a darkly-hidden truth suddenly turns Martin's world upside-down . . .

EUGENE McELDOWNEY

THE FALOORIE MAN

Complete and Unabridged

ULVERSCROFT
Leicester

First published in Great Britain in 2000 by
Review
London

First Large Print Edition
published 2002
by arrangement with
Headline Book Publishing
a division of the
Hodder Headline Group
London

British Library CIP Data

McEldowney, Eugene
    The Faloorie man.—Large print ed.—
    Ulverscroft large print series: general fiction
    1. Catholics—Northern Ireland—Belfast—Social life
    and customs—Fiction
    2. Large type books
    I. Title
    823.9′14 [F]

    ISBN 0–7089–4614–3

Published by
F. A. Thorpe (Publishing)
Anstey, Leicestershire

Set by Words & Graphics Ltd.
Anstey, Leicestershire
Printed and bound in Great Britain by
T. J. International Ltd., Padstow, Cornwall

This book is printed on acid-free paper

This book is dedicated to the memory of
Kathleen and John, Sarah and Isaac, and
to Maura, without whom there would
have been no story.

Acknowledgements

I am always wary of acknowledgements for fear of leaving someone out and making an enemy for life. But some people have to be mentioned.

Mary Maher for constant support and a superb first edit.
Maeve Binchy for setting me on the writing road and for great-hearted encouragement.
Sally Mimnagh for friendship and advice.
Edwin Higel for talent-spotting.
Ciara Considine for steering the whole thing through. And my family for always being there.

Faloorie Man: a mythical figure in a Belfast children's song.

Book One

1

Sarah's stories always had happy endings. I remember as a little boy in short pants sitting with my mother at the kitchen table, the big picture book spread out before us. I recall even now the smell of the ink and the shiny texture of the pages, and Sarah's finger slowly tracing the words as she drew me inexorably into that innocent world where virtue was rewarded and everyone lived happily ever after. Those tales always ended well. All except the story of the Titanic.

Our house was filled with holy pictures. They were in the hall and the front room and the kitchen. They were in the bedrooms. The only place that didn't have holy pictures was the bathroom. Everywhere you went in the house, the eyes of the saints were upon you.

Above the fireplace, in the front room, was a big picture of Jesus with his Sacred Heart exposed and a crown of thorns on his head and a lamp burning. It was plain to see he was in agony. Tears fell down his cheeks. In my bedroom, there was a picture of the Virgin Mary in a blue dress looking beautiful, her hands joined in prayer and her eyes gazing up to Heaven.

There was a picture of the Pope that someone had brought Sarah one time from a pilgrimage to Lourdes. Eugene Pacelli. Pius the XII. He had a thin, pinched face and narrow eyes behind his rimless glasses. I thought he looked cross. I asked Sarah about it.

'Cross? Who says he's cross?'

'He looks cross.'

Sarah bent close to examine the picture.

'He's not cross. He's just sad, that all.'

'Why's he sad?'

'Because he's got all the worries of the world on his shoulders, poor man. He's thinking of all the sinners and all the wickedness. You'd look sad if you had that to put up with. The man's a living saint.'

'Does that mean he's going to Heaven when he dies?'

'Of course he is. To sit forever with God and the holy martyrs.'

'What's a martyr, Mammy?'

'A martyr is someone who dies for the faith. Like Blessed Oliver Plunkett. He's a martyr. Bad men cut his head off and stuck it on a pole over in London.'

My heart missed a beat.

'Why did they do that, Mammy?'

'Because he wouldn't give up his holy religion. So they cut his head off for badness. You can go and see it. It's still there in the church in Drogheda. In a glass case. We'll go on the bus some time.'

I wasn't *really* sure that I wanted to see Blessed Oliver Plunkett's head. So I just said: 'That'll be nice, Mammy.'

I wondered why there were no pictures of happy saints. They all seemed so sad. I supposed it had to do with getting your head cut off and stuck on a pole and stuff like that.

The picture that intrigued me most was called 'Mass in the Penal Days'. It showed a priest offering up the sacred host at a rock in the middle of the country somewhere. There was snow on the ground. People were kneeling, men and women and children saying their prayers. It was easy to see they were poor people because most of them had bare heads and the snow was coming down. They wore shawls. They had no shoes on their feet. And in the valley below, coming to capture the priest, were the Redcoats with their rifles.

I was fascinated by this picture. I couldn't figure out why the Redcoats wanted to hurt the people who were doing no harm, only saying their prayers. I had a strange notion they were the same people who had cut off

5

Oliver Plunkett's head and stuck it on a pole over in London. I asked Sarah about it one day.

She put down the duster she was using to clean the mantelpiece.

'Martin, it's plain and simple. The priest represents the Pope. And they hate the Pope. And they hate his holy church. And they hate us too because we're Catholics.'

'Why, Mammy?'

'Because they're bigots, that's why.'

'What's a bigot, Mammy?'

Sarah let out a loud sigh.

'A bigot is somebody that doesn't know any better. Now run on there and give my head peace.'

But I wasn't satisfied. So the first chance I got, I asked her again.

Sarah said: 'Bigots are people who hate Catholics and when they get drunk they curse the Pope.'

'You mean they use bad words?'

'Terrible words. Words that it's a mortal sin to let past your lips. Words that God could strike you dead for, if he had a mind to.'

'And why doesn't he strike the bigots dead when they curse the Pope?'

'Oh, but he does. In his own good time. Did I not tell you the story about the Titanic?'

I shook my head.

'Well now. It was a big boat they built down at the shipyards one time. It was the biggest boat in the world. And every time they hammered a rivet into it, the Orangemen cursed the Pope.'

I sat still as a mouse. I felt my blood run cold. Sarah stroked my hair.

'But let me tell you what happened to the Titanic. It sank on its very first voyage. Everybody was drowned. All the fancy people in their fur coats screaming for God to help them. But he wouldn't help them. He let the sea drown them. Because of the Orangemen and the way they cursed the Pope.'

I caught my breath and tried to figure out this momentous thing my mother was telling me. I thought it was terrible that the Orangemen should curse the Pope in the first place, but then to be drowned as a result. I was filled with an immense wonder and a feeling of pride that I was a Catholic and that God would do such powerful things to punish our enemies.

'Never forget the Mass Rock,' Sarah said, pointing to the picture with the Redcoats coming. 'In the olden days, the people clung to the faith. The priest was hunted. There was a price on his head. But nobody gave him up. Nobody betrayed him. Remember what the

7

people endured in the penal days. Never forget the faith.'

'No, Mammy,' I said. 'I won't.

★   ★   ★

Isaac was Sarah's husband. He was a small, wiry man with a bald patch at the back of his head that looked like a pink billiard ball. He was a soccer fanatic and supported Celtic Football Club. Isaac used to say that everybody was against Celtic because Celtic was Catholic. The referees and the linesmen and the reporters who wrote in the papers all hated Celtic. He said they couldn't stick Celtic because they were the best team in Scotland and nobody could beat them and that made the Blue Noses sick as parrots.

I tried to picture these people with blue noses and I couldn't figure it out. Isaac said it was just an expression people used about the Rangers team because they hated Celtic and they played in blue jerseys.

It seemed to me that everybody hated us because we were Catholics; the Redcoats and the bigots and the Orangemen and now the Blue Noses.

Isaac said: 'You'll learn soon enough, son. There's only two sorts of people in this world. Celtic supporters and everybody else.'

Isaac was a member of the Ancient Order of Hibernians and kept a green sash in a wardrobe in his bedroom and paraded up the Falls Road every St Patrick's Day with a ceremonial sword across his shoulder. He always seemed to be cheerful. I used to hear him singing in the morning in the bathroom as he shaved himself.

I am the wee Faloorie Man, a rattling
   roaring Irishman.
I will do whatever I can, for I am the
   wee Faloorie Man.

Isaac worked as a porter in the City Hospital. He would tell me about all the jobs he had to do.

'Oh, it's dangerous work, Marty. I have to collect all the blood and guts when they've finished cutting people up. Some days the operating theatre is swimming in blood and the surgeon will say: 'Get me Isaac McBride. He's the only man can handle this.'

'And I have to collect it all in a bucket, bits of people's legs and arms and I have to put it in the furnace before I can have my tea. And when I'm finished for the night they hose me down with disinfectant in case I pick up any germs.'

I didn't know what germs were but I didn't

9

like the sound of them. They made me think of Germans, and I knew they were bad people because I heard the adults say they dropped bombs on the city during the Blitz and killed hundreds of people.

I thought that Isaac had a grand, important job, even if I didn't fancy the idea of cleaning up all that blood. He used to bring home bundles of comics that got left behind in the children's wards. Beanos and Dandys and Hotspurs and Wizards.

Every morning before he went to work, he would come into my bedroom with an egg and butter beaten up in a cup and soldiers of toast.

'Get that into you. That'll put hairs on your chest.'

I'd sit up and wipe the sleep from my eyes. I didn't want hairs on my chest, but I loved the taste of eggs and toast and I didn't want to displease Isaac. He'd sit on the edge of my bed and I'd dip the toast in the egg and it tasted lovely.

'Did you not hear the news?' he would say. 'Celtic won again. They beat Rangers three nothing. Charlie Tully scored two goals. What do you say to that?'

I knew all about Charlie Tully because Isaac had told me. He was the greatest footballer in the world. He used to play for

10

Belfast Celtic before he went to Glasgow.

'Two goals, Marty. Ran rings round the whole Rangers' defence. Blue Noses didn't know what hit them. Oh there's joy in the Vatican today.'

'That's great news, Daddy.'

'Great? It's sticking out, so it is. They're going to win the League. You mark my words.'

And he would dance around the room with his scarf stretched out between his two arms singing the Celtic song while I mopped up my egg.

For it's a rare ould team to play for.
And it's a rare ould team to see.
And if you know their history,
It's enough to make your heart grow
    saaad.

Isaac worked Monday to Friday, from nine o'clock in the morning till six o'clock at night. On Saturday, he had a half day and finished at one o'clock, when he would come home and put his wage packet on the table for Sarah. She'd sit down with a little smile on her face and open it. I'd watch her count the green pound notes and the silver coins. When she was satisfied, she'd push a pound note back across the table.

11

'There's your pocket money, Isaac.'

'You're one decent woman, Sarah,' he would say and put the money in his pocket. Then he would sit down to his dinner. Sarah always made a special dinner on Saturday, soup and bacon and cabbage and potatoes with the butter melting on them.

'Mother of God,' Isaac would say. 'You wouldn't get better than this in the Grand Central Hotel. Didn't I marry the right woman?'

And he would wink at me, as if we were partners.

'Yes, Daddy.'

'It's very important to marry the right woman, Marty. Marry the wrong one and you'll be ruing it till the day you die.'

I didn't know what he meant, but it sounded important. Everything Isaac said was important.

When he was finished eating, he would take out a paper packet of Wild Woodbine cigarettes and flick at his lighter. Isaac said it was made from a bullet cartridge brought back from the War. Then he would go upstairs to get washed. I'd hear him slopping around in the bathroom, humming and singing. He would come down again dressed in his Sunday suit, white shirt, blue tie, hair oiled, shoes shining.

'Are you going out?' Sarah would say.

I used to wonder why she asked, because Isaac did the same thing every week.

He would bunch up his mouth and blow air through his lips.

'I thought I might take a wee dander round to Logue's and catch up on the news.'

'And what time will you be back?'

Isaac would look at his watch.

'Och, I shouldn't be late.'

Then I'd hear the door close and Isaac would be off to Logue's public house on the Crumlin Road.

Sarah used to take herself to bed early on Saturday nights. She would say she wasn't feeling great. It took me a long time to figure out the connection between those early nights and Isaac coming home around midnight after the pubs had closed, bumping into the furniture and knocking Sarah's holy pictures off the walls.

★ ★ ★

There were five mills down Brompton Park; big barrack-like buildings with tall chimneys. They dominated the district. All day long you could hear the clatter of the looms and smell the flax on the air. The mill horns would shriek when the shifts changed, and I would

13

press my face to the window and see lines of mill girls linking arms as they went off to work. They carried milk bottles full of tea. The mills provided a lot of employment, but it was mainly for women. It was dirty work and the wages were bad and people kept having accidents. You would see women with the sleeve of their coat pinned up where they had lost an arm in a machine. If a man worked in the mill, he wasn't regarded as much.

There was a lot of unemployment then, when the War had ended, and if you had a good job people looked up to you. Much of the talk out on the street was about whose father had the best job.

'My Da's got a start on the docks and he's earning £5 a week and me Ma says we're going to have beef for our Sunday dinner and ice-cream for afters,' one boy would say:

'That's nothing,' another would say. 'My Da's starting on the Corporation and he's getting me a bike for my birthday.'

When they talked like this, I kept quiet. I knew Isaac had a good job and never got laid off work like other fathers. He always brought his wages home to Sarah and we had everything we wanted. So I kept my mouth shut.

When the good weather came, a lot of the

men found work as labourers on the building sites. They would go home on the summer evenings with cement dust on their faces. Their wives would rush out and buy clothes for all the family.

Kids would boast: 'My Da has a great job. He has to climb a ladder with a hod of bricks on his back and he's earning £6 a week.' Or: 'My Da has to work the concrete mixer and push a wheelbarrow full of cement and you want to see the muscles on him.'

The work that most fathers had was unskilled. It was badly paid and insecure. There was a handful of craftsmen, like plumbers and fitters, and they had steady jobs and went to work in overalls with their toolboxes under their arms.

One of the few self-employed men was John Rea. He lived across the street from us and drove a big black taxi. He was very proud of his taxi and spent all his spare time polishing it.

'I'm my own boss, Isaac,' he would say, 'and I please myself. I doff my cap to no man.'

'It's the only way to be, John. Nobody ever got rich working for somebody else,' Isaac would agree.

A lot of the men had no work at all. I'd see them sitting on the front steps smoking

Woodbines and passing the time of day with the neighbours going up and down the street. Mr McHenry was the father of twelve children and his wife was always going into the hospital to have more. On a hot day, he would take a big armchair out and stretch in the sun and Mrs McHenry would bring him bottles of beer. It used to drive Sarah mad. When I asked her why he didn't work she would say, 'Why should he? Sure isn't the State keeping him?'

Willie Toner was a chimney sweep and lived beside us. He used to say to Isaac that it was all the fault of the Orangemen who kept the good jobs in the shipyards for themselves and wouldn't let a Catholic breathe fresh air if they could help it.

Isaac would nod his head wisely and say: 'You never spoke a truer word, Willie.'

The man with the best job in the district was Spa Doherty's father, Harry. He went to work every day in a suit and drove a car. It was the only car on the street, apart from John Rea's taxi. Harry Doherty always had plenty of money and his wife always had new clothes. One day, I asked Spa what his father did and he said he was an insurance man. When I told this to Sarah, she snorted.

'Is that what he calls it? Insurance man, my eye. He's nothing but a bloody tick-man.'

'A tick-man?'

'He's a collector for a money-lender.'

This was all new to me.

'What's a money-lender, Mammy?'

'A money lender is a man who lends money to poor people who've got in trouble and makes them pay back twice as much. He's the sort of man Our Lord drove from the temple. Money lending's a sin.'

But Harry Doherty didn't look like a sinner to me. I thought he had a great job. He was always laughing and telling us jokes. He used to give me and Spa money for sweets. And on Sunday afternoons, when he wasn't working, he'd let us sit in the car. We would take turns holding the steering wheel and pretending to drive.

Every couple of months, a group of men from the district would go off to England to work in the factories in Birmingham and Coventry. They would leave their wives and families behind and send back money every week. Kids would boast that their fathers were earning hundreds of pounds and were going to take them to England to live and they'd never want for anything again.

Then at Christmas, the men would come home with new suits and strange new accents. They would be in great demand in the pubs around Hooker Street and Brookfield Street till the money was gone and they'd go back again to England.

Our next-door neighbours were the McAllisters and they had six children. Bobby was the same age as me and we used to play marbles together. One day Maggie McAllister announced that her husband, Barney, was going to England. Sarah was delighted for her.

'He's landed a job as a bus conductor in Manchester. The digs are all lined up and everything. He'll be able to send us £10 a week.'

This was enormous money and everybody was happy for her. Sarah said Maggie would be able to get on her feet now. Barney McAllister left in May and as Christmas approached Sarah said, 'I suppose we'll be seeing Barney again, any day now. There'll be turkey and plum pudding. You must be looking forward to it.'

Maggie shook her head.

'He's not coming. He says the money's great over the holidays. There's lashings of overtime. He's going to stay and save up the money and then he'll come home at Easter.'

But Easter arrived and Barney didn't. I heard Sarah say to Isaac there was something fishy going on next door. When I asked her about it, she got cross and told me not to be poking my nose into things that didn't concern me.

Barney didn't come home the following Christmas either. In fact, he never came home at all and Bobby McAllister never saw his father again.

★ ★ ★

Everybody went to Mass on Sunday morning, for if you didn't it was a mortal sin and you could burn in Hell for all eternity. From half-past-six, you could hear people moving up our street for the first Mass and this would go on every hour until one o'clock. Sometimes there would be several Masses going on at the same time all over the church at side altars and lady chapels. Isaac used to say that the prayers going up from Holy Cross chapel alone would convert half of Russia in one go.

Sarah would get up before seven o'clock and put on the yellow camel-haired coat that she wore for special occasions, and off she'd go up the street. Sarah always took Communion, so she'd be fasting since midnight. Isaac would lie on in bed.

Shortly after eight o'clock I'd hear the key in the lock and the sound of Sarah bustling about in the kitchen. This lovely cooking smell would begin to creep up the stairs till eventually it filled the whole house.

I'd get up and go down to the front room where Sarah had laid out the Sunday breakfast. There'd be plates of black pudding and fried soda bread and these lovely eggs. And sitting in the middle of the table, covered in a woollen cosy, was a big pot of black tea.

'Eat up,' Sarah would say and push my chair closer to the table. 'You're a growing boy. Growing boys have to eat.'

I didn't need Sarah to tell me. Her Sunday breakfast was the best meal of the whole week, better even than the stew she made on Thursdays with minced meat and carrots and onions, and almost as good as the Christmas dinner. I'd eat the black pudding first and then the fried bread. I would save the egg till last. I would spear it with my fork and watch the yellow yolk run all across the plate and then I'd get a slice of bread and butter and mop it all up.

About half-past-ten, Isaac would stir and we'd hear him splashing about in the bathroom. Isaac never sang on Sunday mornings. He'd come down the stairs in his suit and tie, his face sad and his eyes red. He'd go straight to the cupboard and take down the bottle of lemonade he had brought home the night before. Sitting at the kitchen table, he would pour out two glasses, one for him and one for me. Isaac never ate any breakfast and he hardly spoke. If I asked Sarah about it, she'd say he wasn't well, Sunday morning was his bad morning and not to be annoying him. Isaac and I would finish the bottle of lemonade. Then he'd belch, take my hand and at five to eleven we'd start off for the chapel.

It stood at the top of our street, just across the Crumlin Road, a great, big, stone building with two steeples and bells that used to ring out all over Ardoyne. The eleven o'clock Mass was a short Mass and Isaac said that suited him fine for God could see into the hearts of men, you just had to look at the Parable of the Publican and the Sinner. I didn't know what he was talking about, but if Isaac said it, then it had to be true.

The Mass was usually over in half an hour. The church would be packed, people standing along the side aisles and at the back and some even standing outside on the porch. The priest who usually said this Mass was Father Brendan. He was young and would race through the prayers. Isaac called him 'Speedy' and said he was a man after his own heart.

But sometimes the Mass would be said by Father Benedict. If he was on, Isaac would scowl. Father Benedict was old and he had a strange accent that the altar boys couldn't understand. He used to ramble over the sermon and forget what he was saying. When Father Benedict was taking it, the eleven o'clock Mass could go on for nearly an hour.

Isaac would sit through this and his face would grow pale. Little beads of sweat would slowly break on his forehead until they ran down his cheeks like rain. His lips would move as if he was saying his prayers, but if I listened close, I would hear him mutter, 'Get a move on. For the love of God and His Holy Mother, would you get a move on and put me out of my misery.'

There were times when Isaac wouldn't be able to get up till twelve o'clock and this was the High Mass. It had bells and incense and the choir singing and it was followed by Benediction. It lasted for over an hour and the holiest people in the district went to it.

The High Mass made Isaac very cross. He would sit beside me in the pew nearest the door, clutching his hands tight to stop them from twitching, and his face would be the colour of soap.

Isaac would shiver every time the altar boys rang the bell. When the choir sang, he would groan. I would watch him twist and turn till the last prayer was said and the priest had blessed all the people and the Mass was finally over. When at last we got outside the door, Isaac would be shaking. He would stand for a moment drawing deep breaths of air and then he would take out his handkerchief and wipe the sweat from his face. He would turn to me and say, 'Do you know what it is, Marty? There'll be no Purgatory for me when I die, for God knows I've done all my suffering on earth.'

Out would come the crumpled packet of Woodbines. Isaac would select one and pull the cartridge lighter from his pocket and light up and take a deep draw and say, 'That's better. With a bit of luck, I might last till dinner time.' He would take my hand again and we'd go down the big steps to the Crumlin Road and our visit to Aunt Minnie McCrory.

*   *   *

Aunt Minnie was Isaac's sister and she lived in a house in Chatham Street with her husband Paddy who used to be a sailor and had been all around the world on a boat. Aunt Minnie was a rebel and she had given all her five children rebel names.

The eldest boy was called Patrick Pearse McCrory. He was fifteen and had left school and was working with the milkman on his float. He used to ruffle my hair and give me marbles he found on his milk round and I looked up to him and thought he had a brilliant job, riding around on the milk float and leaving bottles of milk at people's doors.

The next boy was Wolfe Tone McCrory, then Robert Emmet who was my age. The baby was called Kevin Barry. There was a girl who was a bit older than me, called Betsy Grey.

Isaac said there had been trouble with the priest when they went to get Patrick Pearse baptised. The priest had objected, saying he didn't think it was a good idea.

'Good idea?'

Aunt Minnie was outraged.

'Aren't I the child's mother and entitled to call him what I want?'

'But Mrs McCrory. You have your obligations to consider.'

'What do you mean 'obligations'? Patrick Pearse was a patriot. He was in the GPO in 1916 and shot by the English. If I want to call my son after him, that's my business.'

The priest took her aside and lowered his voice and said: 'Mrs McCrory, you have to think about his future.'

'His future?'

'His job prospects. How's it going to look

when he grows up, if he applies for a job in the shipyard or Mackie's foundry and he gives his name as Patrick Pearse McCrory? In a town like this, Mrs McCrory, you'll be handicapping the poor child for life.'

'Is that all you're worried about?' Aunt Minnie said indignantly. 'Well I'll tell you how we'll fix that. If you won't baptise him, I'll take him next Sunday to the Presbyterians down the Woodvale Road and I'm sure they'll not turn him away. And that'll solve the problem about the job, for then he'll be a Protestant.'

The priest sighed and glanced at Uncle Paddy who shrugged his shoulders and looked up at the ceiling where God was sitting on his throne surrounded by his angels.

'You're a tough woman, Mrs McCrory. I hope you realise what you're doing.'

And he proceeded to say the prayers over Patrick Pearse's bald head and induct him into the ranks of the One Holy Catholic and Apostolic church.

★ ★ ★

Aunt Minnie was small, like Isaac, but round and plump with a fresh schoolgirl's face. I thought she must be the boss in her house, for Uncle Paddy was afraid of her. When we

25

came in the door she would take a good look at Isaac and depending on his condition she would say:

'You're looking bravely.'

Or 'You're quare and failed, this morning, Isaac.'

'Och, Minnie. I got a bad pint in Logue's last night and my head's not right.'

'Tsk, tsk, tsk. Will you never learn?' Aunt Millie would say. 'You look like you've been put through the mangle. I'd say another clean shirt should do you.'

Then she'd turn to me and take her purse out of her apron and give me a threepenny piece, and say: 'Away you with Robert Emmet and get some sweeties. And remember to hold hands when you're crossing the road.'

And Robert Emmet and me would head down Chatham Street to Skinny Lizzie's shop and we'd buy liquorice and sherbet and caramels. Then he'd take me round to Herbert Street to a fella he knew called Willie Dobbin, who had a goldfish in a glass bowl and would sometimes let us feed it if we gave him a gob-stopper.

When we got back to Aunt Minnie's, the three adults would be drinking tea. Isaac would be in much better form. Sometimes he'd even be singing again:

Come back, Paddy Reilly to Ballyjames-
   duff.

He would take my hand and we'd start for home, and sometimes I'd catch that strange, sweet smell on his breath, the same smell I used to get when I passed the open door of Kilpatrick's pub at the bottom of Hooker Street.

Sunday was the most boring day in the whole week. There was nothing to do. The picture houses and the shops were all closed. Some of the parks were open but the swings were locked and chained. Isaac said it was all the fault of the Bible Thumpers who ran Belfast Corporation. He said they wanted everybody down on their knees saying their prayers. They were determined that nobody was going to enjoy themselves if they had anything to do with it. His solution was to go for a walk.

After we'd had our dinner, he would get up from the table, stretch his arms and take out his Woodbines. They came in paper packs of ten and were untipped. Spa Doherty's mother, Teesie, smoked the new tipped cigarettes but Isaac wouldn't hear tell of them. He said it was just a trick by the tobacco companies to rob people of their last bit of tobacco. Sarah would be clearing away the dishes and plates from the table and taking them into the kitchen to wash them in the big sink. Isaac never lent a hand. He had his own jobs. He looked after the garden and did the heavy lifting work and fixed anything that got broke.

Isaac would sit for a while, puffing happily on his cigarette and looking out the window. Then he would turn to me. 'What do you think, Marty? Will we go for a bit of a dander?'

I'd be all excited.

'Yes, Daddy.'

'Where will we go?'

'Up the fields.'

'Right. A dander's just the thing. It'll shake up the puddins.'

'What's puddins?'

Isaac would laugh.

'Puddins is what's in your stomach, son. There's miles of them. They need to get a good shake-up every now and again. Otherwise they get costic.'

'What's costic, Daddy?'

Isaac would scratch his head.

'Costic's when your pudding gets all clogged up and your mother has to give you syrup-of-figs for a good cleaning-out.'

Sarah would go tsk, tsk tsk from the kitchen.

'Don't be talking like that in front of the child, Isaac.'

'Well, he's the one asking the questions, Sarah.'

Because he worked in a hospital with doctors and nurses, Isaac was regarded by the neighbours as an authority on medical matters and he liked to give his opinions on the mysteries of the internal organs.

But this sort of talk made me uneasy. I touched my stomach and all I could feel was Sarah's dinner. I thought of the black puddings, she had cooked for breakfast. They came in a fat string like sausages, tied with twine. I wondered if my stomach was full of black puddings.

It was all very mysterious, but much of what adults said was and if I asked too many questions, Isaac would tell me to run on there and give his head peace.

He would get up from his chair near the window and begin to whistle. He would take a comb from his pocket and run it through his hair, carefully combing over the bald patch at the back. Then he would crush out the withered stump of his cigarette and take his coat from the peg behind the door.

We would walk down the garden path to the gate and I'd hold his hand and we'd start up the street on our dander. I loved these walks with Isaac. They made me feel grown-up. I loved the smell of tobacco from his clothes and the conversations we'd have and the things he'd point out to me.

We had a number of walks, depending on the mood Isaac was in and the state of the weather. They nearly all involved open fields, for Ardoyne at that time was almost countryside. We'd go up the Crumlin Road, past the Forum picture house and stop at Collins's shop for ice cream. Then we'd walk up Ardoyne Road, past Everton school on our way to Ballysillan. At the top of the road, an old woman kept goats and chickens. We'd stop and look at the goats, tethered to a line by a length of rope to prevent them wandering.

'Goats are the boys, all right,' Isaac would say. 'Did you know they can eat anything, old shoes, tin cans? They'd even eat a man's shirt off the clothes line if they got half a chance.'

I looked at the goats with renewed interest, the straggly beards dripping from the narrow chins, the glazed eyes that made me think of the devil, the sharp, pointed horns on the billy goats.

'Would they hurt you, Daddy?'

Isaac shrugged.

'They might. If you annoyed them.'

'Would they kill you?'

'Och, I don't think they'd kill you. But they might give you a right puck with them horns.'

'What does she keep them for?'

'For the milk.'

'But I thought milk came from the cows.'

'So it does. But you can get it from goats too. Goat's milk is better. It's full of vitamins. It's very good for the pipes.'

'What's pipes, Daddy?'

'Pipes is what's in your chest, son. It's what you breath through.'

It sounded very complicated. I looked at the old woman's cottage with the honeysuckle climbing up the wall and the wild roses in bloom and thought how it must be brilliant to wake up in the morning with the smell of the fields and the fresh eggs from your own hens and milk from the goats that was so good for the pipes.

If we had time and the weather was good, we would walk past Ballysillan fields and up into Ligoniel. This was a little mill village, much smaller than Ardoyne, only a handful of streets with a tall mill chimney poking up in the middle of it all. It sat on a hill so we were usually out of breath when we got there, but Isaac said it was worth it for the view. He would take off his coat and wipe his face with a handkerchief and begin to point things out.

31

The whole city lay before us. You could see the factories and the spires of the churches and the river Lagan curling into Belfast Lough past rows of small terraced houses where they clustered together along the main roads. You could see the cranes of the shipyards and the white dome of the City Hall.

'Can you figure out our house?' Isaac would say. 'I'll give you a penny if you can find it.'

I would look down on the confusing jumble of rooftops and spires, the occasional flash of sunlight on water.

'I'll give you a clue,' Isaac would say. 'Start from here and work your way back.'

I would follow his advice, tracking my way down the Crumlin Road till I had located the spires of the chapel.

'Now where's Butler Street?'

I'd point.

'That's right. Now how do you get from Butler Street to our street?'

'Through Herbert Street.'

It was an exciting game. I'd trace along Herbert Street and through the gap to Brompton Park, then I'd count the chimneys till I came to our house.

'There.'

I'd point with excitement. I could just

make out John Rea's big black taxi parked on the street outside his door.

'Boys a boys,' Isaac would say. 'You're a smart wee buck, so you are. When you grow up, you're going to get a big, fancy job sitting on your arse doing nothing all day and everybody'll be talking about you.'

I'd nestle close to him and bask in his admiration and hold my hand out for the penny he had promised.

★ ★ ★

Sometimes Isaac's Sunday walks would take us to the brickyard. This was a waste-ground which ran from Ardoyne as far as the Oldpark Road. On top of the brickyard, there was a pitch-and-toss school.

Isaac didn't approve of pitch-and-toss. He didn't approve of gambling of any kind. He said gambling was an addiction which had brought many a poor man to ruin. Men had lost their entire week's wages and their wives and children had to go hungry. It was far worse than drinking, for a man could only drink so much till he fell down, but a gambler could lose his whole fortune on the turn of a card.

He always hurried past the pitch-and-toss school but I would peek anxiously at the men standing in the circle as the coins went spinning in the air. I'd wonder if any of them had lost their week's wages and I'd think of the children crying with the hunger when their Daddies came home with their pockets empty because they'd lost all their money at the pitch-and-toss.

Most of the times when we went to the brickyard, it was to watch the football. At the bottom of the hill where the gambling took place was a cinder pitch and all through Sunday, matches would be played between local teams. Hundreds of people would come to watch. Isaac's favourite team was Crumlin Star and he knew all the players because they would drink with him on Saturday nights when he went to Logue's pub.

We would sit on the hill overlooking the pitch and Isaac would give me a commentary on the game.

'Look at your man. He's got two left feet.'

I'd look closely but the man's feet seemed all right to me.

'Look at that big eejit standing there with his two arms the one length.'

And I would hold out my own arms and check to see if one was longer than the other.

'That referee's blind.'

And I would wonder how a man could referee a football match, if he couldn't see. It was all very confusing. But I didn't care. Just sitting here with Isaac talking about the football was good enough for me.

One afternoon, when we had been there for a while, I saw Isaac rummaging in his pockets. He had a worried look on his face. He went through one pocket and then another, till at last he turned to me.

'Do you know what it is, Marty? I think I've left my fags behind.'

'What are you going to do, Daddy?'

'I'll have to go to the shop and get some more.'

'Will I come with you?'

'No. You stay here till I get back. I won't be long.'

I settled down to wait. All around me, men were shouting encouragement to their teams and for a while I was content to watch the game. But when Isaac didn't return, I began to get uneasy.

It was the first time he had left me alone like this. I had no way of knowing how much time had passed, but it seemed that he was gone a long while. I scanned the faces of the crowd, watching to see if he was coming back. But there was no sign of him.

I was getting worried. Maybe something had happened to him. Maybe he'd had an accident. Maybe he'd been knocked down by

35

a car and taken to the hospital.

I stood up and began to struggle through the crowd. I started to run, stubbing my toes against stones and tufts of grass. I thought of Isaac on a stretcher in the ambulance with the blood pumping out of him. I ran as fast as I could till at last I came to Jamaica Street.

And there was Isaac, standing outside Billy O'Carroll's shop, talking to Artie McDaid.

The two men stopped when they saw me coming. Isaac put out his arm and scooped me up.

'What's the matter, Marty? Where are you off to in such a big hurry?'

I felt the hot tears well in my eyes. I buried my head in his shoulder and began to cry.

'What's the matter, son? You can tell your Daddy.'

'I thought you were hurted,' I said. 'I thought maybe you were dead and were never coming back.'

★ ★ ★

The people who lived on the other side of us from the McAllisters were called Toner and they had a tree in their back yard. It was the only tree I can remember in the district. Willie Toner said it reminded him of his days as a boy when he was growing up in the fields of Armagh. He said that trees were good for you, because they put oxygen back in the air.

Willie Toner and his wife Lizzie must have been about sixty. She was always dressed in a black cardigan and smelt of snuff. In the summer, they made candy-apples from syrup and sold them to people for a penny each.

Willie Toner was an even bigger rebel than my aunt Minnie McCrory. He used to say that the Catholics would never get their rights till the English had left Ireland for good and we had a nation once again. Every Easter, he hung a green, white and orange flag from his window in memory of the Rebellion in Dublin.

'Up the Rebels,' he would shout as he put the flag out and all the kids in the street below would cheer. 'Ireland unfree shall never be at peace.'

I didn't understand any of this, but it made a big impression on Isaac.

'I admire a man who stands up for his principles,' he would say. 'Willie Toner's got spunk.'

But Sarah didn't like anything to do with flags and bands and stuff. She said they brought nothing but trouble. She said the world would be a far happier place if all the flags were put on a bonfire and burnt.

'Willie Toner's just a stupid ould eejit. Sure

wasn't he an air-raid warden during the War and if that's not the next best thing to being in the British army, what is?'

But Isaac said the War was different, for the Germans were trying to bomb the hell out of us and Willie was only making sure that people didn't get killed. He said the Orangemen could wave their flags and march with their bands and if it was all right for them, then it was all right for us too.

'The Orangemen's one thing,' Sarah would say. 'And we're another. If the peelers come round, they'll soon make him take it down again.'

'Let them try,' Isaac would mutter. 'And we'll soon see how many real Irishmen there are in this district.'

★　★　★

Willie Toner was a chimney sweep. And his two sons, Seanie and Hughie, were chimney sweeps too. They cleaned all the chimneys in the district and rode around on bicycles with their brushes sticking out the back and their faces black from the soot. There was a daughter called Mamie and she had a girl called Eileen who was my age. Eileen didn't seem to have any daddy that I could figure out and if I asked Sarah about it, she would tell me to give her head peace and not be asking awkward questions.

One evening, after Isaac had come home from work, there was an awful commotion outside our house and I could hear Eileen Toner screaming: 'Mammy, Mammy. I'm killed. I'm killed.'

Isaac ran out onto the street at once. I went with him. Eddie Russell, the ragman, was standing on the pavement, wringing his hands and jumping up and down. His cart was turned over and Eileen was lying under one of the shafts. She was screaming blue murder and Eddie Russell was telling anybody who would listen that it wasn't his fault.

'Honest to God. I didn't even see her. One minute she was on the cribpath and the next minute she's under my cart.'

Isaac bent down and gathered Eileen in his arms. He took her to her own house and I followed, afraid that something terrible had happened.

'Mother of God,' Lizzie Toner cried when she saw Eileen. 'The child's been murdered. Somebody send for the ambulance.'

Mamie appeared and started to cry and soon the whole house was in uproar.

'There, there now. It's all right, Mrs Toner,' Isaac said. 'She got knocked down by the handcart. Her knee's grazed, that's all.'

'That blackguard, Russell,' Lizzie spat. 'I'll swing for him. He'll never get another rag off me, the longest day I live.'

'She's going to be all right,' Isaac insisted. 'There's nothing to worry about. Have you got any disinfectant in the house?'

Mamie disappeared into the kitchen and came back with a bottle of Dettol and a box of plasters.

Eileen started screaming louder and I thought she was going to bring the roof down.

'Am I going to die and go to Heaven?'

'No you're not,' Isaac said. 'You're going to be grand.'

'Thank God you were here, Isaac,' Lizzie Toner said, sticking a pinch of snuff up each nostril. 'And you a medical man that works in the hospital.'

Isaac smiled, and I could see he was pleased with himself.

'Och, it was nothing Mrs Toner. Sure I'm well used to dealing with emergencies.'

'She might have had to get the leg off. That blackguard Russell and his handcart. Wait till I get my hands on him.'

She starting abusing the ragman again till she saw me standing in the doorway.

'And that wee fella of yours that's a credit to you and Sarah.'

She reached into her cardigan and took out a threepenny piece.

'There are you are, Martin. Get yourself sweeties.'

★ ★ ★

I was playing marbles out on the street with Bobby McAllister and he said to me: 'Did you know girls have no mickies?'

I thought I was hearing things.

'No mickies?'

'That's right.'

I stared at him amazement.

'But if they've no mickies, how do they pee?'

'They pee through their bums. They have to sit down.'

'You're sure?'

'Honest to God.'

Girls had no mickies and peed through their bums. I couldn't believe it.

'How do you know?' I said.

'I saw our Gemma getting ready for bed. And when my Ma had our wee Mary, I used to look when she was changing her nappy and she'd no micky either.'

'I don't believe you,' I said.

But Bobby McAllister had sown a doubt. The thought that half the people I knew were walking around with no mickies obsessed me. I went to sleep that night, thinking of all the girls I knew and trying to picture them with no mickies and it was a terrible thought.

A couple of days after this, I met Eileen Toner out on the street. She was skipping rope outside her front door.

'Is your knee better?' I asked.

'Yes,' she said. 'Your Daddy fixed it. Your Daddy's awful smart.' She pulled up her dress to show me where the plaster had been and I caught a glimpse of her white knickers.

A sudden idea came to me. There was an air-raid shelter outside her house that had been built during the War for people to hide in during the Blitz.

'Come into the shelter,' I said.

'What for?'

'I want to check something.'

She dropped the skipping rope and followed me in. It was dark inside but my eyes soon got accustomed to the light.

'Eileen, lift up your dress again.'

She laughed, but did as I asked, as if it was some game.

'Now, take down your knickers.'

Eileen reached for her drawers and pulled them down.

My heart leaped in my mouth. What Bobby McAllister said was true. Eileen Toner had no micky. Instead there was this thing like a scar between her legs. I felt a strange excitement, tinged with horror.

'How do you do your wee wee?' I said.

Eileen looked at me as if I was mad.

'I sit down,' she said.

I kept this information to myself for about a week, but I couldn't get it out of my head. Maybe Bobby McAllister had got it all wrong. Maybe Eileen Toner was deformed. I decided to find out once and for all. There was one person who would know for sure, and that was Isaac.

One evening as he was finishing his tea, I said: 'Daddy, is it true that girls have no mickies?'

Isaac slowly put down his knife and fork.

'Who told you that, son?'

'Bobby McAllister.'

'He did, did he?'

'Yes. And I know Eileen Toner has no micky.'

'How do you know that?'

'I brought her into the air-raid shelter and got her to take down her knickers.'

Isaac slapped his thigh and started to laugh.

'You're a clever wee buck,' he said. 'No doubt about it.'

'But is it true?'

'Well,' Isaac said. 'Not really, son.'

He scratched his head and looked at Sarah. Her face had gone red.

'Remember that time Eileen got knocked down by the handcart?'

'Yes, Daddy.'

'Well, I didn't tell you this. But she got her micky cut off.'

Suddenly everything made sense. Girls did have mickies after all and Bobby McAllister was wrong.

'And will it grow back again?'

Isaac scratched his head once more.

'It will, son. But these things take time.'

I felt enormous relief. Isaac patted my head.

'Away you now and play yourself. And stay out of that air-raid shelter.'

I felt a warm glow. Isaac was the best and the smartest Daddy of them all and I was proud of him.

★ ★ ★

Once a month, on a Thursday afternoon, Isaac got a special half-day and he would take me down the town. This was a great adventure and involved getting a tram outside the chapel.

On these occasions, he was usually paying a bill or looking for some tool he needed but it always turned into an excursion. I loved these trips and if Isaac happened to mention earlier in the week that there was a chance we might be going, I'd be all excited until Thursday arrived.

He would come home as usual around half-past-one and have his dinner. When he was finished, he'd get up and walk to the window to see what the weather was like. I'd watch him anxiously, not daring to speak. Then he would turn to me and say: 'It's looking a wee bit changeable. Skiff of rain on the way. But I think we'll chance it. What do you say, Marty?'

'Yes, Daddy. I think we will.'

'Dead on,' Isaac would say. 'Let the dog see the hare.'

He'd rub his hands together and take out his Woodbines, while Sarah got me ready. For these trips, Isaac would get dressed up the way he did for his visits to the pub or to Mass. He would go up to the bathroom and we'd hear him whistling and humming while he shaved and got washed. Then he'd come down with his good suit and tie on.

'You never know who you might bump into,' he would say. 'It pays to put your best side out.'

I couldn't understand this strange talk. It was like the dog and the hare. What did it mean? How could you bump into people if you were looking where you were going as Sarah was forever telling me to do? And what was this best side he was talking about? And how did you put it out? I couldn't make any sense of it. Isaac was always coming out with words like this; smart, adult talk that I couldn't understand. But I kept these words in my head and sometimes, out on the street when I was playing with other boys, I would drop one of his phrases just to see the effect.

The tram journey was a big part of the enjoyment. The trams ran on steel tracks sunk into the road and sparks shot out from the overhead wires as they moved along. There was a lot of jangling and shunting and it all added to the excitement.

The driver sat in the front where the passengers got on. He had a neat uniform with silver buttons and a cap and a big wheel for guiding the tram. I thought it was a great job, maybe even better than Isaac's, although I never said this. The driver always winked at me whenever we boarded and said: 'What about ye?'

The tram for the city centre left the depot up on the Ardoyne Road and when it came, it would slide to halt with a clanking noise and Isaac and I would get on board. I could never make up my mind where to sit;

downstairs near the door, where I could watch the driver work the controls, or upstairs where I could look out the window and see the city pass by.

If there were no seats near the driver, we would climb the stairs to the top deck. The tram would rattle down the road past the dark mills and the courthouse and the gaol. I would look at the rows of barred windows sunk into the gaol wall and wonder who was in there. I imagined men in chains, the way I had seen in picture books. I tried to think what bad things they might have done and whether there were any murderers.

After the gaol, we'd go flying past the Mater Hospital and Carlisle Circus and St Patrick's Chapel and before you knew it we'd be in Royal Avenue. Here there were more trams and new, red trolley buses and crowds of people going in and out of the fancy shops.

Isaac always got off outside the Central Library. This was a big building with steps leading up to the front door. There were lumps missing from the walls which Isaac said were bullet holes caused by the German bombers during the Blitz. I'd look at them, trying to imagine the German planes zooming down Royal Avenue and the people fleeing in panic before them as they shot everyone in sight.

We would wander around the shops while Isaac searched for whatever it was he'd come into town to buy. 'Why don't we take a dander round to Smithfield and see if there's any bargains?' he would say. And he'd take me by the hand and lead me through a maze of streets, till at last we came to Smithfield Square.

This was the highlight of the trip. Smithfield was an indoor market, which ran between North Street and Castle Street. It was surrounded by pubs. As we went past, you could see into the dark interiors, the big mirrors above the polished counters, the dark wood, the barmen in their long white aprons, the strange smell of Guinness and cigarette smoke.

I would sometimes see groups of men sitting up at the counter, black pints of porter in their hands and their duncher caps pushed back on their heads. This was the sort of place where Isaac liked to go on Saturday afternoons, drinking pints and smoking his Woodbines and talking to his pals about football. This was obviously the place where men went. I decided when I grew up this was where I would come as well.

The market itself was a dusty place with a funny smell that I'd sometimes get at the back of Sarah's wardrobe, not like the fancy shops in High Street or Royal Avenue. But it was full of wonderful things. There were three aisles with stalls selling carpets and old clothes and second-hand books. There was a pawn shop with a sign saying: JOE KAVANAGH. I BUY ANYTHING. It had a suit of armour in the window and a stuffed gorilla and an old gramophone and china dogs and a Japanese helmet. Isaac said a man once sold his artificial leg to Joe Kavanagh after Conlon's pub wouldn't give him another pint because he hadn't any more money.

I thought about this for a long time, trying to figure out how a man with one leg could get about and what he'd tell his wife when he got home.

Isaac would spend hours in Smithfield. He would start at the first aisle and work his way along, picking up items that caught his attention, examining them and putting them down again. These were usually ornaments with bits broken off them, which Isaac said were antiques.

If he was interested in something, he would study it for a long time, trying to make up his mind. He would put it down and lift it up again. He would turn it sideways and look under it.

'How much are you looking?'

The owner would give a price.

'Would you run away and chase yourself. Do you think I came up the Lagan in a bubble?' Isaac would say.

The owner would bring the price down a bit.

'Are you codding me?' Isaac would say. 'Sure it's falling apart. I'd be doing you a favour, taking it off your hands.'

The owner would come down a bit more and they would argue for a while till they reached a price. Then the owner would quickly wrap the ornament in an old copy of the Irish News before Isaac could change his mind.

Isaac would have a gleam in his eye.

'You couldn't watch those fellas,' he would say as we went round to Royal Avenue to catch the tram for home. 'They think they're cute, but they'd have to get up quare and early in the morning before they'd catch me.'

We'd get off the tram near the Forum picture house and go into Freddie Fusco's and get fish and chips for our tea.

'Your mammy will love this,' Isaac would say as we made our way down Brompton Park with his purchase stuck under his arm. 'Women love to be surprised, Marty. They love to get presents.'

Sarah would take the ornament from its wrapper 'It's lovely, Isaac. But you shouldn't be wasting your money,' she'd say.

He would shrug. 'Och, it's nothing. Just a wee thing I picked up in Smithfield. It's got an arm broken off but I can easy fix that with a bit of glue.'

She would clear a place on the sideboard and wipe Isaac's present with a feather duster and place it in a nice position beside the holy pictures. Then a few weeks later, when Isaac was at work, I would see her leave it out for the binmen.

When I asked her why she was throwing out Isaac's nice ornament, she would give me a strange look and say, 'What you don't know, doesn't do you any harm.'

Isaac never complained, so I supposed he didn't mind.

★ ★ ★

One day when we were down the town, Isaac took me to the City Hall to pay the electricity bill. This was the finest building in Belfast. There was a nice garden in front with flowers and a big statue of this fat woman holding a big round ball and staring down Royal Avenue. Inside there were more statues and pictures of men with beards and whiskers and medals pinned on their chests and chains around their necks.

The minute Isaac entered the City Hall, he lowered his voice. There was a hush in the place like you'd find in the chapel and men standing around in uniforms like the tram drivers wore, with their hands behind their backs. They gave you a dirty look if you talked.

Isaac took me into the electricity office. There were two queues; a big, long one and a shorter one. The long one had all these people; women with headscarves carrying babies, and men with mufflers and duncher caps. Isaac joined the short queue. When he came to the hatch, he pushed his bill in.

The clerk lifted it and then he looked at Isaac and studied him above his glasses.

'Brompton Park?' he said in a loud voice. He had an angry face and little squinty eyes.

'Yes,' Isaac said.

'That's Glenard. Glenard's the other queue.'

'The other queue?'

The clerk looked at Isaac with his angry face.

'Are you deaf or something? This queue's for people that pays their bills in full. People that's paying part use the other queue.'

'But I *am* paying in full.'

The man looked at the bill again and then he pushed it back to Isaac.

'Don't argue with me,' he said in a sneery voice. 'I've never seen anybody from Glenard that paid their bills in full.'

'Well, you're seeing one now.'

The clerk's face went red.

'Are you giving me cheek? Glenard's the other queue.'

Isaac turned. Everybody in the long queue was looking at him. One of the men in the tram driver's uniforms came hurrying across.

'Along you go, now,' he said, 'Don't you be causing any trouble or we'll put you out.'

I began to get frightened at the way they were treating my Daddy.

'I just want to pay my bill,' Isaac protested.

The well-dressed people in the queue behind him were starting to mutter. The man in the tram driver's uniform took Isaac by the arm.

'You heard what Mr McFettridge said. Glenard's the other queue. You cause any trouble and we'll get your electric cut off.'

Isaac allowed himself to be led away. His face was all embarrassed. I felt sorry for him. I wished I was a man so I could hit the sneery clerk a good box and make his nose bleed. But he was ignoring us now. There was a smile on his squinty face, as if he was delighted with himself.

'Next please,' he said.

2

When I wasn't with Isaac, I was with Sarah. She was always busy; washing and cleaning and ironing and baking. She always wore a pinafore, except when she was going to Mass or somewhere important when she wore her camel-haired coat. I'd sit in the warm kitchen and watch her smooth out the dough with her big rolling pin and put it in the baking dish. Sometimes she would put in currants and raisins. Other times she would chop up apples or rhubarb and make tarts. She would put in a special piece for me and when it was baked, she would put the kettle on for tea and we would sit at the kitchen table and she would take out the big picture book.

'Once upon a time,' Sarah would begin. Her finger would trace the words and I'd snuggle close and smell the lovely fresh smell off her as if she had just washed herself all over with scenty soap. She was taller than Isaac and skinny and had cheeks like rosy apples.

When the winter drew in and the rain would batter against the window-panes, Sarah would make cocoa and toast and we'd sit together beside the fire. She'd tell me stories out of her own head. Mostly these were tales about the fairies but sometimes I would say, 'Tell me a ghost story, Mammy.'

'Ghost stories will only give you nightmares.'

But I would coax her until she told me the tale of Galloper Thompson, the headless horseman who appeared every midnight on the roof of York Street mill.

'Is it really true, Mammy?' I would say, breathless with fear.

'Of course it's true.'

'And would he take you away?'

'Not if you're a good boy. No harm will come to you if you say your prayers and obey your Mammy and Daddy.'

And I would hold her hand tight and listen to the wind whistling in the chimney pot and think how lucky I was to be safe and warm with Sarah while we waited for Isaac to come home for his tea.

Isaac did the same thing every night. He would come home shortly after half-past-six, take off his coat and hang it behind the door. Then he would go up to the bathroom to get washed. Meanwhile, Sarah would be busy getting his dinner ready.

Isaac would come down again and push his chair up to the table and rub his hands together. He would look at whatever Sarah had prepared and say, 'My God, Sarah. You've surpassed yourself again.'

She would smile and say, 'Well, an empty sack can't stand, Isaac.'

'You've never said a truer word.' And he would tuck in and while he was eating he would tell me all the interesting things that had happened at work.

When he was finished and Sarah had cleared away the table and washed the dishes, we would all kneel down and say the family Rosary.

Sarah led the prayers. The first Joyful Mystery. The Annunciation. She would start into the Our Father and then the Hail Mary. Isaac would mumble the responses, rushing the prayers in an effort to get it over quickly so that the words rattled round the little room like gunfire.

Holymarymotherofgodprayforussinnersnowa-ndatthehourofourdeath . . .

He would lay heavy emphasis on 'Amen'.

Sarah would start off again.

Hail, Mary full of grace the Lord is with thee, blessed art thou amongst women . . .

Isaac would shift on the hard floor as if in pain, but as we neared the end of the prayers his face would brighten. Sarah would pause briefly and announce another prayer for the Pope's special intention and Isaac would groan.

'The Pope doesn't need prayers, Sarah. He's got more prayers than he can handle.'

But Sarah would just ignore him and start into another Our Father and Isaac would have to follow. When she had finished at last, Isaac would fish out his Woodbines and cartridge lighter from his pocket, sighing loudly in relief.

★ ★ ★

One evening, Sarah said to me, 'I think it's time you went to school and got out from under my feet.'

Isaac was sitting near the window, reading about Celtic in the Belfast Telegraph. He peeped out from behind the paper.

'Could he not wait a wee while longer, Sarah? Sure he's only four and a half.'

But Sarah said: 'He's big enough and ugly enough and the sooner he starts the better.'

I didn't mind going to school. Most of my pals were there already. The school was called Holy Cross and it was round in Butler Street. I could see it from the back windows of our house across the mill dam, where the big white swans came to nest every summer. There was one school for boys and another for girls.

I was already able to recognise some words and Sarah had also taught me how to write my first name with single letters and how to count to twenty. So I had no fear about going to school.

The following Monday she washed me carefully. She scrubbed my nails and combed my hair and put me into my best shirt and trousers.

'Remember. You call the master Sir and you keep your mouth shut. You don't speak till you're spoken to. And if you want to go to the toilet, you put your hand up. All right?'

'Yes, Mammy.'

'This isn't the street you're going to.'

Then she took me by the hand and we walked the short distance to Butler Street to meet the school principal. He was a tall man in a tweed jacket with a row of pens in his breast pocket. His name was Mr Elwood. We went into his office where he took out a bundle of papers and began asking questions.

'Name and date of birth?'

Sarah told him and he wrote it down.

'Any illnesses we should know about?'

'He had the chicken pox when he was a baby.'

'Anything like epilepsy? Anything he's allergic to?'

Sarah shook her head.

'Any special medication he requires?'

'No.'

Mr Elwood put down the pen and for the first time, he looked at me.

'We don't stand for hooliganism in this school and we don't stand for bad language. Any boy using bad language will have me to deal with. Understand?'

Sarah gave me a shove.

'Yes.'

Mr Elwood waited. I felt Sarah shove me again and remembered what she had told me earlier.

'Yes, Sir.'

Mr Elwood nodded and turned back to Sarah.

'He can start tomorrow. He can go into Senior Infants. The school will be finishing for the summer holidays at the end of June. It's only a couple of months. It'll break him in.'

★   ★   ★

I was delighted with myself. Most people starting school went into Babies, but I was going into Senior Infants with the big boys. When I told Bobby McAllister, he said it mightn't be such a good idea because Senior Infants was harder and if you got things

60

wrong, they slapped you.

School started at nine o'clock. Sarah had me up at eight with a big breakfast of porridge and a boiled egg but I could hardly eat any of it for the excitement. She had gone out the previous afternoon and bought me a new leather school-bag with my name written on it. She'd also got me a pencil case with pencils, an eraser, a ruler and a jotter.

Our teacher was called Mr O'Reilly. He didn't look as old as Mr Elwood. Sarah left me at the door and Mr O'Reilly brought me in and put me sitting beside a boy from Highbury Gardens called Charlie Pigeon. He had a big ugly dollop of snot dripping from his nose and smelled as if he'd pissed his pants. I spotted some people I knew from our street; Paddy McKenna, who had a stiff leg and walked funny and was about eight, and Locky Power, whose Da was a conductor on the trams.

I sat nervously into the desk, trying to take in my new surroundings. The room was small and bright. On one wall there was a big map of the world and a press with books and jotters stacked in a neat pile. There was a crucifix above the blackboard with Jesus hanging on it and a big window that looked out over the school yard.

Mr O'Reilly introduced me to the class.

'This is a new boy. His name is Martin McBride. He's only four-and-a-half so I don't want any of you older guys teaching him bad habits.'

The class laughed and immediately Paddy McKenna put up his hand and said: 'Please, Sir. I know him. He lives in our street.'

'Right, McKenna,' Mr O'Reilly said. 'You can look after him.'

As soon as Mr O'Reilly turned his back to write something on the blackboard, Charlie Pigeon leaned over and whispered: 'What does your Da do?'

I told him and he said: 'That's nothing. My Da's in the circus.'

'The circus?'

'Aye. He tames the lions and sometimes he rides the elephant. Have you any brothers and sisters?'

I shook my head.

'Not even a baby?'

'No,' I said.

'I've got eight brothers and ten sisters. All my sisters work in the mill. I've a brother in the army and another in the navy and another in the US Marines. My Ma's sixty and my Da's sixty-five.'

This sounded very old.

'Are you not scared they're going to die?' I asked.

'Not at all. My Da says he'll live to be a hundred. He drinks a bottle of whiskey every day and eats ten pig's feet for his breakfast.'

I was very impressed.

'Ten pig's feet?'

I heard the class grow silent and slowly looked up to find Mr O'Reilly staring at me.

'Stand up, McBride.'

I did as he said. I felt my face burn. Everybody was watching me.

'McBride. In this class you keep quiet. No one speaks unless I say so. Do you understand?'

'Yes, Sir.'

'What were you talking to Pigeon about?'

'His Da, Sir. He's a lion-tamer in the circus and sometimes he rides the elephant and he's sixty-five and drinks a bottle of whiskey every day and eats ten pig's feet for his breakfast.'

I heard a giggle go up among the other boys. Mr O'Reilly tried to keep his face straight.

'Does he now? And I'm sure he has pickled onions with them as well.'

Another laugh went up around the room. Mr O'Reilly waved the class to be quiet.

'McBride. One thing you should learn. Pigeon is a great storyteller. He knows the most amazing stories. Pigeon, sing that song you know for the class.'

Charlie Pigeon stood up and began to pipe in a screechy voice.

> They were baggy at the knees, they
>   were full of bugs and fleas.
> Those ould woolly drawers that me
>   granny used to wear . . .

Everybody laughed. When he had finished Charlie sat down again, well pleased with himself.

'You see, McBride. Pigeon is a born entertainer. His stories are even better than Grimm's fairy tales. But I wouldn't believe everything Pigeon tells me, if I was you. Now sit down and while you're in this class you'll only speak when you're spoken to. Do you understand?'

'Yes, Sir.'

'Ask the class, what I'll be if you disobey me.'

'Fit to be tied, Sir,' they chirped.

★ ★ ★

For the rest of the morning, I kept my mouth shut. Mr O'Reilly wrote letters on the blackboard and we had to copy them into our jotters. Mr O'Reilly came round the class and leaned over our shoulders to look. Every so often he would stop and help a boy, taking his hand and guiding the pencil slowly across the page. When he came to me, he looked at my work and nodded.

'Did you do this before?'

I told him about Sarah and how she read me stories from the picture books.

'Very good,' he said and moved on.

At eleven o'clock, we had a break for milk and to go to the toilet. Paddy McKenna took my hand and showed me where it was.

'I'll look after you,' he said. 'And I'll take you home after school.'

We had another break for lunch and then we all lined up and filed back into class. I was beginning to feel tired. Mr O'Reilly gave us cards with holes punched in them and coloured threads that we wove through the holes to make patterns. Then he gave us paper and crayons and asked us to draw a picture. I drew a man in the Celtic football strip.

About half-two, he took a big picture book out of the press and everybody got excited. He clapped his hands.

'Put your pencils and jotters away.'

There was a scramble to do as he said. Then Mr O'Reilly opened the picture book and began to read us a story about a man called Sinbad the Sailor. It was a wonderful story about all these strange lands. I was totally wrapped up in Mr O'Reilly's story when suddenly a loud clanging noise started ringing all over the school.

Mr O'Reilly closed the book and the class stood up. He blessed himself.

'In the name of the Father and the Son and the Holy Ghost. Hail Mary, full of grace . . . '

The class stumbled through to the end.

'Amen,' Mr O'Reilly said. 'Class dismissed. Go home safely and God willing, I'll see you all in the morning.'

★   ★   ★

I quickly got used to school. Every morning at a quarter-to-nine, Paddy McKenna would hobble up to our door. Sarah would give us both a ginger-snap biscuit and we'd walk round to Butler Street with our schoolbags on our backs. We'd play around the yard for a bit, the smaller boys at one end and the big boys at the other. Then at nine o'clock, the bell would ring and we'd form up in a line and march into class.

Every boy had to sit at the same desk all the time. Before class began, we would stand up and Mr O'Reilly would say the morning prayers. Then we'd sit down and Mr O'Reilly would take out a big roll book and call out each boy's name. We had to answer '*Anseo*', which was the Irish word for 'Present'. Mr O'Reilly would tick off each name and then put the roll book away and class would begin.

Mr O'Reilly's classes weren't all reading and writing. One day he brought in frog spawn and put it in a big fish bowl. Everybody crowded round to look, but all we could see was this green stuff floating there. It looked like the tapioca that Sarah gave me sometimes after our Sunday dinner. Then one morning, the frog spawn had bloomed into tadpoles and they swam all around the bowl like little black berries with their tails twitching.

Day by day, I watched the tadpoles as they grew legs and their skin changed to yellow and suddenly the bowl was full of baby frogs. I could see their eyes watching me when I looked in the bowl.

One day, Mr O'Reilly said it was time to let them go. We all formed in a line and marched round to the mill dam. Mr O'Reilly told Paddy McKenna to hold everybody back and he emptied the bowl into the dam and the frogs all swam away.

Mr O'Reilly called it the cycle of nature. He said it was just like the trees or the flowers. Old life died and new life took its place. When he said that I felt sad.

He had a gramophone and some days he would play records of these men with big deep voices singing operas. Other times, it was this music with orchestras that none of us had ever heard before. Mr O'Reilly called this classical music. He said it was the most beautiful music in the world and if you listened carefully, you could hear the angels singing.

We all listened carefully but we couldn't hear any angels, just these drums going boom-de-boom-de-boom and violins screeching and Danny Fitzgerald said if you listened to that stuff long enough it would give you a pain in your arse, so it would.

Mr O'Reilly also held quizzes which he called General Knowledge.

'Can any boy tell me why the chapel bells are on top of the church?' he asked one day.

Charlie Pigeon's hand shot up.

'Please, Sir. In case somebody steals them.'

Mr O'Reilly smiled.

'Well now, Pigeon. They might go in for that sort of thing round in Glenard where you come from, but I don't think the good people of Butler Street would want to steal the chapel bells.'

The class sniggered.

'I meant the Prods, sir. The Prods would steal them.'

Mr O'Reilly frowned.

'No, Pigeon. I don't think the Protestants would want to steal our chapel bells. They've got their own fine churches and their own bells.'

'They would, Sir. Me Ma says the Prods would steal the eyes out of your head, Sir. She says you couldn't trust them as far as you'd throw them.'

'Your mother's a bigot, Pigeon, and you can tell her I said that.'

'A what, Sir?'

'A bigot.'

'What's that, Sir?'

Mr O'Reilly turned back to the class.

'Think, boys. Why are the chapel bells on top of the church?'

Another hand went up.

'So that everybody can see them, Sir.'

'Good try,' Mr O'Reilly said. 'But incorrect.'

He tapped a ruler into the palm of his hand.

'The answer is simple if you think about it. C'mon now, think hard.'

I struggled to figure out the answer. Why were the bells on top of the church? And suddenly it seemed so obvious. I put up my hand.

'Please, Sir. So that everybody can hear them.'

Mr O'Reilly beamed.

'Of course, McBride. Full marks. The bells are on top of the church so that everyone can hear them. The higher up they are, the wider the sound travels. If there was a boy singing in the next street, you wouldn't hear him. But if he was standing on top of the roof, then you'd hear him.'

Charlie Pigeon's hand was up again.

'Please Sir, what's he doing standing on top of the roof?'

Mr O'Reilly groaned.

'I think that's enough General Knowledge for one day.'

★ ★ ★

I felt well pleased with myself. Most of the boys in the class were coming on for six. Some were seven and eight. I wasn't even five and yet I knew the answer to a question that had baffled them all.

Later in the school-yard, Locky Power came up to me.

'Somebody told you the answer,' he said.

'No,' I said. 'I worked it out for myself.'

'Somebody told you. You're a show-off. You're just looking for attention.'

'That's not true.'

'Yes, it is. You're just a show-off. You're

70

sucking up to O'Reilly.'

I felt like crying at the unfairness of it all but I fought back the tears. I had figured out the answer for myself like the teacher had asked, and now I was being accused of being a show-off. I pushed past Locky Power, but I filed the experience away. From then on, I only answered questions when Mr O'Reilly asked me directly.

★ ★ ★

Lunch break was half-an-hour. The teachers went to a room beside Mr Elwood's office and made tea. Those boys who lived near the school would go home but most of us stayed in the school-yard and played games and ate our sandwiches.

Every morning, Sarah would cut up two slices of bread for me, or sometimes a bap which she got from Andy Molloy's shop at the top of the street. She would put in different things like tomatoes, or cheese, or sometimes sliced eggs. I liked eggs best. Sometimes she would put in an apple and a scone as well.

I began to notice that some of the boys had only bread and butter in their sandwiches. Some had bread and jam. Sometimes boys would have no sandwiches at all.

I was standing in a corner of the yard one day when I saw Joey Graham watching me. Joey lived in Glenard like me, in a house in Etna Drive. As I chewed the bread, I realised he was hungry. I held out the newspaper that Sarah had wrapped the sandwiches in.

'Do you want one?'

Joey Graham grabbed a sandwich and stuck it in his mouth.

'What are they?' he said, munching quickly.

'Cheese.'

'Them's my favourites.'

I offered him another one and he took that too and gobbled it up.

'Did your Ma not make you any?' I asked.

'No. She never got up this morning. They were fighting last night, me Ma and Da. When they have a fight, me Ma stays in bed all day. Does yours fight?'

'No,' I said truthfully.

'Mine fights all the time,' he said.

I told this to Sarah when I got home.

'Poor Joey,' she said and shook her head. From then on, she put two extra sandwiches in my lunch every day.

'Just in case,' she said.

★ ★ ★

I began to understand what Mr O'Reilly meant about Charlie Pigeon. Charlie told lies all the time. But he didn't tell bad lies to hurt people. I think he told lies because it was exciting. It was really just stories he was making up in his head and he was living in them himself.

One day he told me his brother Paddy was in the US Marines and was getting a medal from the President for capturing fifty Japs over in Korea. Another time he said his sister, Hennie, was getting married to a film star and he was going to take her to Hollywood and get her a job in the pictures. Then, when she was rich, she was going to buy a big house with a swimming pool and a motor car and they were all going to live in America.

Some of the things he told me were true. He did have a big family. One day, after school, we were walking home along Flax Street and Charlie said: 'Why don't you come round to our house and play?'

Sarah had always said I was to come straight home from school, but since Highbury Gardens was the next street, I couldn't see any harm in it.

Charlie's house looked just the same as ours. It was in the middle of a long street with black roofs and smoking chimneys. But some things were different. The paint was peeling

73

off the front door and there was a window broken that somebody had fixed with a piece of cardboard.

The first thing I noticed when we got into Charlie's house was this funny smell, like the smell you got in Smithfield. The hall was filled with bags. So was the front room and the kitchen. They were everywhere, stuffed with rags and old clothes and shoes, so that you could hardly move.

This girl was sitting in the middle of it all. She had a cigarette hanging from her mouth and she was sorting out the rags. She looked up when we came in. 'You're home early, Charlie,' she said. 'Who's that with you?'

Charlie told her I was Marty McBride.

'Hello Marty. I'm Jeannie. Did ould O'Reilly slap you today?'

I said No and she laughed.

'I suppose you're hungry?'

Charlie said he was. Jeannie threw the end of her cigarette into the fireplace and squeezed between the sacks into the kitchen. I noticed a baby sleeping in a pram by the window and another baby with a dirty nappy playing on the floor.

'What's she doing?' I whispered to Charlie.

'She's getting the rags ready.'

'What for?'

'The market. Me ma's got a stall.'

I knew what the market was. It was a big place down the town where you could buy second-hand clothes and odds and ends. Sarah used to bring me there sometimes on a Friday morning to get fresh eggs from the farmers.

'Does she sell them?'

'Yes.'

'And where does she get them from?'

'Eddie Russell, the ragman.'

I looked around the room. There seemed to be dirt everywhere, in the corners and along the window sills. There was dirt on top of the dresser. Charlie Pigeon's house didn't look like our house at all, for Sarah was always washing and polishing and keeping our house clean.

I looked into the kitchen where Jeannie had gone. I could see plates and dishes stacked on a table and in the sink. There was a jam pot with a knife stuck in the top and a loaf of bread on the table. And hanging from the wall was a cage with a lovely yellow canary. It shook out its features and stretched its neck and started to sing.

Jeannie came back with two slices of bread and butter and gave us one each. 'You'll have to make that do you,' she said. 'There'll be nothing more to eat till Ma gets home.'

She sat back down beside the fire and

continued sorting the rags.

I wasn't sure about eating the bread with all the dirt in the house, and anyway, I wasn't hungry, but I didn't want to offend anybody so I just nibbled it a bit, till Charlie took it off me and ate it himself.

The door opened and a big fella came in. He was wearing a vest and there were all these black hairs on his chest and a tattoo of a heart on his arm.

He winked at us and said, 'Where's my clean shirt, Jeannie?'

'How would I know?' she said. 'Wherever you left it.'

'It's usually on the back of the door, but it's not there now.'

Jeannie rustled among the rags and pulled out a shirt.

'Here,' she said. 'See if that one fits you.'

The big fella examined the shirt and checked the buttons, then he closed the door and went back up the stairs.

We went out to the front and sat on the step. A couple more kids were pushing a broken cart across the grass. I asked Charlie who they were and he said they were his brothers.

'How many's in your family altogether?'

Charlie wiped his nose on the sleeve of his coat and started to count.

'There's me Ma and Da and then there's Frankie, that's him was looking for his shirt. And Jeannie and Hennie and Cissie and Mary. They work in the mill. Then there's our Sadie. She works in Billy O'Carroll's shop. Then there's our Paddy. He's in the Marines. Then there's Billy and Geordie. Then there's wee Annie and the twins. And then there's the baby. How many's that?'

I gave up trying to count.

'Do you all live in the same house?'

'Aye. But Cissie's getting married in August. Her boy's in the RAF and he's got his own plane. He said he'd give me a ride in it some time. She's going to live with him in England.'

'Where does everybody sleep?'

Charlie gave me an odd look.

'In the bed.'

'And is there enough room for everybody?'

'Sure. There's loads of room.'

I wasn't convinced. I tried to figure out how everyone could manage in the tiny house and how they moved around in the rooms filled with rags. Where did they all eat? How did they all wash themselves? How did they get to sleep, cramped together in the little rooms? I felt a sneaking fascination for Charlie Pigeon's family. All those brothers and sisters, all the excitement, all the drama,

77

all the wonderful adventures of their lives. I had only myself and Sarah and Isaac. Secretly, I envied Charlie Pigeon.

When I got home, I said to Sarah: 'Why is there not more of us?'

'More of us? Are you joking? If there was more of us, Isaac's money would never stretch.'

'But everybody else has brothers and sisters and I've only got myself.'

Sarah was knitting. She put down the needles and the wool on the chair beside her.

'Are you lonely?'

'Sometimes.'

She cuddled me close.

'But you've got Isaac. He takes you everywhere. And you've got me.'

'I'd love a brother or sister,' I said.

Sarah picked up the knitting again and the needles went clack, clack, clack.

'Would you not get one, Mammy? Please? I'd help you with it, so you wouldn't have to do all the work.'

But Sarah was no longer interested.

'I'll see,' she said.

I knew she would do nothing about it. Whenever Sarah said 'I'll see', it meant nothing was going to happen.

★ ★ ★

78

One day, as we were coming home from school, I asked Paddy McKenna why he walked funny and why a boy of eight was in Senior Infants and not in Second Class where he belonged.

'I got polio,' he said. 'And I had to stay in hospital.'

This was something new.

'What's it like?'

'It makes you sick. And it hurt my leg. I can't bend my knee. Look.'

He rolled up his trousers and showed me the wasted knee.

'I can bend the other one, but I can't bend this one. That's what the polio done.'

'How did you get it?'

He shrugged.

'I don't know. The doctors think I got it from the water.'

'The water?'

'Aye. They think the germs are in the water. But they don't know for sure. I'm better now, but I can't bend my knee.'

'Maybe you'll be able to bend it when you grow up.'

Paddy McKenna shook his head.

'I don't think so.'

★ ★ ★

After Christmas, there was a new boy in the class. He was small and shy and he huddled in his new blazer as if it was going to swallow him up. Mr O'Reilly introduced him.

'This is Gerard Boyle. I want you all to make him welcome.'

Charlie Pigeon leaned across and whispered: 'I know him. He lives round in Holmdene Gardens. He used to go the Sacred Heart school. He's an orphan.'

I knew what an orphan was. A boy with no mother and father. Every week Sarah gave me sixpence for the Orphans' Home in Kircubbin.

'But why is he not in the Home?' I asked.

'These people adopted him. But they're not his real Ma and Da.'

I looked at Gerard Boyle again. He sat quiet, afraid to look sideways or make a sound. I felt sorry for him. No mother or father. Adopted. It seemed to me the worst possible thing that could ever happen to you in your whole life.

★ ★ ★

Towards the end of June, we had our last day before the summer holidays. Mr O'Reilly said everybody was to ask their mother to send in something special and to bring our own cups

80

and we'd have a party.

Sarah baked buns and put them in a bag and Isaac gave me the money to buy a bottle of American Cream Soda. That was my favourite lemonade.

After he said the prayers and read the roll, Mr O'Reilly said we weren't going to have any lessons today. Instead, he was going to read us a story. He got down his big story book and told everyone to remain silent. Then he told us the tale of Gulliver's Travels.

This was a brilliant story about this man who sails in a ship and finds himself in a land where everybody is a giant. Then he sails again and finds himself in a land where everybody is a midget.

When he had finished reading, Mr O'Reilly asked each boy what he was going to do for the summer holidays. Most of them were doing nothing. One boy said he was going to Bangor on the train. Charlie Pigeon said he was going to America to see his brother, Paddy, who had just got a second medal from the President for capturing another fifty Japs and the top Jap general. He said the President was sending them the money and his Ma was getting a new fur coat.

I said I was going to Portstewart to stay in Mrs McMahon's boarding house. It was something we did every year. I didn't think it was anything special, but I could see some of the boys looking at me with envy when I told Mr O'Reilly about the swings and the paddling pool and the boats in the harbour.

After the break, we had the party. Mr O'Reilly put a big table cloth over his desk and laid out all the cakes and buns and apples and oranges that people's mothers had sent in. He made a speech. He said we were the best class he had ever taught and he was proud of us, but time marches on and next year we wouldn't be infants any more but would be First Class. He said he'd miss us all, especially Pigeon, who kept us entertained all year, and he called on him to sing us a song.

Charlie stood up and cleared his throat and everybody laughed. Then he sang:

My Aunt Jane, she called me in,
She gave me tea out of her wee tin.
Half a bap, with sugar on the top.
And three black lumps out of her wee
    shop.

We all clapped and Mr O'Reilly said we could have as much to eat and drink as we wanted but to behave like Christians and not be pushing and shoving.

We stood around Mr O'Reilly's desk and filled our cups with lemonade and ate cakes and buns and barmbrack and Charlie Pigeon put up his hand and said: 'Please Sir, Joey Graham has a bigger cup and he got more lemonade than me.'

Mr O'Reilly said for God's sake would you ever stop arguing. You should all be happy to be going on your holidays. Then somebody told a joke about Paddy Irishman, Paddy Englishman and Paddy Scotchman. We all laughed and Joey Graham stuffed his face so much, he was sick all over his jersey and Mr O'Reilly had to take him out to the toilets to clean him up.

Then the bell rang for three o'clock and we all went home.

3

One day, Sarah said to me: 'I'm thinking of taking you out of Holy Cross. They're not stretching you.'

This wasn't good news. I was happy in Holy Cross. I was in third class and had made my First Communion and Confession.

'Where will I go, Mammy?'

'You'll go to the Christian Brothers.'

This was what I was afraid of.

The Christian Brothers were a religious teaching order and they had a tough reputation. Their school was down the town in Donegall Street. Sarah organised an interview and we went to meet Brother Byrne who was the principal. He was a thin man with bony hands and hairs growing out of his nostrils. He wore this shiny black soutane and a collar like the priests and he spoke with a country accent.

He took us into his office: 'Why do you want him here?' he asked Sarah.

Sarah smiled politely.

'Because I think he'll do better. He'll have to do his Qualifying in a couple of years and I hear good reports about your school.'

Brother Byrne looked pleased.

'We get good results, but the boys have to work hard. We don't put up with slacking.'

He looked at me.

'What's nine times seven?'

'Sixty-three,' I said.

'Let's hear you read.'

He took a book off the shelf and opened it at a chapter and I read aloud for him.

'Very good,' he said. 'Name me a Corporal Work of Mercy.'

'Visiting the sick.'

'General Knowledge. Where does the water come from, that's in the water-taps?'

'From a reservoir.'

'And what's a reservoir?'

'A reservoir is a big lake that collects all the water and then it gets cleaned and is sent out all over the city to people's houses.'

'Do you have Irish?'

'*Tá.*'

'*Caidé mar atá tú?*'

'*Tá mé go mait, go raibh mait agat.*'

Brother Byrne smiled.

'He can start on Monday,' he said.

Next was the business of telling Mr Elwood. He wasn't pleased.

'He's doing very well here. Why do you want to take him out?'

'Because I think he'll do better with the Brothers.'

'The Brothers don't always get good results. They're only interested in the brainy ones.'

'I think he's brainy enough.'

'Very well,' Mr Elwood said. 'But if it doesn't work out, you needn't bring him back.'

And he showed us the door.

★   ★   ★

Brother Byrne put me in Fourth class, which meant that everybody was a year older than me.

'He's bright for his age. He'll be well able for it.'

Our teacher was a man called Brother Delargey. He was tall and his hair stuck out like the bristles on a yard brush. He had a face like a ripe tomato. He taught us reading, writing, arithmetic and Irish history. Brother Delargey was very strong on the oppression that the English heaped on the Irish down all the years. He talked about the Penal Days as if they happened only last week.

He taught us about Red Hugh O'Donnell and Hugh O'Neill and Patrick Sarsfield. He taught us about the Battle of Aughrim, which the Irish should have won, except they were commanded by this Frenchman called Saint Ruth who got his head blown off by a cannon ball in the opening minutes of the battle, so nobody knew the plans. He told us about the traitor Luttrel, who was in charge of the cavalry and deserted the battlefield and left the poor Irish infantrymen to be slaughtered.

'The dead after Aughrim stretched for four miles. Can you imagine it, boys? Dead Irish soldiers covered the fields like sheep. The English took no prisoners. But Patrick Sarsfield sailed for France and joined the French army and got his revenge on the English fighting with the Irish Brigade.'

Brother Delargey filled our heads full of Irish history and the wrongs the English had inflicted on us. He taught us about the United Irishmen and the Rebellion of 1798 and the heroic Presbyterians of Antrim and Down. He taught us about the Famine and the poor people being forced to eat grass because there was no food for them.

He taught us rebel songs, which he said the English had tried to suppress, but they lived on in the hearts of the people because the Irish were indomitable and would never be put down.

At Boolavogue, as the sun was setting,
O'er the bright May meadows of Shelmalier,
A rebel hand set the heather blazing,
And brought the neighbours from far and
    near.
Then Father Murphy of old Kilcormack,
Spurred up the rocks with a warning cry;
Arm, arm, he cried, for I've come to lead
    you.
For Ireland's freedom, we'll fight and die.

Brother Delargey's red face would be even redder from singing. He would smile and say: 'Never forget your country's history, boys. History is what makes us what we are.'

★ ★ ★

Every day, I travelled to school on the bus with a boy called Larry Devine who lived in Holmdene Gardens. He was tough and he knew things.

One day when we were coming home, he said: 'Remind me to show you something when we get off.'

There was a look in his eye.

When the bus stopped, he led me to an entry at the back of the Forum picture house. He looked around to make sure there was nobody about and then he took a magazine

88

out of his school-bag.

'Take a gander at that,' he said.

On the front cover was a picture of a girl in a bathing suit. I felt a warm stirring in my groin.

'Open it,' he said. 'It get's better.'

I turned the pages. There were pictures of girls in bras and knickers and black stockings. They were sitting on the bonnets of cars or in deck chairs in the sun. They were all smiling as if they enjoyed having their pictures taken like this.

One girl had no bra but held her hands over her breasts. You could see a nipple peeping out. They seemed the most gorgeous creatures I had ever seen, all the more exciting because of the bold way they were displaying themselves for the camera.

Larry Devine took the magazine back.

'Is your micky hard?' he said.

I felt my penis straining against my underpants and shook my head.

'You're a liar,' he said. 'Everybody's micky gets hard when they look at dirty pictures.'

★ ★ ★

Of course, I had to tell about it in Confession. I was discovering that Confession was one of the drawbacks to being a Catholic. While it was great that you could go to the priest and have your sins forgiven, once they got you started, they expected you to go every week.

Brother Delargey left nothing to chance. Every Friday afternoon, when school was over, he marched us next door to St Patrick's church and we queued up to tell our sins. There'd be forty of us waiting to go into the dark confession box and bare our souls. I came to dread Friday afternoons.

That week, I knelt and examined my conscience. That meant I had to make a list of all the sins I'd committed since the last time. It was a bit of waste of time for I knew there was only one sin that really mattered. I had looked at dirty pictures and taken pleasure from it. I glanced at Larry Devine, sitting along the row from me, and he grinned back.

My turn came at last. I went into the box. I could hear the priest mumbling forgiveness to the boy on the other side. Then the shutter opened and I could see the shadow of his face in the darkness.

'Bless me Father, for I have sinned.'

'Yes, my child.'

'I told lies, Father. I was disobedient. I used bad words. I was cheeky to my mother . . . ' I went through the usual litany.

'Anything else, my child?'

'I looked at dirty pictures, Father.'

There was a pause.

'In what way dirty, my child?'

'Pictures of women with no clothes on.'

'Where did you see these pictures?'

'In a magazine. Another boy showed me.'

The priest's voice became grave.

'Did you take pleasure from these pictures?'

'Yes, Father.'

'Did you touch yourself?'

'No, Father.'

'Do you ever touch yourself?'

I didn't know what he was talking about.

'No, Father.'

'Tell me, my son. Have you ever been with girls?'

I thought of Eileen Toner and the kiss-and-chase games we sometimes played on the brickyard.

'Yes, Father.'

'Did you touch their bodies?'

I was beginning to sweat now. This wasn't the usual matter of reeling off a list of misdemeanours. It was turning into an inquisition. Outside, I could hear the restless shuffling of the others, waiting their turn. I thought of Brother Delargey. He'd be wondering exactly what sins I'd committed that were taking so long to tell.

'I kissed them, Father.'

'I asked if you touched their bodies.'

'I put my arms around them.'

'Their bodies, child? Their bodies?'

I didn't know what he meant.

'I held their hands.'

'Did you touch them intimately?'

I didn't know what intimately meant, so I just said: 'I don't think so.'

There was another pause.

'My son. Your body is the temple of the Holy Ghost. You must never defile it by impure thoughts or acts. You must never touch yourself or another person in an impure way. Above all, you must never enter a girl's body unless you are married to her.'

I thought I was hearing things. Enter a girl's body? What in the name of God was he talking about?

'Improper pictures are meant to excite you and looking at them will lead you on to other sins. Promise me you won't look at such pictures again.'

'I promise, Father.'

'And refrain from bad company. Bad company can be the occasion of sin.'

'Yes, Father.'

'For your penance say a decade of the Rosary.'

I heard him start the absolution and I sighed with relief. The shutter closed and I was out in the church again. I was certain that all those eyes looking at me were seeing into my soul.

* ★ ★ ★

This business of entering a girl's body intrigued me. I couldn't figure it out. Where were you supposed to enter her in the first place? Eventually I went to Larry Devine. He just laughed.

'He means a ride.'

'A ride?'

'Yeah. It's what your Ma and Da do. When your Ma has a baby in her belly, your Da has to stick his micky into her to make it come out.'

'But where does he stick it?'

Larry Devine looked at me as if I had two heads.

'For God's sake. He sticks it in her snatch and he wiggles it around and that makes the baby come out.'

This was truly amazing information.

'Her snatch?'

'Yeah. The thing between her legs.'

I was horrified. I felt sure Larry Devine was making this up. I could never imagine Sarah

93

and Isaac doing something like that. Not in a million years.

★ ★ ★

Aloysius McVeigh was my best pal. We called him Aly because Aloysius was too hard to say. We used to go for rides on our bikes together over the brickyard and down Butler Street and all around the district.

I had been at Sarah for months to get me a bike but she would say: 'Bikes are far too dangerous. What's going to happen if you fall off and crack your skull? You'll look a right sight then.'

But I kept at her.

'Spa Doherty's got a bike.'

'Oh, he would, wouldn't he?' Sarah would say. 'And his Da running around taking the bread out of the mouths of starving children. Why wouldn't he have a bike?'

Eventually I wore her down and Isaac went off to Smithfield and came back with this second-hand Raleigh that had flat tyres and a broken wheel and the chain hanging off. It looked like a wreck but Isaac said it was a bargain and all it needed was a wee job done and a lick of paint.

He got out his tools and started banging and thumping out in the yard. All the time,

Sarah was wringing her hands and saying: 'He's far too young for a bike. I don't like this at all.'

Isaac took me out to the entry at the back and showed me how to put my feet on the pedals and turn the wheels. He held onto the seat till I was able to ride the bike by myself. He showed me how to indicate when I was turning right and left and said: 'When you go out now, remember the Rules of the Road.'

And Sarah said: 'Rules of the Road? Mother of God. What are you trying to do, Isaac? Put ideas in his head?'

Aly had a grandmother and she was very old and she was a religious maniac. She must have been about ninety and she was a bigger rebel than Aunt Minnie McCrory and Willie Toner put together. She was always talking about Henry Joy McCracken and Brave Michael Dwyer and his Mountain Men. She had all these holy medals and scapulars and sacred relics and she was always going around the house sprinkling holy water and scaring the cat.

Whenever I came into Aly's house, Granny McVeigh would grab me with her bony hand and say: 'Are you a good boy?'

'Yes, Mrs McVeigh.'

'Do you say your prayers?'

95

'Yes.'

'Do you say a prayer for the Pope's intentions?'

'Yes,' I would lie.

Granny McVeigh would pat my hand and give me a peppermint.

'Don't forget your prayers, boy. Don't forget your holy religion. You're a Croppy and you should be proud. The Croppies will never lie down.'

I didn't know what she was talking about, but I said Yes.

The first time I called for Aly with my new bike, Granny McVeigh pinned a holy medal on my chest.

She said: 'That medal came the whole way from Knock. It was blessed specially by the Holy Father himself and it will keep you out of all harm. Don't take it off. Do you hear me, boy?'

And she sprinkled holy water on me and watched as I made my wobbling journey down the street, a crowd of kids running behind shouting: 'Hey McBride. Give us a go on your bike.'

★ ★ ★

I was learning that Ardoyne wasn't all Catholics like us. At the top of Berwick Road there were Protestant streets. You knew the Protestant streets because every Twelfth of July they hung out Union Jacks and painted the kerbstones red, white and blue. They would paint the gable walls with pictures of this man on a white horse with a curly wig on his head and a sword pointing.

I asked Isaac about it and he said the man on the wall was King Billy and he was dead years ago and it was all to do with history and very complicated and I'd never be able to make head nor tail of it.

But I wasn't satisfied so I asked Kevin Trainor.

'King Billy was the head of the Orangemen,' he said.

I already knew who the Orangemen were. They were the ones who wouldn't let people get the good jobs in the shipyards.

'And why do they put his picture on the walls?'

'Because he killed all these Catholics at the Battle of the Boyne.'

'What'd he do that for?'

'Because he was an Orangeman and they don't like us. They cut a fella's micky off last week. It was in the paper.'

This was shocking news.

'Cut his micky off?'

'Aye. With a Stanley knife.'

97

'And it said that in the paper? Micky, I mean?'

Kevin Trainor thought for a moment.

'I think it said small intestine. That's the word the doctors use. But they cut it off, all right.'

I didn't know any Protestants but I didn't like the sound of them. People who ran around with Stanley knives cutting fellas' mickeys off couldn't be nice. Bobby McAllister said it was because we believed in the Virgin Mary and they didn't. I found the whole business very complicated, just like Isaac said.

There were no Protestants in our street but Aly said there were Protestants round in Hooker Street. He said their name was Taylor and they went to Everton school and that was how he knew. We decided to go and have a look at them.

I didn't know what to expect, but I wouldn't have been surprised if they had horns on their heads. I remembered what Sarah told me about the Titanic and the way the Orangemen had cursed the Pope and how God let the sea drown them. It seemed to me that these Taylors would be bad pills altogether.

We finally tracked them to the waste ground at Butler Street. There were two of them and they were kicking a football around. They looked exactly the same as us. They had the same scuffed shoes and snotty noses and torn cardigans. There were no obvious signs that they were Protestants. I was disappointed. We took a good look at them and then got on our bikes and went home.

★ ★ ★

Aly McVeigh said: 'I'm fed up going round the same streets all the time. Why don't we go somewhere different? Why don't we go for a spin up to Carr's Glen?'

Carr's Glen was up beyond Ballysillan playing fields. I used to go there sometimes with Isaac on our Sunday walks. To get there, we had to pass the Protestant streets at Berwick Road. As we approached, Aly slowed down and got off his bike.

'Remember,' he said, 'if any Prods catch you and ask you to curse the Pope, you have to say No.'

'What are you talking about?'

'They caught Hughie Lavery last week and asked him to say the Lord's Prayer and he got it mixed up with the Hail Mary and when he got to Holy Mary, Mother of God, they knew he was a Catholic for sure and made him sing

The Sash. Then they hit him because he wouldn't curse the Pope. If you curse the Pope, it's a mortal sin and you go straight to Hell when you die. But if they kill you for not cursing the Pope, you go to Heaven right away and God gives you a special place.'

I didn't like the sound of this at all. I thought about what Kevin Trainor told me about some fella getting his small intestine cut off. I supposed there'd be lots of blood.

'Don't look nervous,' Aly said. 'That's the whole trick. Just look normal.'

I got back on my bike and tried to look normal. I glanced at my jersey and there was Granny McVeigh's holy medal. I might as well have hung a sign round my neck saying I AM A CATHOLIC. So, I took it off and put it in my pocket and with my heart thumping in my chest, we crossed into the Protestant streets.

They were practically deserted. There were a few Union Jacks hanging from the windows and King Billy on his horse on a gable wall. There were a couple of men sitting on their front steps smoking cigarettes just like the men in our street. It took us a few minutes to pass through and then we were in the safety of the playing fields.

Aly laughed and stuck up his thumb. I felt like one of those heroes from the comic strips

I was reading, Dan Dare or Captain Courageous. I leaned on the handlebars and coasted to a halt.

We hung around Carr's Glen throwing stones in the river and watching them make a splash and then it was time to go home.

'Let's go back the long way,' I said.

This meant a detour across the playing fields but it cut out the Protestant streets.

Aly said: 'You're scared.'

'No, I'm not.'

'Yes, you are. You're a scaredy cat.'

'Right,' I said. 'We'll go your way.'

We got back on our bikes. I was annoyed with Aly. It seemed stupid to be putting ourselves in danger a second time just so he could boast about it later. But if I didn't go, I knew he would tell everybody and I'd be shamed forever.

I lowered my head and the first street went flashing by. I felt my heart start to thump again. In the distance, I could see the safe Catholic streets of Glenard and the smoke curling from the little chimneys. I could see the back wheel of Aly's bike and his legs moving in rhythm with the pedals. Then suddenly, I saw him swerve.

I looked up in time to see a bread van move away from the footpath. I pulled hard on the brakes but it was too late. The bike careered out of control and I went smashing into the van. The last thing I remembered was the blue sky and the ground rushing up to meet me like something I'd seen in the pictures.

★ ★ ★

I woke up in the Mater hospital with my leg in plaster and bandages round my head and aches all over my body. Sarah and Isaac were sitting beside the bed.

'Thank God you're all right,' Sarah said. She put her arms around me and hugged me. 'It was the holy medal saved you. Where is it?'

I tried to think but my head was confused.

'It must be lost,' I said.

'Well, you're one lucky boy,' she said and took something out of her pocket. 'Nellie McCabe's just back from Knock and guess what she brought me?'

She held up another holy medal.

★ ★ ★

I was a hero on the street. Aly had told everybody I'd got run over while trying to escape from a gang of Protestants who wanted to cut off my small intestine because I wouldn't curse the Pope.

'We'll get the bastards,' Kevin Trainor said.

One of the big boys, Brian Quinn, ruffled my hair and said: 'Don't worry about them. They're only a crowd of yella-bellies.'

People wanted to write their names on my plaster. Eileen Toner wrote E L M and drew a heart with an arrow in it and said she'd be my girl, if I liked. I told her I was too young to have a girl.

Paddy McKenna came hobbling up to me and said: 'You and me's the same. We've both got bad legs.'

'Mine's getting better,' I said.

Paddy nodded. 'I suppose you're right.'

Bobby McAllister said I shouldn't be walking till my leg was better but I could referee the football games and if the peelers came I was to hold the ball, for they'd hardly take the ball off a fella with a broken leg who'd just got run over with a bread van. Spa Doherty's Da came along and said I was a brave wee buck, so I was, and put his hand in his pocket and gave me half a crown. I wondered why I hadn't got my leg broke long ago.

★   ★   ★

All the time, I was wondering about why I didn't have any brothers or sisters. Everywhere I looked in Ardoyne, I saw big families. The only other boy who had no brothers or sisters, was Gerard Boyle and everybody knew he was adopted and felt sorry for him.

But the big families were nearly always poor and the kids wore hand-me-down clothes and they were always going around hungry. I began to think that maybe Sarah didn't want any more children because they cost too much money.

One day I said to her: 'Would you not even get me a wee brother? Just to keep me company? Everybody else has brothers and sisters and I've got nobody.'

Sarah looked at me. I thought she was sad. She took out a handkerchief and blew her nose.

'Martin,' she said, 'I never told you this before, but now you're old enough. You do have a brother and sister.'

'Where are they?'

'They're up in Heaven. They're watching over you. They're your wee guardian angels.'

I knew what that meant. It meant they were dead.

'What happened, Mammy?'

'They just came too soon. That's what happens sometimes. They weren't ready for this world. So God took them back to Heaven.'

'Do they have any names?'

'Yes. Your sister is called Margaret. And your brother is called Peter. Margaret is fourteen now and Peter is twelve. And they're up there in Heaven praying for us every day.'

I looked at Sarah and I could see the big tears starting in her eyes. Whatever this was about, it was making her sad and I didn't want that, so I kissed her cheek.

'That's great news, Mammy,' I said.

4

At the start of the new school year, Brother Delargey made a little speech: 'Boys, this is a very important year. This is one of the most important years of your lives. Because this year, boys, we sit the Qualifying.'

He took out his big leather strap and laid it on the desk for all to see.

'The Qualifying is your passport to success. If you get the Qualifying, you go to grammar school, and that opens the door for all the good, well-paid jobs like the bank and the civil service. It even opens the door of the University itself where you can go on to become doctors or lawyers or engineers. Or even, if God pleases to send you a vocation, a priest or a Christian Brother.

'Now, boys, the people in power in the Government would be delighted if you failed the Qualifying. They want to keep you down, just like they kept your poor parents down. They want you to have the lowly jobs while their own crowd in the Orange lodges and the Masonic Order keep the best jobs for themselves.

'They don't want to see a Catholic boy

getting on. Nothing gives them more pain. They'd love for you to emigrate to England or America. They'd even pay your fare, just to see the back of you.'

He brought the strap down hard and the desk rattled and we all sat up straight.

'But we're not going to please them, are we boys?'

'No, Sir,' we carolled.

'We are not, boys. We're all going to pass that Qualifying. Even if I have to tan the skin off the stupidest boy in this class, we're going to pass that exam and spite them. We're all going to pass the Qualifying and woe betide any boy who gets in my way.'

He worked us like slaves. Compositions, Essays, General Knowledge. Geography, History, Addition, Subtraction, Division. We learnt off the multiplication tables. We learnt the capital cities of the world. We learnt verbs, adjectives, nouns and pronouns.

He got hold of previous exam papers and every month we sat the mock Qualifying and every month he marked the papers and told us who had passed. He concentrated on the weaker students, keeping them back after school and going over the mistakes they had made till they got it right. Brother Delargey was a man with a mission.

One day Larry Devine said to me: 'Fuck

this for a lark. I'd rather emigrate.'

All this studying meant I had hardly any time for my pals. Sarah was well pleased. Kids would come to the door and ask if I was coming out to play football and she would say: 'He can't come out. He's studying for his Qualifying.'

But at weekends, I got a chance to relax. On Saturday afternoons Aly and I would go to the matinee in the Forum picture house. It was four pence to get in and the place would be in uproar while everybody waited for the Big Picture to start. The commissionaire was called Paddy Mallarkey and he was a tall, thin man with a bristly moustache.

He would run around, grabbing kids by the ears and hauling them back to their seats. He would curse and swear. 'Jesus Christ,' he would shout. 'Can yiz not sit still? Yiz are like a flock of sparrows. I'd have an easier job minding mice at a crossroads.'

Eventually, the lights would dim and a cheer would go up. As the credits started to roll, a hush would come over the cinema. Paddy Mallarkey would take out his Woodbines and lean over the back rail and shout: 'Yiz have been warned. Anybody moves from their seats again and they're out on their arse.'

Afterwards, we would go to Freddie

Fusco's chip shop and buy a bag of chips and a bottle of Coca-Cola. Freddie got a juke-box that winter. It was a big silver machine with shining chrome and flashing lights. You could play a record for six pence or three for a shilling. A lot of the bigger boys started hanging around Freddie's. They wore these tight jeans and long jackets that came down to their knees. They grew their sideburns thick and called themselves Teddy boys.

One Saturday afternoon we were eating our chips when a Teddy boy put money in the juke-box and this wonderful music came out. I asked Aly did he know what the song was and he said it was called 'Heartbreak Hotel' and the man who was singing it was Elvis Presley. I had discovered rock 'n' roll.

At night, after I finished my homework, I would scan the dial on the radio looking for a station that played this exciting music. One of the boys in school had a record-player and some evenings I'd go to his house and we'd play Elvis Presley and Little Richard and a new singer who was coming along, called Buddy Holly.

Sarah hated it. She said it was immoral. She called it the devil's music and said it was created by evil men in America to corrupt the youth and lead them astray. Brother Delargey hated it even more. He said it was a plot to destroy our own native culture, which everyone knew was among the finest in the world, you just had to look at John McCormack. He said any boy who mentioned rock 'n' roll in his class could expect six of the best.

Everybody started wearing jeans like the Teddy boys, and I was going around in these baggy flannel trousers which were regulation school uniform. I was ashamed to be seen in them. So one day, I asked Sarah to buy me a pair of jeans and she almost had a fit. She said jeans were low-class and only suitable for gather-ups and no child of hers would ever be seen in such a corner-boy outfit as long as she had breath in her body.

Isaac said: 'Och, now Sarah. Sure, they're all wearing them.'

Sarah said they could all put their hands in the fire but that didn't mean I had to do it too.

But I kept at her till she gave in and reluctantly took me to a shop in North Street and I got my first pair of jeans.

★ ★ ★

The winter wore on and into the spring. The days lengthened. The daffodils, which Isaac had planted in the front garden, began to push through the earth. I watched the sparrows build nests under the gutters of the house.

Brother Delargey was driving us like a lunatic. As exam time approached, he began to bring us in on Saturday mornings. We'd be the only people in the cold, empty school. It was an odd feeling, huddled together in our desks, repeating verbs and participles and clauses after Brother Delargey, while outside the window traffic roared along Donegall Street.

Exam day came. Part of the examination was an intelligence test and then came the main exam. There were two papers. One in English and the other in Maths.

I was confident about the English paper, because my compositions always got good marks. I was less confident about the Maths paper, but Brother Delargey had told us to answer every question and to watch the clock so we didn't run out of time. I took his advice and finished the paper with minutes to spare.

After the exam was over, we had to wait for the results. The school regime changed completely and Brother Delargey was like a different man. The leather strap was put away. Instead of lessons, we got more Irish history. The great battles we had won, Patrick Pearse and the men of 1916 and the sacrifices they

111

had made that Ireland would be free. He even took us to the pictures to see *The Song of Bernadette* and everybody cheered when Our Lady appeared.

On the day of the results, we trooped into class and sat nervously at our desks. Boys nudged each other and said: 'Cheer up, for God's sake. It's only a bloody exam. It's not the end of the world.' But each of us knew it could be. Brother Delargey came in and it was easy to see he was well pleased.

'Boys,' he said. 'I have great news. We've got the best results of any school in Belfast. Out of the forty boys who sat for the Qualifying, thirty-two have passed.'

He licked his lips.

'This is the best result the school has ever achieved and I'm proud of you all. You've shown them that a Catholic boy from the back streets of Belfast is a match for any boy in a swanky blazer that goes to Methodist College.'

And he proceeded to read out the names of those who had passed. My name was among them. I felt a wonderful wave of relief. I couldn't wait to rush home to tell Sarah and Isaac.

I looked around the class. A few boys had their heads down and were close to tears. Larry Devine was among them. I went up to

112

him afterwards in the school yard.

'I'm sorry you didn't pass,' I said. 'Maybe you can repeat it next year.'

He tried to smile.

'Not everybody can pass. They have to fail so many, otherwise they'd say it was all a fix.'

'I'm still sorry,' I said and put my arm around his shoulder but he pushed it away.

'It doesn't matter. I don't want to go to the grammar school anyway. All it'll be is more bog-trotters like Delargey beating the shite out of you. Our Jim's getting me a job in the mill when I'm fourteen.'

★ ★ ★

I woke one morning in August to hear Isaac singing from the bathroom:

*I am the wee Faloorie Man, a rattling
    roaring Irishman.
I will do whatever I can, for I am the
    wee Faloorie Man.*

Downstairs was the smell of eggs cooking for breakfast. I looked at the clock beside the bed and saw that it was already ten past eight. I cursed myself for sleeping in. This was the morning I had been looking forward to all summer, the morning we went to Portstewart for our two weeks' holidays.

I wiped the sleep from my eyes and pulled on my clothes. The previous night, Sarah had left out a clean shirt and a new pair of jeans. I looked into the bathroom and Isaac was standing in front of the mirror with his shaving razor in his hand and his face covered in soap.

He turned and winked.

'All set, Marty?'

I told him I was.

'Game ball,' Isaac said and continued shaving.

Downstairs, Sarah was laying out plates of bacon and eggs and fried bread and big thick sausages, but I wasn't hungry. I was too excited at the prospect of the holiday. I sat at the table and she poured a mug of tea.

'Tsk, tsk,' she said. 'Your father always leaves everything to the last minute. John Rea's coming at nine o'clock and he isn't even shaved yet.'

This was all part of the ritual. At five to nine, John Rea would come out of his house and stand at his gate and sniff the air. Then he would walk to the taxi that was already parked across the street from our house. He would give the windscreen a wipe with a cloth and then he'd get into the front seat and drive to the top of the street and turn round and come back down again so that he was outside our door for nine o'clock on the button.

Going on our holidays was the only time we ever used a taxi. In the district, it was considered a frivolous expense, even though John Rea gave us a discount because we were neighbours. But at holiday time, Isaac threw caution to the winds and drove to the railway station in style.

'To Hell with poverty,' he would say. 'We never died of a winter yet. And anyway, you can't take it with you.'

John Rea would open the doors and we would climb in and sit on the plush upholstery and smell the rich scent of the leather for John Rea kept his taxi in tip-top condition. He would take the cases from Isaac and stow them in the boot and then he'd get into the driving seat again and honk the horn and off we'd go.

I often looked into the mirror and watched the wistful faces of the kids standing in the road as the taxi bore us away down the street on our holidays.

'Brave day, Isaac,' John Rea would say as we turned into Flax Street and the towering mill chimneys.

'Thanks be to God, John,' Isaac would say.

'A decent bit of weather makes a holiday, Isaac.'

115

'I think the rest is the main thing.'

'But the weather has to be right. Bad weather can ruin a holiday.'

'Only if you let it. Weather's all in the mind. You know there's some people and they're never happy. They'd complain that the Sahara Desert was too cold.'

'You never said a truer word, Isaac.'

They would chat away while my mind teemed with images: the shining strand at Portstewart, the mist settling on Inishowen Head, divers at the Herring Pond, white sails on the flat sea beyond Portrush. At York Street station, John Rea would pull in at the taxi rank and jump out and open the boot and retrieve our cases. Isaac would give him five shillings and tell him to keep the change. John Rea would shake Isaac's hand and wish us the best and if there was another train due in, he would wait in the hope that maybe he'd get another fare.

Isaac and I would carry the cases into the main hall of the station. It would be bustling with people. We would sit under the clock while Sarah went off to get the tickets.

Isaac would be in high good form. He would rub his hands together and take out his Woodbines and light up and say: 'Everybody needs a break, Marty. The ould horse can only work so hard. There's people spend their whole lives slaving away and they're so mean they wouldn't spend Christmas.'

When the train came in, Isaac and I would go down the platform till we got a carriage to ourselves. The carriages were small and only held about eight people and Sarah had a dread of being stuck with rowdies or gather-ups who might be drunk and sing songs the whole way to Portstewart.

I would loosen the big leather strap that held up the window and look out at the activity around me. It was all part of the excitement. I would watch the guard coming down the platform slamming the doors shut. He would take out his pocket watch and check the time. Then if the signals were clear, he would lift his red flag and blow his whistle and the engine would give a hoot and there'd be a big puff of steam and we'd lurch out of the dark station and into the warm summer sunshine along York Street.

'Get away from that window,' Sarah would say. 'You'll get a cinder in your eye.'

But Isaac would say: 'Give over your foostering, Sarah. Sure the wee lad's on his holidays now.'

The train would rush along the shores of the lough, past Greencastle and Whiteabbey and then it would leave the sea behind and turn inland across the flat pastureland of

117

County Antrim. The air would be filled with the rich smell of cow manure. Isaac would wrinkle his nose and say: 'God almighty. Would you get a whiff of that. Wouldn't that knock your socks off, now.'

More passengers would get on at Ballymena and Coleraine and then it was only a short hop to Portstewart. Isaac would get up and stretch his arms and take the luggage from the overhead rack and then we would get on the bus and ride into town.

We always stayed with Mrs McMahon. She had a big, sprawling boarding house on the Coleraine Road. She was a middle-aged widow with four teenage daughters and they helped their mother with the cooking and cleaning. Every year, we had the same room at the back. It overlooked a shed and a patch of scrawny garden where a few blighted rose bushes struggled to survive.

Mrs McMahon would show us up to the room with the big double bed for Sarah and Isaac and the single for me and then she'd say: 'You'll want to have a wee wash, Mrs McBride and then a wee mouthful of tea, for I'm sure you're parched after the long journey.'

And Isaac would say: 'Go easy with the tea, now, Mrs McMahon. It's a medical fact that tea's not good for the kidneys.'

Sarah would shake her head and Mrs McMahon would laugh and say: 'You haven't changed a bit, Mr McBride. The same ould two and six.'

And she'd go down the stairs and we'd hear her putting on the kettle.

We would have our tea and scones and then we would go for a walk along the promenade and Isaac would fill his lungs and say: 'Can you not smell that sea air? Sea air's a great man for clearing the pipes. Sea air and goat's milk. Boys a boys, I can feel this holiday doing me good already.'

We would walk down as far as the harbour and watch the fishermen taking the boxes of fish off the boats, and then we would go back past Morelli's and Isaac would stop and buy ice-cream cones with nuts and syrup on top.

When we got as far as the Montague Hotel, he would say: 'Do you know what it is, Sarah? I think a bottle of stout wouldn't do me any harm. It would settle me down anyway.'

'Settle you down, Isaac? Is your head cut?'

'It would take the chill off me.'

'Chill? What chill are you talking about? Sure the sun's splitting the trees.'

And Isaac would sniff and say: 'It was only an idea, Sarah.'

★ ★ ★

Mrs McMahon fed us four meals a day. I often wonder how we managed to eat them all and how they didn't kill us. We got breakfast at 8.30 a.m. There was cornflakes or porridge and then a big fry of bacon and eggs and tomatoes and black pudding and fried bread and tea and toast. If you didn't want that, Mrs McMahon would fry you a kipper instead.

At 1 p.m. there was dinner. This was soup and then roast beef or bacon and cabbage or chicken with potatoes and peas and brussel sprouts and carrots. After that there was dessert. Mrs McMahon made her own apple pie. Some days there was ice-cream and bread-and-butter pudding. On Fridays, she cooked fish for her Catholic guests like us, who weren't allowed to eat meat. She always got plaice, fresh from the harbour and cooked it in breadcrumbs.

At six o'clock, she served tea. This was another massive meal. Steak and kidney pie some nights, fish and chips, shepherds pie, ham salads for those who couldn't eat any more. And always big silver pots filled with tea and plates of Mrs McMahon's scones. At nine o'clock, she served supper: tea and more scones. As the week went on, there were fewer takers.

I always slept well at Mrs McMahon's,

because of the sea air that Isaac said was so good for the pipes, or the sheer exhaustion of all the activity that we crammed into the day. Some days we would walk the four miles into Portrush, other days the length of the strand to the Bar Mouth where the river Bann tumbled into the sea. We would watch the anglers fishing for dabs and the big ships puffing out from the Foyle estuary.

We would swim in the Herring Pond or *Port na hAppail*. We would play Crazy Golf. We would sail the dinghies in the marina. We would go into Barry's and Isaac and I would ride the dodgems and the big dipper. After tea we would sit on the summer seat outside Mrs McMahon's house and Sarah would read her book, but after a while Isaac would get restless.

He would stand up and say: 'I think I'll just go and stretch the ould legs. A wee dander is good for the digestion.'

And he would disappear down the road in the direction of the Anchor Bar and when he came back a few hours later, I'd smell the Guinness off him.

★   ★   ★

It didn't take me long to find where the rock 'n' roll was. Beside the cinema on the promenade there was an amusement arcade and it had a juke-box. In the evenings, while Sarah read her book and Isaac stretched his legs in the Anchor Bar, I would make my way down to the arcade. It had a rackety collection of pin-ball machines, but it was towards the shiny juke-box that I gravitated. I would stand nearby and wait for someone with money to play a record. If no one did, I might spend some of my pocket money and play one myself: Elvis Presley or Buddy Holly.

There were two skinny girls from Ballymena who congregated there each evening as well; Avril and Violet.

They smelt nice and used make-up and Avril had her nails painted red with varnish. When I wasn't looking, Avril would push Violet against me and I'd have to put out my arms to catch her. Violet would look into my eyes and Avril would say that Violet was falling for me and they would both have a fit of the giggles.

I would hang around the arcade till it was time to go home and later in bed in Mrs McMahon's, I'd think of Avril and Violet and the things I could do with them up the fields beyond the Coleraine Road. And then I would fall asleep wondering if I would have to tell it all to the priest the next time I went to Confession.

* ★ ★ ★

The same people came to the boarding house
each year so that we all got to know each
other. There were the McCloskeys from
Swatragh, the Mackens from Draperstown,
the McAuleys from Cookstown. They'd have
loads of kids and they would all say Hello to
Sarah and Isaac in their odd country accents.
At teatime they'd talk about all the things
that had happened to them since last year's
holiday.

One Saturday afternoon, while I was
waiting for Sarah and Isaac on the summer
seat, a car drew up outside the house and the
McCloskeys got out with their luggage. They
had a strange new woman with them.

Mrs McCloskey said Hello to me and how
was my Mammy and Daddy and was I
enjoying my holiday. Then they all went
inside the house, Mr McCloskey sweating
under the weight of the suitcases. I sat on,
waiting for Sarah and Isaac to come down.
We were going into Portrush that afternoon
where there was a band parade on. Isaac
loved a kilty band. He said it would be good
fun and a bit of diversion anyway.

From the open window above me, I
could hear snatches of conversation. Mrs
McCloskey was telling the children to behave

123

themselves for they weren't in their own house now and not to be letting themselves down and making a show in front of the other guests.

And then I heard another voice. It must have been the strange new woman who had been with Mrs McCloskey. 'Who's that wee fella down there? The one you said Hello to?' she asked.

'That's Mrs McBride's wee boy,' said Mrs McCloskey.

'Och, sure I know him now. That's the wee boy they adopted?'

Time stopped. I felt the blood singing in my head.

Mrs McCloskey said: 'Ssshh. That's him. Martin he's called. He's a great wee buck. But don't let on, for God's sake. Nobody's supposed to know.'

★   ★   ★

I sat stunned. I saw the cars passing by on the road, people strolling in the afternoon sun, the sea shells that someone had arranged into a pattern in the concrete around the summer seat. I heard the squabbling of the gulls on the roof, the phut-phut sound of a motorboat out in the sea somewhere beyond the harbour. These things must have registered,

124

for I remember them as if it was only yesterday. But that August afternoon, all I could think of were the terrible words I had just heard. I was adopted. Sarah and Isaac were not my real parents. I was adopted, just like Gerard Boyle.

I felt a wild impulse to go back into the house, to confront Mrs McCloskey. Why was she saying these awful things about me? Everyone knew I was Sarah and Isaac's child. And then I grasped at the thought: Maybe I've heard it wrong. Maybe it wasn't me they were talking about at all. Maybe it was some other boy, some stranger from Swatragh who I had never met.

But the words kept echoing in my head and I knew there could be no mistake.

'Och, sure I know him, now. That's the wee boy they adopted?'

'Sssh. That's him. Martin he's called.'

I felt the tears well up in my eyes and I fought to keep them back. I mustn't cry. I mustn't show emotion. I mustn't let Sarah and Isaac know what I had heard. And all the time, the word kept repeating, like a record stuck in a groove. Adopted. Adopted. Adopted. I was different from other children. All these years, Sarah and Isaac had been telling me lies. They weren't my parents at all.

I don't know how long I sat on the summer

seat. I have no recollection of it, just this cold, empty feeling that seemed to go on forever. Eventually, Sarah and Isaac came down from our room and we started for Portrush. I don't know how I made that journey. To this day, I cannot comprehend how I walked with them along the twisting path by the golf course and the sea without blurting out the awful truth I had learned.

We arrived in Portrush. It was filled with friends and supporters of the bands that had come from all over Ulster to take part in the piping competition. I have snatches of memory from that day. I can remember the skirl of the pipes, the neat uniforms, the beefy legs of the bandsmen in their tartan kilts, the shiny leather of their brogues. A group of bandsmen outside the Railway Arms with black pints of porter, play-acting as they posed for photographs; a child crying for his mother; a drunken girl with a broken shoe laughing hysterically as her friends helped her along Causeway Street.

These images are imprinted on my mind, but of my thoughts and feelings, I can remember little. It is as if I was in a state of shock, the way people react when they learn of some terrible tragedy or hear some awful news.

I must have appeared sad or withdrawn, for

I can remember Isaac saying: 'You're not yourself, Marty.'

I shook my head.

'What's the matter with you, son?'

A bitter thought flashed into my mind: I'm not your son. Why do you say that when you know it's a lie?

'He's worn out. That's the matter with him,' Sarah answered. 'All that running around. He's taking too much out of himself.'

Isaac looked at me and pursed his lips. 'Cheer up, Marty. C'mon.'

And he took me into Barry's amusements and paid a shilling for us to ride the Thunderclapper and afterwards he bought me ice-cream while we waited for the bus back to Portstewart.

★   ★   ★

I didn't sleep that night. The conversation I had overheard kept repeating and I couldn't shake it away. I desperately searched for some explanation that would make everything right and put my world together again. And then the doubts that had sneaked in on me over the years would come creeping back, things submerged and hidden. Things I had been afraid to confront lest they should become real.

I examined the facts. I was an only child. I had no brothers or sisters. Sarah and Isaac were older than most parents with children my age. And then there was that rubbish that Sarah had told me about my brother and sister, Peter and Margaret, who had come too soon and were now my guardian angels in Heaven.

Didn't it all make sense? Wasn't it all part of a truth that was so obvious that I should have grasped it long ago? I thought once more of Gerard Boyle, the way he sat quiet and afraid in his desk. The pity I had felt for him, then, I felt now for myself.

I closed my eyes and prayed, harder than I ever prayed before. I asked God to make everything right again. I promised him anything he asked. I would go to Mass every day. I would go to Communion. I would never commit another sin. I begged him to let me wake the way I had woken this morning. Everything in order and in place, our little family intact.

I fell asleep at last, as the first streaks of dawn dappled the window pane. But when I woke, the terrible secret was still there, lying like some dead thing on my chest.

Book Two

5

Somehow, I managed to get through the last days of our holiday till the time came to go home. Maybe I blanked out the information, filed it away in some forgotten part of my brain. I never did the obvious thing. I never asked Sarah and Isaac. Maybe I thought if I didn't ask them, it wouldn't be true.

I watched them carefully now. I tried to catch them off guard, studying their faces for some tell-tale sign that would convince me. In the days that followed, I was torn by emotions. Rage at Mrs McCloskey, anger at Sarah and Isaac, disappointment, bewilderment, self-pity and loss.

They must have noticed, for they paid me more attention. Sarah pampered me, cooked special meals that I liked. Isaac, in his simple way, tried to spoil me. He took me to the pictures in the evenings, something unheard of. He brought home great bundles of comics from the hospital. He gave me money and sweets. He tried, with the small resources he had, to turn me back into the happy boy I had been.

I must have worried them terribly. I

became sullen and disobedient. I took a perverse pleasure in doing things I knew would hurt them. One afternoon, Sarah and I had a raging argument and I made her cry. I felt no sorrow, just a perverted joy that I had wounded her.

Another time, when they were out, I took all the picture books I had carefully collected since childhood and burned them in the fire. I took a penknife and cut my arm and Isaac was aghast. He pleaded with me never to do such an awful thing again.

I became a silent boy. I refused to talk. I went for long periods and held no conversation with them. I took to eavesdropping, listening to whispered intimacies from the top of the stairs. I heard Sarah confide to Isaac that she was going demented with worry about me and what were they going to do?

And Isaac trying to comfort her, saying: 'Och, Sarah. It's just a wee phase he's going through. He's just growing up.'

I felt my heart swell with pleasure at their pain.

Sarah and Isaac grew wary of me that summer. Instead of the discipline that had prevailed before Portstewart, there came a latitude that I had never experienced before.

I lay in bed late in the mornings, came home at night when it pleased me, went for long solitary walks up into the hills above Ligoniel, turned up for meals when it suited me. Sarah's carefully maintained order in the household was turned into anarchy. Yet they never complained.

I began to test them, casually dropping remarks about adoption into our conversation to see their reaction.

'I met Gerard Boyle today. Did you know he was adopted?'

Isaac would glance nervously at Sarah.

'No,' he would say. 'I didn't know that.'

'Oh yes. He's adopted. He's living with these people round in Holmdene Gardens, but they're not his real mother and father. Everybody knows about it.'

'Dear, oh dear,' Isaac would say.

'Why would anybody do that?'

'Do what?'

'Give their child away? Is it because they didn't want him? Or because they couldn't afford to keep him?'

Isaac would look uncomfortable.

'Who knows?' he would say. 'Maybe his real parents are dead. There's different reasons.'

'Like what?'

Sarah would quickly get up from the table and go into the kitchen and say, 'I just baked a nice apple cake, Marty. Why don't I cut you a slice?'

I was convinced now that the conversation I had overheard outside Mrs McMahon's boarding house was true. I wondered who else knew. I thought of Aunt Minnie and Uncle Paddy, searched for clues that would convince me, recounted signs, words spoken in an unguarded moment. I thought of the neighbours, my teachers, the kids out on the street. Maybe they all knew, talked about me behind my back, felt sorry for me, the way I had felt sorry for Gerard Boyle. Maybe the whisper that had gone round the school-room about him had also gone round about me?

I became haunted with thoughts of my real parents. Who were they? I hadn't considered that they might be dead. I wondered if I had any brothers or sisters. I wondered why my parents had given me away. I wondered if they ever thought of me.

One day I said to Isaac: 'Would people give a child away because they didn't love him?'

He gave me a strange look.

'What put that notion into your head?'

'Would they?' I insisted.

'Och, I wouldn't think so.'

'But if they loved him, they'd want to keep him. Isn't that right?'

'I suppose so. But sometimes it mightn't be possible.'

'Why not?'

Isaac took out his Woodbines and flicked at the cartridge lighter.

'Do you know what it is, Marty? You're asking an awful lot of questions these days.'

'*You'd* never give away a child you loved, would you?'

'No, of course not.'

'And if you ever adopted a child, you'd tell him. Wouldn't you?'

Isaac blew out a cloud of blue smoke and took a while to answer.

'Sure,' he said slowly. 'Sure, I would.'

★ ★ ★

In September, I moved to my new school, St Mary's Christian Brothers' Grammar school. It was in Barrack Street, at the bottom of the Falls Road. I had to wear a uniform which Sarah bought for me at a shop in Castle Street; black blazer and badge, grey trousers, white shirt and tie.

All the boys from my old school, who had passed the Qualifying, moved to St Mary's. All except one. Henry McAstocker put his hand up one day and told Brother Delargey that his mother was sending him to St

135

Malachy's College. St Malachy's was the other Catholic boys' grammar school in Belfast. It was run by the priests and it was considered swankier than St Mary's.

Brother Delargey stared at Henry McAstocker for a moment as if he hadn't heard him right.

'St Malachy's College is it?'

'Yes, Sir. Me Ma says it'll be handier.'

'She does, does she?'

'Yes, Sir. She says I won't have to get the bus.'

Brother Delargey's face grew dark. His fingers twitched as they rustled in the folds of his soutane.

'You're an ungrateful whelp, McAstocker. You and your mother together.'

Henry McAstocker looked down at his desk.

'Yes, Sir,' he said.

'After all the work I've put in, slaving to fill your thick skull with enough facts to drag you through that exam. And the minute you pass, nothing will do you but it's off to St Malachy's College. Is that the thanks I get? Are the Christian Brothers not good enough for you, anymore?'

'No, Sir. It's not that at all, Sir.'

'You've got concrete between your ears, McAstocker. It's taken me months of patient work to penetrate it. Well, you can just run off now to St Malachy's College and take your ingratitude with you and before you go, I'll give you something to remember me by.'

And out came the strap and he began to beat Henry McAstocker around the legs while Henry screamed: 'Please, Sir. It's not me at all, Sir. It's me Ma.'

★ ★ ★

We had to study English, Maths, History, Geography, Latin, French, Irish, Physics, Chemistry and Religious Knowledge and we had a different teacher for each subject. The headmaster was a fierce-looking man called Brother Comerford. He wore a long soutane that made a swishing sound as he walked and just to look at him would put the fear of God into you.

On the first day, he made a little speech. He said we should be proud to be going to St Mary's for it was the finest school in Belfast and if we all worked hard and obeyed our teachers we'd pass any exams they cared to throw at us and go on to do great things. He said we should be grateful to be getting the chance of a good education, which was denied to our parents, for education was the key to the future and would open any door.

He said we were to show respect for our teachers at all times and respect for one another and there was to be no jackass behaviour or foul language or we'd have him to deal with, and by God we'd remember it, was that clear?

A voice beside me said: 'Fuck this for a game of soldiers' and I turned to see this small, tousle-haired boy grinning back at me.

Brother Comerford proceeded to allocate us to our classes. The classes were arranged according to age and since I was younger than most of the others, I ended up in Class ID which was the lowest class in the school.

The tousle-haired boy was put sitting beside me. He said his name was Fergus Brennan and he came from the Pound Loney which was at the bottom of the Falls Road.

'Have you been with these bogmen before?' he said.

'The Brothers?'

'Yeah.'

I told him I'd been to St Patrick's in Donegall Street.

'Well, they better not try any hard-man stuff with me or I'll get me Da down to them and he'll soon sort them out. We'll find out who's a jackass then.'

★ ★ ★

138

Most of the teachers had nicknames. They had them before we came to the school and they were handed on from one year to the next. Our Latin teacher was a tall, heavy man called Biffo Brankin. According to Fergus Brennan it stood for Big Ignorant Fucker From Omagh. Mr O'Grady, who taught us French, was called Grinder. Brother Healy was a pale, earnest young brother who taught Religious Knowledge and was known as Dr Death. Mr Breen, who taught us Irish was called Amo, which was short for *amadán*, the Irish word for fool, which was what he called anybody who couldn't answer his questions.

The man who taught us History was called Porky Mulqueen. He was small and fat and had little tiny eyes sunk into his face. He said the thing to remember about History was it was written by the crowd that won, so you always had to be on your guard. He said History reflected the concerns of the ruling class and that's why you never got a mention of the poor unless they were causing trouble, like the Peasants' Revolt. The same thing went for women.

Brother McGrath taught us Physics and Chemistry and his nickname was Gorilla. It was easy to figure out where that came from. He was the hairiest man I had ever seen. He had hair on his nose and sprouting out of his ears and on the backs of his hands and half way up his face and out the collar of his shirt. People said he got like that from carrying out experiments on himself in the lab after school. They said he'd be in there mixing chemicals and drinking them out of test-tubes when no one was looking, just like Dr Jekyll and Mr Hyde.

Gorilla McGrath was the softest teacher in the whole school. He never punished anyone and he never checked homework. He would set us questions to do and the following day he would go through them with us on the blackboard. As he worked out each answer, he would say: 'How many boys got that right?' A forest of arms would shoot up and the Gorilla would smile and say: 'Good boys.'

After a while, most people stopped doing homework altogether and just put up their hands when the Gorilla had worked out the answers on the blackboard for you'd have to be an awful eejit to be doing homework when there was no one checking it.

He said the one thing about Science was, it unlocked the Mysteries of the Universe. It taught us what the world was made of and how it had evolved and developed. He said the world was governed by immutable laws, some of which the scientists were still trying to figure out.

Nearly every teacher said his subject was the most important. Brother Healy said Religious Knowledge was the most important because it taught us right from wrong and if we didn't have religion we'd be no better than savages, worshipping cows and trees and running around afraid of our own shadows.

Mr Breen said Irish was the most important because it was one of the most beautiful languages in Europe and our native tongue and the English had been trying to stamp it out for hundreds of years because language is the badge of nationality and if you take away someone's language, you make them a slave.

Porky Mulqueen said History was the most important because it showed us that nothing ever changed and human nature remained the same and people just kept making the same mistakes over and over again.

The only teacher who didn't say his subject was the most important was Gorilla McGrath. He just kept saying: 'Pay attention boys, and cultivate an inquiring mind. You'll find that Science will unlock the Mysteries of the Universe.'

★　★　★

141

Nearly every day for the first few weeks, I struggled home from school with books. There were books of graph paper, lined books, jotters, Irish dictionaries, French dictionaries, Latin primers, Physics and Chemistry textbooks, History books, poetry anthologies, novels, plays, atlases, books of tables and logarithms. Isaac had never seen so many books outside of a library.

'Boys a boys,' he would say. 'How can your brain cope with all that learning? Does it not get sore?'

Other times he would say that with all the fancy studying, I would surely end up with a nice soft job and be able to sit on my arse all day and order people around and draw down a big fat salary.

He took a great interest in my new education. He would lift the books from the table and turn the pages and examine them and screw up his face in puzzlement. But even though I was proud and flattered, I discouraged his attention and treated him coolly.

One Saturday afternoon towards the end of September, he went down to Smithfield and came back with several lengths of timber. He spent the rest of the afternoon locked away in my bedroom and I could hear him sawing and hammering and banging in nails. Then he called me up the stairs.

Near the window, he had built a desk and above it several shelves to hold my books. I could see he was pleased with his handiwork.

'What do you think?'

'It's not bad.'

'Not bad? It's stickin out, so it is. Look at that. Solid as a rock.'

He gripped the desk and shook it to show how well he had put it together.

'It's good,' I said.

Isaac smiled. He plugged in an electric fire and the bars gave off a nice, warm glow.

'There you are, Marty. When you're studying hard, your brain needs a steady temperature. You'll be nice and cosy here. Specially with the winter coming in.'

★   ★   ★

One morning in March, I woke with this sticky mess all over my pyjama pants. I'd been having a dream about some girl I'd seen in a film. She was taking her clothes off, piece by piece and just as she was about to remove her bra, I felt this wonderful release of pleasure which shook my whole body and caused me to wake with a start.

I wasn't sure what had happened, but I knew it was a nice warm feeling and I had

143

enjoyed it. I also had a vague notion it might be wrong. When I heard Sarah leaving the house for early Mass, I went into the bathroom and rinsed out my pyjamas and left them in the hot press to dry. The next time I went to Confession, I told Father Gabriel about it.

He sat quietly for a moment and then he said: 'Did you make this happen yourself?'

I wasn't sure what he meant so I said No.

'Did you touch yourself in any way?'

'No father. Sure I was asleep.'

'What age are you, my child?'

'I'm twelve, father.'

'Do you understand the facts of life? Has anyone talked to you about these things? Your father, perhaps?'

'No, Father.'

Father Gabriel paused and then he said: 'My child, you're growing up. Sometimes these things happen unwillingly, without any action on your part and that is not a sin. But if you do anything to make it happen, that is a sin. It's called masturbation. It's the sin of self-abuse.'

'Is it a mortal sin, father?'

'It may be.'

'And this stuff that came out, father? What's that?'

I could hear Father Gabriel coughing.

'It's fluid, my son. Your body is producing it. It's perfectly normal. It means you're becoming a man.'

'Right, Father.'

Father Gabriel paused and then he said: 'Say three Hail Marys for my intentions. And my child, ask your father to tell you about the facts of life.'

I left the confessional in a bit of a daze, as if I had learnt too many things in the space of seconds. I was becoming a man; my body was producing this fluid stuff. If it came out by itself, it was all right, but if I made it come out in some unexplained way, it was the sin of self-abuse which was a new sin that nobody had ever told me about and wasn't mentioned in the Ten Commandments. Finally there were these facts of life that I was to ask Isaac about.

Whatever they were, I realised they were not the sort of things I could get Isaac to explain. I had caught the edge of hesitation in Father Gabriel's voice, as if he was uncomfortable talking about it himself. Whatever these facts of life were, they were obviously a bit unsavoury and if I was going to find out about them, I would have to do it some other way.

I couldn't ask Fergus Brennan or Danny Morgan or some of the wise guys in the class who seemed to know all about these things, for if I did that, I'd be a laughing stock. After all, Father Gabriel had said I was becoming a man, which meant I was supposed to know this stuff myself. And then one Saturday afternoon at the matinee in the Forum, a strange thing happened.

I'd gone on my own that day and I remember that I sat in a row near the back. The main feature was a comedy. About half way through, a girl came in and sat beside me. I didn't recognise her in the dark but she looked older than me. On the other side of her was a younger boy who I took to be her brother.

This girl was plump and had blonde hair and she seemed to be enjoying the film very much. She kept laughing out loud and slapping her knee. Every now and then, I would catch her glancing slyly at me. And then, as if by accident, instead of slapping her own knee, she slapped mine. I felt an instant rush of pleasure. Her hand rested on my knee for a second; then it was gone.

I sat still, staring straight at the screen, hoping her hand would return. Beside me, I could hear her laughing out loud. Minutes seemed to pass and then her hand touched my knee again. This time it remained. I felt the pleasure return. Her hand lingered for a

146

moment and then it began to travel up my thigh.

I caught my breath. The girl didn't turn her head, didn't look at me, but I could feel her fingers working at the buttons of my fly and her hand moving inside my pants. At once I felt my penis swell.

I couldn't believe what was happening. We sat side by side watching the screen, not looking at each other and all around, people were laughing at the film. I was afraid to move in case she would stop. I felt a pleasant warmth move from the pit of my stomach. I felt her fingers caress my penis and then begin to pull the skin back, slowly and gently.

She took my hand and placed it on her own knee, then guided it up her leg and pushed my fingers inside the elastic of her knickers. Her legs tightened on my hand and I heard her sigh and move closer so that her head was almost touching mine.

I don't know how long we sat like this, but I remember hoping it would never end. I didn't care if anyone saw us or if Paddy Mallarkey came and shone his torch on us. I just wanted this beautiful feeling to continue.

It ended suddenly. I felt this tickle start in my groin and then this enormous surge of pleasure and I was pumping out fluid, the way I had done in the dream.

It seemed to be everywhere, all over my underpants and jeans. She withdrew her hand and took out a handkerchief and wiped herself clean. Then she took my hand off her leg and sat up straight as if nothing had happened. No one spoke a word.

When the film ended and the lights came on, she turned to me and smiled. She looked about fourteen or fifteen, an ordinary-looking girl with wispy, blond hair. She ushered her brother before her and together they left the cinema.

I went back the following Saturday and sat in the same seat but she didn't return. I thought about her for weeks; waited for the weekend to come round so I could go back to the Forum and find her. But I never saw her again. I felt a kind of loss. But I also knew that I had learnt one of the facts of life that Father Gabriel had talked about. And I had discovered masturbation.

★   ★   ★

In the months following, I learnt the rest of it and in an odd way Gorilla McGrath was responsible. He was taking a class in Biology and talking about plants. He said that plants were just like human beings, they needed to feed and drink and breathe. And of course, they needed to reproduce, otherwise they would die out entirely and there'd be no more of them left.

He said that plants reproduced in different ways, some used water and wind. Some used birds. Birds? This was amazing. For the first time since I'd sat in his class, the Gorilla had caught my attention.

He said flowering plants reproduced by using colour and scent which attracted insects like bees. The bee crawled around the flower searching for nectar and as it did so, it collected pollen from the stamen. The Gorilla said that the bee then flew off to another flower where the pollen from the first plant got brushed onto the stigma, thus fertilising the second plant and ensuring reproduction.

I wrote down as much of this as I could and that afternoon, instead of going home, I went to the Central Library in Royal Avenue and up the stairs to the reference section. I asked the woman behind the desk for an encyclopaedia and the Oxford dictionary.

I felt a bit guilty, afraid that she would somehow read my mind and maybe ask me what age I was and what I wanted these big books for. But she didn't seem to mind.

The place was quiet as a church. Rows of schoolkids sat at the long desks, studying or doing homeworks. After a few minutes, a man

149

in a porter's uniform brought me the books I had asked for. I sat forward and opened the dictionary. I started with 'fertilize'. It said: Make fertile or productive, fecundate. 'Fecundate' sounded promising so I looked that up. The dictionary said: 'make fruitful, impregnate'. 'Impregnate' sounded like pregnant which was what a woman was when she was going to have a baby, so I knew I was on the right track.

I looked up 'impregnate'. It said: 'make (female) pregnant; fill, saturate'. But the dictionary didn't give any indication how this was supposed to be done. I could see I was going round in circles.

I opened the encyclopaedia and went to the index at the back and looked up 'impregnate' there. It referred me to another section and when I turned the page, I knew at once that I'd found what I was looking for.

My eyes almost popped out of my head. Under Reproduction, there were pictures, diagrams, strange words I'd never come across before like ovary, uterus, vagina. There were words like testes, sperm, ovulation, menstruation, orgasm. I glanced up to see if the woman behind the desk might be watching but she was busy attending to somebody else, so I took a deep breath and started to read. On page 304, I got my answer. Under the heading Coitus and Fertilisation, I read the following:

During sexual intercourse or coitus, the erect penis is inserted into the vagina and rhythmical movements lead to orgasm and the ejaculation of semen.

It was what Larry Devine had told me that time in the school yard at St Patrick's. This was what a ride was. Only Larry Devine had got it all wrong. He said it was to make the baby come out. Now I knew it was to put the baby in.

I read till the library closed at eight o'clock. I went back the following night and the night after that and by the end of the week I had devoured that encyclopaedia. There was nothing about reproductive organs and the business of making babies that I didn't know.

Suddenly, I felt important. I would look at people in the street like someone who has got the Knowledge. I wondered at how naive and innocent I had been. And I knew it was all because of Gorilla McGrath. He had spoken the truth. Science really did unlock the Mysteries of the Universe.

★   ★   ★

151

Now that I had learnt the facts of life, I was anxious to try them out. But first I had to find a girl to practice with. I would hear Fergus Brennan boasting at school on Monday mornings about what he got up to with girls over the weekend. The way he told it, his weekends were one long sex orgy.

'I was with this one I met at the Jig and she nearly ate me alive,' he would say. 'I was at her for two solid hours and she still wanted more. Look, I've got love-bites all over my neck.'

And he would pull down his collar and show me these red marks like something that Dracula would leave and I'd be jealous as hell. I'd go around all day fantasising about Fergus Brennan and his girls and wondering what I was doing wrong because I was getting nothing at all. When he talked like this, I would encourage him, hoping I might pick up some tips about how to get started.

'The secret is to get them to relax. They like to pretend they're nice and proper but underneath they're smouldering volcanoes of lust. It's a scientific fact that women are randier than men. It's all to do with the propagation of the species.'

I'd go down to the library again and get out the encyclopaedia but I could find nothing about smouldering volcanoes of lust, just

152

sections on ovulation and pregnancy, so I asked him about that.

'Oh yeah,' he said. 'You have to be careful. Get them up the pole and there'll be hell to pay. The best thing is to wear a frenchie.'

'A what?'

'A French letter. It's like a kind of balloon. You put it over your dick.'

This was amazing.

'And where do you get them?'

'In the chemists. But you have to be eighteen. You could ask an older guy to buy them for you.'

I knew it was useless. What was the good of having frenchies when I'd no one to practice on? I kept thinking of the girl in the Forum cinema and some nights in bed, I'd get so worked up, I'd take an old sock and commit the sin of self-abuse. Then I'd have to go to Confession and get the head eaten off me by Father Gabriel or one of the other priests who were dead set against self-abuse. You could have gone in and told them you'd just murdered somebody and they wouldn't have been half as upset. Father Alexander was the worst. He was an old man and nearly deaf and I hated going to him, but sometimes he'd be the only priest on duty and I'd have no option.

'Do you know what you're doing to

yourself?' he would roar. I'd be terrified that everybody waiting outside would hear.

'You're polluting your body. You're polluting your mind. You're destroying your very brain, itself. Do you want to end up like a vegetable?'

'Oh no, Father.'

'Then stop this dastardly practice at once, or you'll live to regret it.'

'Sometimes I can't help myself, Father. These thoughts come into my head and I just have to do it.'

'Don't talk nonsense. You don't have to do anything you don't want to. Why, people have been martyred, people have died the most horrible deaths, people have had their fingernails torn out with pliers and branded with red-hot pokers and all they had to do to save themselves, was deny their religion. And did they do it? No, they did not.'

'Yes, Father.'

'So the next time these thoughts come into your head, banish them at once. Can't you take a cold shower?'

'We don't have a shower in our house, father.'

'Well take a cold bath. Or sit down and read something wholesome. Have you ever read *The Lives of the Saints*?'

'No, Father.'

'You can buy a copy from the Catholic Truth Society at the back of the church. I strongly recommend it. And sleep at night with your hands outside the blankets.'

'Yes, Father.'

★ ★ ★

Spa Doherty was big into self-abuse. He said he sometimes did it to himself five times a night and he was worried he was going blind.

'I can't stop it. I keep thinking of Gina Lolabrigida and those gorgeous big jujubes on her and I just have to pull my wire. It's like a compulsion. I think I'm addicted to it. And then, when I wake up in the morning, the room's all hazy.'

His eyes looked ok to me.

'Maybe you need glasses,' I said.

'I'm going blind, I tell you. Because of the wankin'.'

'Who told you that?'

He gave me a look of despair.

'Nobody has to tell me. It's a well-known fact. That's what it does to you. And now I can't stop and I'm going blind and I'll be walking around with a white stick for the rest of my life and everybody'll know what done it.'

This got me worried. The first chance I

had, I was back down in the Central Library with the encyclopaedia. I reread the whole section on Reproduction and I couldn't find anything that said self-abuse made you go blind. But I didn't like to take any chances, so I laid off it for a while.

Then one afternoon, I met Eileen Toner coming home. She was wearing her school uniform, short skirt and white knee socks, and I noticed she had suddenly grown up. She had a nice pair of legs on her. But most astonishing, she had breasts. I could see them plainly through her school blouse, nestling like two white globes inside her bra. I could even see the bra straps. I'd never noticed her breasts before. How had I missed them? Surely they hadn't sprouted on her overnight?

We walked along together and later I saw her out on the street with some of her friends. She had changed into jeans and a sweater and I could see the swing of her hips and her nice, round ass. But the thing that impressed me most were those breasts, poking through her sweater like two juicy melons.

That night I lay in bed and I couldn't keep my mind off her. I remembered Father Alexander's advice and tried to focus on people getting their fingernails pulled out and being branded with red-hot pokers. But all I could think of were Eileen Toner's breasts. I imagined myself handling them. What did they feel like? What were they like to touch?

Then it came to me. Eileen Toner was the girl I was looking for. She was the obvious one to practice on. She had fancied me since we were kids. Ever since the time I got her to take down her drawers in the air-raid shelter. All I had to do was ask her to go for a walk, or take her to the pictures or something, and surely she'd be delighted to let me put my hand inside her bra and feel her big white tits.

I felt my penis straining against my pyjamas at the thought of all the dirty things I would do with Eileen Toner. Maybe she'd even let me take her knickers down again and have a ride and then I'd be able to talk to Fergus Brennan like we were members of the same club. In the end, I couldn't stand it any more. There was no way I could get out of bed at this hour of the night and have a cold bath, so I thought: 'Hump Father Alexander. Here we go again' and reached for a sock. I fell asleep dreaming of Eileen Toner and her wonderful breasts.

I spent weeks working out a strategy. I had never asked a girl out before and wasn't sure what the drill was, so I asked Fergus Brennan what I should do.

'Take her to the hop,' he said.

'But I can't dance.'

'You don't have to be able to dance. All you have to do is hold her tight during the moody numbers and whisper in her ear. That'll get her started.'

There was a dance every Sunday night in the Ardoyne Hall beside the chapel, but I wasn't sure if I was old enough to get in. I decided to chance it. If I wore my jeans and turned my collar up and slicked back my hair, I might pass for fifteen.

I waited till Saturday afternoon and I saw Eileen Toner coming up the street. I caught up with her. She was wearing a flounced party frock and stockings and white high-heeled shoes and she had her hair tied up in a pony-tail. I thought she looked marvellous and I wondered why I had neglected her all these years.

'What are you getting up to?' I began.

'Oh, different things.'

'Like what?'

'Oh, you know. Girls' things.'

'I thought maybe you'd like to come to the dance with me tomorrow night.'

I knew she'd say Yes right away. I knew she'd jump at the chance. But she just smiled.

'I can't, Marty. I'm otherwise engaged.'

'What does that mean?' I stammered.

'It means I've got something else to do.'

'Well, what about next week?'

'I don't think so.'

'You don't think so?'

'No.'

We'd arrived at her gate.

'See ya,' she said and walked up the path to her front door.

I was dumbfounded. I stood gawking as she took out her key and let herself into the house. She didn't even look back.

* * *

This setback was a terrible blow to my morale. I tried to figure out where I had gone wrong. Perhaps I had been too casual, not delicate enough. A worse thought struck me and filled me with horror. Maybe there was something not right with me. Maybe I'd got bad breath or something.

I went home at once and locked myself in the bathroom and brushed my teeth till my gums bled and studied my face in the mirror. I squeezed out every pimple and blackhead I could find.

I struggled to find some rational explanation for Eileen Toner's rejection. And then it came to me. She was playing hard to get. That's what girls did so that you wouldn't think they were too keen. This thought encouraged me and I determined to try again.

Every evening, after school, I hung around the street, waiting for a chance to speak to her. But she seemed to have disappeared. I decided I'd write her a note and get one of her friends to deliver it. Surely that would work?

I sat in my bedroom and agonised over that note. Dear Eileen, I wrote, then scored it out. That sounded too cold and formal. Eileen, looked better. Then I changed my mind and decided to go for something groovy. That's what impressed girls. I knew it from the films I saw in the Forum.

This calls for something soft and romantic, I thought. So I wrote a nice long letter all about roses and moonlight and how my broken heart was aching for her from afar. This was bound to do the trick. I put it in an envelope and gave it to her friend, Mary Bannister. I was confident now. By the weekend, Eileen Toner and me would be rolling in the long grass up the Crow's Glen. But there was no response.

A few days later, I met Mary Bannister on the street.

'Did you give her my note?'

'Yes.'

'And what did she say?'

'She said would you ever catch yourself on.'

'What?'

'She says she doesn't want anything to do with you. She says you're too immature.'

I was devastated. Immature? I went home and locked myself in the bathroom again and took down Isaac's razor and practised scraping at the fluff on my chin. I looked at myself in the mirror, pulled faces, tried to look tough and nonchalant. I rehearsed put-down lines and smart talk, phrases I could use the next time I met Eileen Toner.

I was obsessed with her, thought about her day and night. No matter how hard I tried, I couldn't keep Eileen Toner out of my mind. I decided to try once more. This time, I'd surely succeed. I'd sweep her off her feet with my smart-guy talk and later when she was madly in love with me, I'd make her pay for what she was putting me through.

I waited till Sunday night about seven o'clock. I got all dressed up in my jeans and casual jacket and hung about at Larkin's wall. Some of the older guys were already heading up the street towards the dance. After a while, I saw Eileen Toner come out of her house. I decided to follow her and have it out face to face.

I hurried after her, but as she approached the gap with Herbert Street, I saw that someone was waiting. He was wearing a long draped jacket with a velvet collar and buckled shoes. I heard them laughing as he put his arm around her shoulder and kissed her cheek and as they started to go, I caught his face in the lamplight. It was Locky Power.

I couldn't believe it. Eileen Toner and Locky Power. I felt as if my world was falling apart. I turned into the shadows and my heart was filled with grief. As I slunk away, I could hear their laughter and it followed me the whole way home.

6

All of a sudden, Sarah and Isaac seemed dowdy and old-fashioned. I'd look at Sarah in her flowered pinafore or Isaac in his cardigan and slippers and think how slovenly they had become. I was beginning to feel ashamed of them. I tried to discourage my friends from calling to the house in case they might see them.

Once, Aly McVeigh called unexpectedly. I heard his knock at the front door, but before I could answer it, Isaac came bouncing down the stairs in his shirt-sleeves and braces. He was singing one of his come-all-ye's.

When Aly was gone, I flew into a rage.

'Don't do that again.'

'Do what?'

'Sing that ould rubbish stuff when my friends are around.'

He stared at me.

'You must be joking, Marty. What's wrong with a wee song?'

'It embarrasses me. That's what's wrong. Don't do it again. I don't like it. And put your jacket on. Look at you. You look like a scarecrow.'

The words were out before I could stop myself and immediately I regretted them. But it was too late. I saw that I had wounded him. He turned away and his face was red and his eyes lowered like an animal's.

'I never knew there was any harm in a wee bit of a song,' he said.

Sometimes, in his fumbling way, Isaac would make a gesture of reconciliation. After tea, when he had settled down to read the Belfast Telegraph, he would turn the pages and say: 'I see Celtic's after getting a new striker. Maybe he'll be just the boy they need. What do you think, Marty? Put a few balls in the onion bag?'

But I would just grunt and say nothing.

One Sunday, when he was getting ready to go out for his walk, he stopped at the front door and turned to me.

'It's a brave day,' he said and pointed to the cloudless sky. 'Why don't you come with me? The fresh air will do you good.'

I could see the coaxing look in his eyes.

'I have to study.'

'You can study too much, Marty. Sure a wee dander won't do you any harm.'

'I can't go,' I said firmly.

Isaac just shrugged and patted his pocket to make sure he had his Woodbines.

'It's not that long ago, you were near dead

to go for a walk with your ould Da,' he said sadly and closed the door.

Isaac was smoking too much and he had developed a cough. I used to hear Sarah arguing with him in the kitchen. She'd say, 'For God's sake, Isaac. Would you never give up them cigarettes? Sure they have the chest torn out of you.'

'Hush now woman, and don't be foostering,' Isaac would reply.

One morning, after he had gone to work, I found a few spots of blood staining the white rim of the washing bowl. I felt a wave of revulsion. Isaac was turning into a real slob. He couldn't even shave now without cutting himself.

Every year we had the school mission. A priest would come from somewhere and talk to us for a week about God and Sin and being good Catholic boys who'd be a credit to the saintly men of the Christian Brothers who were striving might and main to give us an education. After the first year, when we were all greatly impressed, the novelty wore off and we took the whole business in our stride.

But this year, we got someone different. Father Begley hit the school like a tornado towards the end of November. The priest was young and had his hair in a crew-cut which was very much the fashion at the time. He wore a nicely-tailored black suit and polished shoes and he sat on the edge of the desk in a relaxed manner that none of our teachers had ever done before.

'You look like a right crowd of black-guards,' he began and someone sniggered in the back row. 'I suppose some of you are smoking cigarettes and drinking? What?'

He glanced around the class and boys tried to look away.

'I suppose some of you are out every night chasing women, instead of doing your homework?'

There was a sort of embarrassed hush and I saw Danny Morgan and Fergus Brennan grinning like monkeys.

Father Begley leaned forward. 'You guys can't fool me. I know what you get up to. Sure, I used to do it myself when I was your age.'

He began to grin himself. We stared at him. None of us had ever come across a priest like this before. With his cropped hair and natty suit, he could have been at home with the Teddy boys in Freddie Fusco's chip-shop.

'I suppose you're into jiving and rock 'n' roll. You there.' He pointed at me. 'What's your name?'

'Martin McBride, father.'

'Who's your favourite singer?'

'Elvis, father. And Buddy Holly.'

'Ah, poor Buddy. He died too young. If he'd lived, he would have been better than any of them. Better even than Elvis. How many boys in this class have had a drink?'

Nobody put up their hands.

'You expect me to believe that?' Father Begley tut-tutted in mock exasperation. 'Fourteen years of age, most of you, and nobody's had a drink yet?'

There was another giggle and I saw Danny Morgan slowly raise his hand.

'Please, Father. We had a party in our house one night and somebody left a half-bottle of stout and I finished it off.'

'Did you get drunk?'

'No, Father.'

'Just as well or your Da would have reddened your arse for you.'

Everybody in the class laughed.

'Boys, all this is normal. Nobody expects you to be plaster saints. You are at an awkward age. You feel strange desires and you want to experiment and find things out for yourselves. You don't want to be reading about these things in books or seeing them on the films. You want to be doing them yourselves. Isn't that right, boys?'

'Yes, Father.'

'No one is perfect. Some of the greatest saints were also the greatest sinners. They did terrible things. But they came back to God in the end and he forgave them. Look at Saint Paul, he *persecuted* the early Christians. He thought it was his life's work to stamp out the teachings of Christ.

'Look at St Augustine. He was a terrible sinner. Anything you care to mention, St Augustine did it. He once prayed for God to make him pure, but not just yet. You see he wanted to live a good, clean, Christian life, but he didn't want to give up the sins of the flesh and the devil. And that's perfectly understandable. Those sins are very pleasurable, that's why people commit them. Because they're easy. Just think about it. It's easier to commit sins than to live a good life.

'People sneer at the boy who is trying to live a good life. Trying to keep God's commandments and obey his parents and keep himself pure. But I'll tell you one thing, it takes more guts to keep the commandments than to break them. Any fool can commit a sin, but it takes a brave boy to turn his face away and say No.'

★   ★   ★

This continued for a week, an hour every day before we broke up for the afternoon. Father Begley would come in and he would sit on the edge of the desk and tell us jokes or talk about rock 'n' roll, just like he was one of us.

We had never heard a priest talk like this. He didn't go on about the Faith and the Mass Rock and the Penal Days and all the persecution we'd suffered down through the centuries because of our religion. He didn't keep mentioning Hell and damnation and burning for all eternity. Instead, he talked about compassion and the poor and the underprivileged. He spoke about Christ's sacrifice on the Cross and his great love for us all. He said what mattered was making the effort, trying to live a Christian life. Everyone would fall. It was getting up again that mattered.

By the end of the week, he had won over all but the most hardened cynics. Danny Morgan said: 'I think it's all a bit of a cod. He's trying to get on our good side. He's just like all the rest of them, only he's much cuter.'

But Fergus Brennan said: 'What are you slabbering about, Morgan? Good side? He'd hold his hand on his arse a long time before he got on your good side, for it's well seen you haven't got one.'

Everybody laughed.

On Friday, we went to Confession with Father Begley in Brother Comerford's study. I waited my turn with the other boys till the time came to go in. Father Begley was sitting behind the desk with his purple stole on. I went to kneel down, but he waved his hand and told me to sit.

'Is there anything bothering you, Martin?'

I ran over the routine sins and then I told him about self-abuse.

He listened sympathetically and said: 'The boy who doesn't mention that sin, is a boy who's not telling the truth.'

'I can't help it, Father. I keep getting these thoughts. Is it a bad sin, father?'

He made a steeple with his fingers.

'Well, there's no such thing as a good sin. How often do you do this?'

'It depends, Father. Sometimes every night.'

'Have you ever committed an impurity with another person?'

'Once, Father. But I confessed it already. Mostly it's just in my head.'

He nodded.

'Impurity is a very selfish sin. You could get a girl pregnant. You could ruin her life and your own life. You could bring an innocent little child into the world. It's also a sin of

170

habit and like all habits, it can be broken if you try. Remember what I said about it being easy to commit sin and hard to be good?'

'Yes, Father.'

'There are things you can do. Avoid the occasion of sin; the places and the companions who lead you into sin. Give them up. Why don't you take the hard road for a change?'

'I will, Father.'

'In the end, that's what separates the men from the boys. Make the effort, Martin. You can do it if you try. God wants you to be good. He wants to see you in the Kingdom of Heaven. But he has given you free will so that you can choose for yourself between Good and Evil. Choose Good. That's the smart thing to do.'

'Yes, Father.'

'And pray. Prayer is a great comfort when you face temptation.'

'I will, Father.'

'Is there anything else you want to tell me?'

I paused for a moment. I wondered if I should unburden myself of the terrible secret I carried about with me. I wondered if I should tell him that I was adopted and about the resentment I felt against Sarah and Isaac. But in the moment that I hesitated, the opportunity was lost. I saw him looking at me

171

and I shook my head.

'No, Father.'

'All right, Martin. You can kneel down now and I'll give you absolution.'

★ ★ ★

That Sunday I went to Mass with Isaac. After I had received Communion, I put my head in my hands and prayed hard. I asked God to give me the strength to be good. I had been greatly impressed by Father Begley and was determined to follow his advice, to avoid the occasion of sin, to pray, to set myself a new routine.

After Mass, I asked Isaac if we were going to visit Aunt Minnie, but he said No, he wasn't feeling great, so we just went home and had our dinner. He sat for a while near the window, reading the Sunday paper and flicking at the pages with no real interest. I thought he looked down, not his usual perky self, so I asked him if he wanted to go for a walk.

'Boys a boys,' he said and tried to smile. 'That's not like you, Marty.' But he took his jacket from the back of the chair and we went down across the brickyard and watched a football game for a while and then we came home.

I stuck tight to my good resolutions. Every night before I went to sleep, I knelt at the side of the bed and said my prayers. I did the same first thing in the morning when I got up. If a bad thought came into my mind, I banished it with a toss of my head. If a boy in the school yard began to tell a dirty story, I turned and walked away. I went to Confession every Saturday afternoon and Communion on Sunday morning.

I began to think before I said or did anything for fear it would give offence or injure someone. I avoided gossip and scandal. I did my homework faithfully, listened attentively in class, went out of my way to be kind to people, particularly Sarah and Isaac who I had hurt so much in the past. They noticed, because one day Sarah said to me: 'There's a quare change come over you, this last while, Martin. Sure it's not so long ago, we could hardly get a civil word out of you at all.'

But there was a price. Some of my classmates began to sneer. I would see them whispering as I approached and looking at me as if I was odd. I would see boys nudging each other and smirking. It hurt me. I had to keep repeating Father Begley's words. This is what separates the men from the boys.

Most of all, I refrained from self-abuse. I

avoided all occasions of sin; magazines, films, company, even advertising hoardings. If I saw an advert for women's lingerie, I looked away. If I saw a good-looking girl on the street, I turned in the other direction. I hadn't realised before how difficult this was, for temptation seemed to be everywhere, even in the most innocent places.

One Saturday afternoon, I decided to visit the Ulster Museum at Stranmillis. I hadn't been there since primary school. Mostly it was displays of old farm implements and the history of the linen industry, but in one room I found an exhibition of paintings, some of them nudes. My eyes were drawn instinctively to them and I felt my heart thump. I turned immediately and walked out, but that night in bed the memory of those paintings returned and I had to close my eyes and pray hard before they went away.

I got hold of a copy of *The Lives of the Saints* and read it from cover to cover. I discovered that the saints came from all walks of life. Some of them had been aristocrats who forsook their worldly goods to follow Christ, some had been peasants. Some had been martyrs who had died terrible deaths for their faith, others had toiled in leper colonies and among the poor. Reading *The Lives of the Saints* inspired me and I determined to try, in my small way, to emulate them.

I also got the idea of penance from that book, of mortifying my body for the sins it had led me into and as a reparation to God for the injury I had caused him. I would fast, skipping breakfast in the morning, sometimes going without lunch as well. I inflicted pain on myself, digging my fingernails into my flesh till it bled, going without sleep till my eyelids would droop with fatigue. I decided to pray more. I began with one decade of the Rosary each morning and evening and then two decades so that soon I was saying a full five decades of the Rosary. I also prayed during the day, at the Angelus bell at noon and at six o'clock.

I began to set myself tasks: be kind to three people a day; give away pocket money to charities and to beggars in the street; do small household chores for Sarah; avoid stepping on cracks in the pavement.

Without realising, I was slipping into obsession. I began to see the world as a vast source of evil and temptation. No matter where I turned, evil was lurking. Everything was contaminated, everything was dragging me down. Even at Sunday Mass, bad thoughts would creep into my mind. If I was to succeed in avoiding sin, I would have to isolate myself. I thought of becoming a priest, of dedicating my life to some far mission field where I would work among the sick and dying.

I prayed more and more, sometimes rising at six-thirty a.m. to kneel at my bedside. If the saints could do it, why couldn't I? I began to develop a nervous tic, from shaking bad thoughts from my head. One day I stood up in class and told Gorilla McGrath that I hadn't done my homework. He stared at me in amazement, as did everyone else.

'Why are you telling me this? I haven't even asked you.'

'Because I wanted you to know. I didn't want you to think I had done my homework when I hadn't. My silence could be interpreted as a lie.'

Gorilla rubbed his chin and looked at me closely.

'Why didn't you do it, anyway?'

'Because I was too busy.'

'Doing what?'

'Praying.'

I could hear a gasp from the rest of the class.

'All right,' Gorilla said. 'Now you've told me. Sit down.'

I was convinced now that I was in a permanent state of sin and my eternal soul was damned no matter what I did. I would wake in the morning and the first thing I felt was a terrible burden of guilt and hopelessness. At times, I hadn't the strength to continue. I would lie in bed exhausted, as if I hadn't slept at all.

I developed a phobia about cleanliness. If I touched something, I would immediately feel that I had picked up germs. Unless I washed my hands, I would pass these germs to someone else and they might get ill and die. I would be responsible and that would be a sin. I washed constantly, sometimes twenty times a day, never feeling that I was completely clean.

I went to Confession more and more often. If I stepped on a crack on the pavement, I believed it was a sin, because I had broken my word to God that I would avoid them. One Saturday morning, I went to Father Gabriel and he listened patiently to what must have sounded like the ravings of a madman.

He gave me absolution, but I was no sooner out of the confessional, when the thought occurred to me that he hadn't understood me properly and I had made a bad confession and now I'd committed a further sin. So I joined the queue once more and waited my turn.

'Bless me Father. It's ten minutes since my last confession.'

Father Gabriel sat quietly and listened while I tried to explain what was tormenting me.

'You're the boy who was in here a while ago?'

His breath smelt stale in the confines of the little box.

'Yes, Father.'

'My son, you have made a perfectly good confession. You must stop torturing yourself. These things you believe are sins, are not sins at all.'

'But you don't understand, Father.'

Father Gabriel took a deep breath.

'My son, I have been a priest for forty years. I have listened to thousands of confessions in my time. Believe me, I understand. Say one Our Father and one Hail Mary, and pray for my intentions.'

'Yes, Father.'

But I still wasn't satisfied. I was still in a state of sin, even after two confessions. I wanted to be told that I had done wrong, to be told I was a worthless sinner, to be spoken to harshly and given a stiff penance. So I took myself across the brickyard to the Sacred Heart church.

Father McEvoy was the priest on duty and I had never talked to him before. I went into the Confessional and waited till the latticed

178

grill slid across. Then I unburdened myself to him, told him about the two previous confessions, explained that Father Gabriel hadn't understood me.

He talked for a long time, tried to put my fears to rest in the strange country accent that he had and for penance gave me Three Our Fathers and Three Hail Marys. I came out of the box feeling that I was at last clean and had been forgiven and my soul was pure. But the following morning, I woke once more with the terrible burden of guilt lying on my chest like a weight, and by noon, I was in a state of sin again.

My condition got steadily worse. I was driving myself relentlessly, never at peace. The nervous tic had now become so automatic that I went about constantly shaking my head. One by one, my friends dropped away. All but faithful Aly, who called to the house regularly until one day I told him not to call again. This was the cost I would have to bear for trying to live a good life and I offered it up to God.

* * *

Isaac's cough had gotten worse now so that it convulsed his chest and brought up great gobs of black phlegm. He went around with a

179

handkerchief always close to his mouth, but he continued smoking, despite Sarah's threats and admonitions. I was so concerned about living a good life and avoiding evil that Isaac's condition had passed me by, but my situation had not escaped him.

'Marty, you know what it is? I think you're not well.'

It was a Saturday afternoon and we had just finished dinner. Sarah was in the kitchen washing the dishes but I could hear her stop every so often to listen.

'I'm OK.'

'No you're not. You're not sleeping right. I hear you up in the middle of the night walking around the house.'

To lie to him would be a sin, so I said nothing.

'And there's something else. You never go out with your pals anymore. You're always locked in your room. You're behaving odd.'

He looked into my face and I suddenly realised how old and drawn he had become.

'It's just, Da, I'm trying to be good and it's very hard.'

'Maybe you're trying too much.'

'You can't try too much. You have to try all the time. The Devil is always lurking, waiting to drag us down.'

He gave me a queer look.

'Do me a favour,' he said. 'I never ask for much.'

'What?'

'Come with me and talk to Father Denis.'

It was a dull day. The sky was heavy with rain clouds and the top of Divis Mountain was green and brown through the mist above Crow's Glen. Isaac and I walked together up the empty street, hardly speaking; diplomatically, Sarah had remained behind.

Father Denis lived with the other priests in the big stone monastery beside the chapel. There must have been about twenty of them and they were called the Passionist Fathers. They wore long black soutanes that swirled around their ankles like skirts and on their breasts was a badge of Christ's heart with a cross on top.

The monastery was set back from the road and hidden by trees. There was a circle of green lawn and steps up to the front door. Isaac stabbed a finger on the bell and looked about. I could see he was uneasy. He took out his packet of Woodbines and removed a cigarette, then changed his mind and put the packet away again. After a while, the door was opened by an elderly brother in sandals.

'We've come to see Father Denis,' Isaac explained.

'Is he expecting you?'

'He is, indeed.'

'Come in and wait in the parlour.'

I had never been inside the monastery before. I could smell polish and mildew. There were portraits on the walls of rectors and saints and a picture of Jesus with a red light burning under it, like the one that Sarah had. The brother showed us into a room with a big table and chairs and we settled down to wait.

'Were you talking to Fr Denis?' I asked at last.

Isaac hung his head.

'I was.'

'About me?'

'Yes.'

'Why?'

'Because I care about you.'

I didn't know what to say. Part of me was angry that Isaac had done this without my permission. But part of me was also glad. He took out his handkerchief and coughed into it for a long time. Then he wiped his mouth, folded the handkerchief neatly and put it away in his pocket.

'The ould chest,' he said apologetically. 'It's giving me gip.'

I looked at him and he shrugged.

'Marty, don't get upset. Sometimes talking to people can be a great help.'

The door opened and Father Denis came into the room. He was a slight man with sandy hair and small, bright eyes like a bird. He had a belt around his soutane and a crucifix stuck down the side. He glanced at Isaac and then at me.

'You're Martin?' he said in a soft voice.

'Yes.'

'I'm pleased to meet you.'

Isaac got up and slid awkwardly towards the door.

'I'll just wait outside and let you two get on with it.'

'As you please, Mr McBride.'

When he was gone, Father Denis said: 'Your father tells me you're going through a wee bit of trouble.'

I started to explain.

'I'm trying to be good, father, but everywhere I look there's sin and temptation. It's very hard.'

'Your father tells me you get up in the middle of the night to pray.'

'But God expects us to pray.'

'He also expects us to sleep. You're studying for your exams. When are you taking them?'

'June.'

'You should be sleeping. You need your rest.'

'I pray for all the sins I've committed. To ask God's forgiveness.'

'What sins have you committed?'

'Sins of self-abuse.'

'But you've confessed them?'

'Yes.'

'So they're forgiven.'

'But I don't want to commit them again. I want to lead a good life, the way God wants.'

Father Denis smiled.

'Martin, God doesn't ask people to do the impossible. He only asks us to do our best.'

'I am doing my best, Father.'

'What other sins do you commit?'

I told him about walking on cracks in the road, about washing my hands, about the impure thoughts that came into my head everywhere I went. I told him about the constant battle I waged from my first waking moment to stay good in a world that was contaminated with evil.

When I was finished, Father Denis sat for a while and didn't speak. Then he said: 'What age are you?'

'Fourteen.'

'You're going through a tough time in your life. Have you any older brothers?'

'No, Father. I'm an only child.'

'I think you're a very good boy. I think God would be proud of you. But I also think

184

you've suffered enough and I don't think God would want that. Did you ever hear of scruples? Did any of your teachers ever mention those?'

'No, Father.'

'I think you're suffering from scruples. It happens to boys your age. It happens to boys who are trying to be good. They try too hard, harder than God intended.'

'But you must try, Father.'

'Of course you must try. But look at the things you think are sins. Walking on cracks, washing your hands all the time. God never said those were sins. As for impure thoughts. Every boy has impure thoughts.

'You know, Martin, there are different degrees of sin. Some sins are more serious than others. Telling a white lie isn't as bad as murdering someone. Missing your prayers now and then isn't as bad as causing worry to your mother and father.'

'You think I'm making them worry?'

'I'm afraid you are. You're worrying them sick. They're distracted about you.'

I lowered my head.

'I'm sorry, Father. I didn't mean to hurt them.'

'Of course not. You don't do it deliberately. But their pain is real, nevertheless.'

'What should I do?'

'I think you should ask yourself what will cause the least harm. If all this praying in the middle of the night is upsetting your parents, maybe you should stop. If trying to be good is making you sick, then maybe you shouldn't try so hard. You should ask yourself what God wants. Do you think He wants you to be sick?'

'No.'

'Neither do I. God is a loving God. He doesn't want you waking up each morning feeling the way you do. He knows you've fought a good, hard fight. I think God would want you to slow down now and concentrate on your studies. I think he'd like you to pass your exams and make your parents proud.'

'Yes, Father.'

'I think He'd want you to go out with your friends and enjoy yourself now and then. He'd want you to stop torturing yourself. You know, always thinking about sin is not healthy. Instead of seeing the world as a sinful place, why don't you look at all the beauty that's around you? God made that too, and He made it for us to enjoy.'

'I know.'

'So, why don't you enjoy it?'

'I will.'

'Stop thinking of sin all the time. You're too young. You don't know what sin is yet. Just say your prayers in the morning and in the evening before you go to bed. That's more than enough. If some of the people I know prayed that much, I'd be delighted.'

Again he smiled and I found myself smiling with him.

'Go to Confession once a week. That's all. Whatever you've done can wait for a week. Everybody in this life has a duty to someone. Your duty is to your parents. Think before you do something. Ask yourself if it's going to hurt them. Do you understand?'

'Yes, Father.'

'You can come and see me anytime you want. Just ring the bell and ask for me. I'll always be here. And tomorrow, when I say Mass, I'll offer it for you.'

'Thank you, Father.'

'Now kneel down and we'll say a short prayer together.'

★ ★ ★

That meeting with Father Denis was a turning point. But breaking the habit of months wasn't easy. It was almost as hard as being good. Now, I had to make a deliberate effort to walk on cracks, to stop rushing to the bathroom sink each time I touched something. And I was still assailed by bad

187

thoughts, more so than ever, as if the Devil had redoubled his assaults. I had to learn to let them pass over me, and each time, I waited in dread for God to strike me down.

Every Sunday, after dinner, I went to see Father Denis in the monastery. We'd talk and he'd review my progress and then he'd hear my Confession and give me absolution. Every time I left, I felt a lighter tread in my step.

One Saturday afternoon, I called for Aly and we went to the Forum cinema together and afterwards to Freddie Fusco's chip shop. I hadn't been in there in almost a year. We ate chips and drank Coca-Cola and listened to rock 'n' roll on the juke box. It seemed like old times.

Fergus Brennan came up to me in the school yard and said: 'Fuck me, McBride, I was worried about you, there. I thought you were having a wee fit or something.'

'I wasn't well,' I said, 'but I'm better now.'

One morning, I woke about seven o'clock and looked out of my bedroom window. The sun was streaming over the little rooftops of Ardoyne. I could see smoke curling from the chimneys as far as the Crumlin Road. The swans were back in the dam behind our house and the buds on the tree in Toner's yard were curling into leaf.

I stood by the window, listening to the

rattling hum from the mills and watching the sparrows quarrelling in the eaves. I knew that something was different. And suddenly, I realised that the weight had gone from my chest and for the first time in months, I was happy.

7

Isaac was getting worse. Most mornings, I would hear him coughing in the bathroom. He seemed to have a perpetual cough now and the handkerchief was never far from his mouth. One day when I was putting clothes in the wash basket, I noticed one of his handkerchiefs and it was stained with blood.

'Get yourself seen to, Isaac. For God's sake. Before it's too late,' Sarah would chastise him.

'Och, Sarah, would you give over with your bargeing. It's just a wee cough. It'll get better itself.'

'It's your chest and it won't get better unless you get it seen to. It's them bloody cigarettes. They're going to be the death of you.'

Isaac seemed to shrink. My Daddy who had once seemed so powerful, was now a shell. His flesh had withered, his chest collapsed, his hands looked like claws. The skin on his face had become pale and drawn.

The morning came when he couldn't get up for work. I could hear him coughing and hacking in the bed and Sarah going in and out of the bathroom and running water in the sink. She came into me with a distracted look.

'Your Daddy's not well. You'll have to go to Toner's and ring for Doctor Caldwell.'

I got dressed and went next door and asked Lizzie Toner if I could use her phone.

'Poor Isaac,' she said. 'I thought he was awful failed.'

Dr Caldwell came in his car soon after eleven o'clock. He took off his coat and went upstairs to see Isaac. After a while, he came down again and he looked grave.

'We'll have to get him into hospital, Mrs McBride. How long has he been like this?'

Sarah was wringing her hands and crumpling her pinafore in a ball.

'Months, doctor.'

'The man's sick. Why wasn't he seen to?'

'He wouldn't let us.'

Dr Caldwell closed his bag with a snap and put his coat on.

'Is he going to be all right?' Sarah asked.

I waited for his reply. I could feel a knot tighten in my chest.

'I don't know, Mrs McBride. He'll have to see a specialist. The sooner we can get him into the hospital, the better.'

The ambulance came for Isaac at mid-day. He was able to walk and had shaved himself and put on his Sunday suit. Sarah had got a bag together with pyjamas and a towel and soap and a couple of books for him to read. I helped him down the path and as we approached the waiting ambulance, his fingers gripped my wrist and he pulled me closer. I could smell the cigarette smoke from his clothes. He lowered his voice and whispered: 'You'll have to look after your mother, Marty. She's an awful woman to be worrying.'

He climbed into the ambulance like a sick old man. Sarah got in beside him and I watched them drive away up the street. As I turned to go back into the house, I saw that some of the neighbours had gathered. Maggie McAllister touched my arm.

'He'll be all right,' she said. 'God is good. They'll just bring him in and do some tests. The next thing you know, he'll be home again. You tell your mother if there's anything she needs, just come to me.'

I went back into the empty house. Sarah had left the radio on in the kitchen and I turned it off. Suddenly the rooms that had always been lively and filled with chatter, fell silent. I gathered my bag and left for school.

★ ★ ★

When I got home, Sarah was sitting by the fire with Aunt Minnie McCrory and they were drinking tea. I could see from the redness around their eyes that they had both been crying.

'How is he?' I asked.

'He's in the sanatorium.'

'Did they say what's wrong with him?'

'They think he's got TB.'

'Is that serious?'

The two women exchanged a glance.

'It could be. The silly ould eejit wouldn't listen to me. He should have got himself seen to long ago.'

That weekend, Sarah and I went to visit him. He was in Musgrave Park Hospital and we had to get two buses; one into the city centre and then another one out the other side. Sarah packed a brown paper bag with fruit and bars of chocolate.

When we checked at the reception desk, the nurse asked us to wait. She picked up a telephone, rang somebody, and a few minutes later a young doctor appeared. His face was long and serious. He took us into a room and introduced himself.

'Mrs McBride, I've bad news. Your husband's got tuberculosis.'

Sarah's hand shook and she bit her lip.

'Is he going to get better?'

'It's too early to say, but it's highly contagious, so I'm afraid you won't be able to visit him in the ward.'

'Does that mean we can't see him?'

'Not in the ward, Mrs McBride. We can arrange for his bed to be brought to the window and you can talk to him from outside.'

Sarah stood up and I could see she was having trouble keeping herself under control.

'I brought him some wee things. Is it all right if I give them to him?'

She held out the paper bag with the fruit and chocolates and the doctor looked inside.

'That's fine, Mrs McBride.'

'Where do we go?'

'If you'd just follow me.'

He took us through the main hospital. I could see the wards, the long lines of beds and white sheets, people sitting up or chatting in groups, nurses in starched uniforms coming and going. As we passed ward after ward, I kept wondering which one was Isaac's and suddenly I realised I had a terrible need to see him again.

The doctor opened a door and we were out once more in the hospital grounds. There were rows of aluminium huts, their curved roofs glinting in the afternoon sun.

'Mr McBride's in the isolation unit,' the

doctor explained. 'Number Nine.'

We trotted behind till we came to a window, where he left us. Inside I could see more beds. I looked at Sarah. There was nowhere to sit, just the rough gravel path, so we stood and waited till a nurse came and opened the window. I could see two porters wheeling a bed and suddenly there was Isaac, propped up on pillows and looking very tired. He wore a grey hospital dressing gown and there was stubble on his chin.

Sarah stood for a moment, uncertain what to say.

'Are they looking after you all right, Isaac?' she asked.

He nodded.

'Did they say how long you'll be in for?'

'No, they didn't say.'

'So what do you do all day?'

'Och, they wake us up in the morning with a cup of tea and then we get our breakfast. They have me in and out for tests all morning and then it's time for our dinner.'

His chest shook and he coughed into the handkerchief and wiped his mouth.

'Did they not give you something for that cough, Isaac?'

'They gave me tablets, Sarah, but they don't seem to be any damn good.'

Sarah shook her head.

195

'If only you'd gone to see the doctor when I told you, Isaac.'

He tried to smile.

'Listen to her, Marty. She's always bargeing. Sure the way they're looking after me in here, I'll be as fit as a fiddle when they let me out.'

We talked for about ten minutes before the nurse came and said they'd have to take Mr McBride back now. Sarah handed him the brown paper bag and waved goodbye and the nurse closed the window and drew the curtains.

On the way to catch the bus into town, she was close to tears. I put my arm around her.

'He'll be all right,' I said.

She turned to look at me.

'Oh, Marty. The isolation unit. It's an awful lonely place. I can't bear the thought of him in there, all on his own.'

Sarah said she was going to bake something for Isaac and every afternoon when I came home from school, the house was warm with the smell of stewing apples. She made tarts and cakes and scones and a barmbrack with currants in it. Aunt Minnie McCrory brought two bottles of Ross's lemonade and a tattered Western comic with a picture of a cowboy on the cover. On Saturday, we set off to see Isaac again.

He was looking better this time.

'Marty, did you see where the Russians are after putting a fella up in a spaceship?' he said.

It had been all over the radio and the newspapers. Everybody was talking about it.

'I saw that.'

'What will they be at next, I wonder? You know something? It's not a good sign. You can't be up to them Russians. They're cuter than a bag full of monkeys. I used to hear the old people saying when the Russians water their horses behind Cavehill, it'll be the end of the world.'

He looked at Sarah who was standing beside me on the gravel path outside the window.

'How are you, love?'

'I'm grand, Isaac. How are you?'

'Och, I'm all right.'

He turned to me again, excited this time.

'Guess what, Marty? There's a fella in here from Sandy Row and he's a Blue Nose and I'm having great fun sticking it into him about Celtic.'

'Can you keep up with the results?'

'Sure, haven't we got the wireless and we get the paper sent round every night.'

'So, you know Celtic beat Hearts last week?'

'Course I do. Two nothing.'

He chuckled and rubbed his hands.

'They're going to win the League, Marty. You mark my words.'

'Everybody's asking for you, Isaac,' Sarah said. 'All your old pals. And Father Gabriel's saying a Mass for you.'

'Is that so? Well, then I'm bound to get better.'

Isaac laughed but it grew into a cough and the handkerchief came out. Sarah and I watched as he struggled to draw breath, his chest wheezing and grunting like an organ.

'What are the doctors saying, Isaac?'

'Och, you know doctors, Sarah. Getting information out of doctors is like pulling teeth.'

'Did they say how long you're going to be in for?'

'They said I'm making progress and with a bit of luck I'll be home in a couple of weeks.'

We talked like this for a while and then it was time to go. Sarah reached the bag in through the window.

'I baked you a few wee things, Isaac, and Minnie sent you a couple of bottles of lemonade.'

He took the bag and looked into it.

'Och, I miss your baking, Sarah.' He paused and then he said: 'Is there any chance you could bring me a couple of Woodbines the next time?'

'Woodbines?' Sarah looked shocked. 'You're not supposed to be smoking, Isaac. That's what's doing it to you.'

But Isaac simply shrugged.

'They're all smoking in here. I asked the doctor and he said it was all right.'

'The doctor said it was all right for you to smoke?'

'Sure, he did.'

Sarah gathered herself together. She didn't looked pleased.

'All right, then,' she said. 'If that's what the doctor says.'

She was quiet on the way home on the bus. She just sat and looked out the window at the big houses and the traffic passing by. When we were getting off at the City Hall, I asked her what was wrong.

'Smoking,' she said. 'And him bad with TB. If the doctor says he can smoke, then he must be worse than I thought.'

★ ★ ★

Sarah and I had to go to Durham Street clinic for tests because the doctor said with the TB being so contagious it was better to check. We got the results after a week and

199

they were clear. We continued to visit Isaac and then, one Saturday morning in May, Sarah got news that he was coming home. The hospital said they would send him in an ambulance, but she wouldn't hear tell of it.

'He's coming home in a taxi,' she said and went straight across the street to talk to John Rea.

She was excited. I was sent round to tell Aunt Minnie and any neighbours I happened to bump into, while Sarah fussed about the house.

'I've got to have the place looking well for him,' she said and began dusting and polishing, even though the house was already shining. She kept looking at the clock as she worked, and at ten to eleven she went upstairs, put on her camel-haired coat and got herself all dickied-up for the visit to the hospital. I was to stay behind and wait for the McCrorys and anybody else who turned up to welcome Isaac home.

At five to eleven, I saw John Rea come out of his house and stand admiring his taxi. Then he got in and drove up the street and turned and came down again and at eleven o'clock he was sounding the horn outside the door. Sarah kissed me on the cheek.

'Maybe you could light the fire,' she said.

'Warm the place up for him. Could you manage that?'

'Sure,' I said.

'And maybe you'd run round to Tessie Donegan's and see if she's got a card or something we can put up on the mantel-piece.'

Then she was gone out the door and down the garden path and climbing into the taxi and they were sailing down the street. I was excited myself, although I tried not to show it. I had missed Isaac while he was in hospital. I made up the fire like Sarah had asked, then went round through Herbert Street to Tessie Donegan's newsagent's shop on the Crumlin Road to pick a Welcome Home card for Isaac. There wasn't much to choose from for they all had pictures of country cottages with roses clinging round the door, or of cats sitting in a window and silly verses inside. I picked one that I thought he might like.

'Who's coming home?' Tessie Donegan asked as she put the card in a paper bag.

'My Daddy,' I said.

'Was he away somewhere?'

'He was in the hospital.'

'And what was wrong with him?'

'He's got TB,' I said.

Tessie Donegan's expression changed.

201

'Och, I'm awful sorry to hear that. Your Daddy's a great character. You should be proud of him. But if they're letting him home, sure he must be all right.'

And she handed me the card and refused to take any money for it, saying the McBrides were always good customers and it was a small thing to give a card for Isaac who was one decent man and would never pass you in the street without saying Hello.

When I got home, Aunt Minnie was waiting on the doorstep with Uncle Paddy. She'd brought a cake and Uncle Paddy had a brown bag that made a noise as if it had bottles inside.

'It's just a dozen of stout and a bottle of sherry for the women. Sure, poor ould Isaac hasn't had a sniff of a bottle of stout for the past two months, God help him. And anyway, it'll build him up.'

We trooped into the house and Uncle Paddy put the bottles in the kitchen. Aunt Minnie started filling the kettle and putting out cups and saucers. I heard a knock on the door and when I opened it, Maggie McAllister was standing there with a plate of sandwiches.

'I thought I'd spare your poor mother,' she said. 'She'll have her hands full with your Daddy coming home.'

'Come in, Maggie,' Aunt Minnie said, 'And have a wee mouthful of tea. Isaac will be home any minute now. In a taxi, if you don't mind. Didn't Sarah go and book John Rea.'

Maggie McAllister came in and then Willie Toner and Lizzie, and Chucky Clark and a couple of Isaac's old pals from the street. By the time we heard John Rea's taxi, the house was full and all the chairs were taken up and there was only room to stand.

I saw him get out of the taxi and start up the path to the house. Sarah had brought an overcoat for him even though it was a mild day, and it seemed to swallow him up. He looked such a tiny figure as he walked unsteadily on Sarah's arm with John Rea guiding him from behind. When he came through the front door, everybody stood up and Uncle Paddy began to sing 'For He's a Jolly Good Fellow', and they all joined in. Isaac just stood with his jaw hanging open, looking from one face to another.

'Here, Isaac, sit up to the fire,' somebody said. 'Sure you'll need the bit of warmth after the hospital.' The big armchair was pushed up beside the grate and Isaac was helped into it.

'Boys a boys,' he said. 'What are yous all doing here?'

'We're having a party, Isaac, to welcome you home.'

'A party?'

'We all missed you, Isaac,' Maggie McAllister said. 'The place hasn't been the same without you.'

She passed round the plate of sandwiches and Aunt Minnie cut up the cake and Uncle Paddy gave out bottles of stout and glasses of sherry for the women. Lizzie Toner said that Isaac had never looked better and it must have been all that good fresh air up there in Musgrave Park Hospital and would anybody mind if she had a pinch of snuff for sherry didn't agree with her. Somebody poured a bottle for Isaac and he licked his lips and sniffed it like it was a glass of wine.

'Boys a boys,' he kept saying. 'Boys a boys.'

John Rea asked Uncle Paddy to sing another song and he cleared his throat and stuck out his chest and sang 'Oh, Let me Like a Soldier Fall'.

Everybody clapped and Willie Toner said what was wrong with them, could they not sing a good rebel song? Chucky Clark said he would try a few bars of 'Johnson's Motor Car' but he hadn't sung it for a long time and if he forgot the words, they'd have to help him out. Sarah frowned but said nothing. Chucky Clark finished the song and drained his bottle of stout and

Willie Toner said they weren't writing songs like that any more, good Irish songs that people could be proud of and Uncle Paddy gave him another bottle of stout and somebody asked Isaac to sing.

'Och no,' he said. 'Sure I wouldn't be able for it.'

'Ah come on, Isaac,' they said and I could see he wanted to be coaxed.

'All right,' he said at last. He wiped the froth from his mouth and in a cracked voice, he started to sing:

When first to this country, a stranger I
   came,
I placed my affection on a maid that
   was young.
She being young and tender, her waist
   small and slender,
Kind nature had formed her, for my
   overthrow.

The room fell silent and Isaac turned to Sarah where she was sitting near the kitchen door and he raised his glass to her.

On the Banks of the Bann, where I first
   beheld her,
She looked like fair Juno or a Grecian
   queen.

Her eyes shone like diamonds, her hair
softly twining,
Her cheeks were like roses or blood
drops in snow.

Everybody applauded and John Rea said that Isaac had a fine tenor voice and Lizzie Toner said you'd pay good money and you wouldn't hear better in the Opera House. I looked over to Sarah and she was quietly weeping into her handkerchief.

★ ★ ★

We put Isaac to bed in the wee room off the kitchen so he wouldn't have to climb the stairs except to use the bathroom. He lay in bed most of the day. In the evenings, he got up, put on his dressing gown, and sat beside the fire reading the *Belfast Telegraph* or listening to the radio.

Once a week, Dr Caldwell came in his car and examined him. If Isaac needed anything he would write out a prescription and I would take it up to the chemist's.

He had good days and bad days. The medicine that Dr Caldwell gave him seemed to clear up his cough and some mornings I would hear Isaac singing to himself in the room next door:

*I am the wee Faloorie Man, a rattling
roaring Irishman.
I will do whatever I can, for I am the
wee Faloorie Man.*

But gradually, he got weaker and the periods spent in bed got longer. One Saturday after breakfast, Sarah put on her coat. She said she was going down the town and she wouldn't be long. I was studying hard now for the Junior Certificate exams, so when she had gone, I took out my books and sat in a chair near the window where I could talk to Isaac. Sarah came home about one o'clock with a coy look on her face.

'I've got a surprise for you, Isaac,' she said.

'A surprise?'

'Something you'll like.'

'What is it, Sarah?'

'You'll just have to wait.'

Isaac glanced at me and he raised his eyes to Heaven.

'God, almighty, Marty. Did you ever encounter such a woman, perplexing a man like this, and him in his sick bed?'

But I could see that he was pleased.

At half-past-three, a delivery van stopped outside our house and two men in overalls got out, carrying boxes up the path. Sarah jumped up and opened the door.

'Mrs McBride?'

'That's right.'

I could see Isaac sitting up in bed straining to hear what was going on.

'We've got your television set here, missus. Where do you want it put?'

Sarah led them through the house and into Isaac's room.

'Mother of God,' he said. 'A television set? What do we need a television set for?'

'It's for you, Isaac.'

'But it must have cost a fortune.'

Sarah said: 'Tsk, tsk. Don't you be fussing about that. I got a good price and I got a discount because I was paying ready cash.'

She looked delighted with herself as the men hammered tacks and installed plugs and wires and then went up on the roof to put up the aerial. When they came back down, they went into Isaac's room and pushed a button. A football match came on. They adjusted the picture quality and showed Isaac how to switch it on and off, how to raise the sound and get the second channel.

Isaac looked at Sarah and said: 'Och Sarah, dear, you shouldn't be wasting your money on me.'

'Sshhh, Isaac. It's money well spent,' she replied.

Isaac was intrigued by the television. All day long, he sat in bed watching programmes about nature and history and current affairs. When I came home from school in the afternoon, he would shout from his room: 'Hey Marty. Do you know what is the Seventh Wonder of the World?' or 'Marty, Did you know that a camel can go for four weeks without a scrap of food? Can you imagine that? Four weeks without even a chew of grass? Sure, its stomach must be sticking to its ribs with the hunger.'

But most of all, he loved the sports programmes on a Saturday afternoon. He'd get the *Irish News*, spread it out on the bed after breakfast, and go through the television listings. Then he'd tune in to a football match and he'd be in his element.

Sarah preferred game shows, like 'Take Your Pick', where contestants competed for prizes of furniture and cash. Sunday nights she would buy a bag of sweets and sit with Isaac to watch 'Armchair Theatre'. They'd pretend they were young again, out for an evening in the front row of the Ritz picture house.

★ ★ ★

One afternoon, Isaac said: 'Sarah. Do you know what it is? I could murder a pint of stout.'

I was sitting near the window reading a book. Sarah gave me an uneasy look.

'Why don't I get Marty to run down to the off-licence?' she said. 'And get you a couple of bottles?'

'Och, Sarah dear, you don't understand. It's a pint I want. Sure, stout was never meant to be put in bottles. Bottles are full of gas. They just give me a sour stomach.'

A look of concern passed over Sarah's face.

'You wouldn't be able for it, Isaac. You're supposed to stay in bed.'

'Woman dear. There you go fussing again. I'm well able for it. And sure the wee dander will do me good.'

I could see Sarah was confused. I put down the book.

'I could go with him,' I offered.

Isaac's eyes brightened.

'There you are,' he said. 'God never closes one door, but he opens another.'

Sarah wrapped him in his overcoat and scarf and we started up the street. Every couple of yards, people stopped him to say how fresh he was looking, and how he was well-mended. I could see he was pleased to be out of the house again. Bucky Stewart said he looked like a million dollars, so he did, and sure it wouldn't be long now before he was back working, for it was amazing the things they could do in hospitals these days.

We went through Herbert Street and along Hooker Street. Isaac had to stop every so often and lean on a window sill to catch his breath, but I could see he was determined to make it to the pub. Eventually we came to the Crumlin Road and there was Logue's, squat as a packing case at the corner of Disraeli Street.

I had never been inside a pub before. When I pushed open the door, I was met by this warm smell of beer and cigarette smoke. I could see a long counter and tables and chairs and a group of men watching television at the end of the bar.

They turned to look at us.

'Well, Mother of God,' one of them said. 'If it isn't Isaac McBride.'

They gathered round and offered their big calloused hands for us to shake. I helped Isaac up onto a stool at the counter and he took out a ten-shilling note. The barman put down a glass he was polishing and said: 'Isaac. It's great to see you.'

'Give them all a drink, Hughie,' Isaac said and pushed the money onto the counter. The men stood around and drank their pints and

211

Isaac raised his glass and said: 'What would you do if the kettle boiled over?'

'Fill it again,' somebody said and they all laughed. They asked him how he'd got on up in the hospital and did he see the way Celtic were milling all before them and surely they were a cinch to win the league this year. Isaac finished his drink and took out more money.

'The same again, Hughie. And whatever you're having yourself.'

And while the barman pulled the big creamy pints, Isaac turned to me and said: 'What about you, Marty? Would you not take a wee drink with me?'

I didn't know what to say but before I could reply, Isaac spoke to the barman: 'Give him a glass.'

I took a drink of the stout. It tasted bitter but I swallowed it down and felt a warm glow in my stomach. Out of the corner of my eye, I was aware of Isaac smiling proudly at me.

We stayed for half an hour and then it was time to go. Isaac's cronies came to the door to see us off. When we got to our gate, he paused. He drew a deep breath and I could hear his chest wheezing and creaking.

'Let me tell you something, Marty. Never be mean. Meanness is the worst sin of all. No matter what they say about me, there's nobody can claim I didn't do the right thing.'

* * *

I took my first exam on the morning of June 10th. It was an English paper and I did well. I wrote an essay titled 'Youth is Wasted on the Young', in which I defended Teddy boys and rock'n'roll. I answered all the questions with time to spare and then I spent ten minutes going over the paper, correcting any mistakes.

The following day I had History and wrote another good paper. Then in quick succession I had French, Irish, Maths, Chemistry and Geography. These papers were more of a mixed bag but I was still confident.

There was a four-day break before the last two exams, Latin and Physics, so I got into my books and tried to memorise as much as I could.

I took the last papers on June 20th, Latin in the morning and Physics in the afternoon. It was a bright day. Sarah made me special sandwiches, cooked ham and tomato. She put in a couple of scones and an orange. As I was preparing to leave, Isaac called me into his bedroom and squeezed my hand.

'The best of luck, Marty. I always said you were going to be a brain-box. You just go in there and show them what kind of stuff you're made of.'

The Latin paper was easy and I knew I had

done well. At lunchtime, a bunch of us went to the bicycle shed to eat our sandwiches and make a last brush-up for the Physics paper. Then at 2.20 p.m. we closed our books and went back to the exam hall.

When I saw the paper, I felt my heart leap. There were six questions to be answered. I identified five that I could tackle easily and another that I could make a good stab at. I lifted my pen and began to write. I wrote till my hand was sore, dragging out pieces of information half-remembered from classes and text-books. I drew diagrams of plants and the internal organs of the body. I applied the laws of gravity and density. I put down formulae. I paid no attention to the big clock on the wall, just answering one question and moving rapidly on to the next one until at last the paper was finished and I heard the invigilator telling everyone to stop.

I made my way out from the hall, blinking into the sunlight. Gorilla McGrath was waiting. He saw me and asked me how I got on.

'I answered all the questions,' I said.

The Gorilla put his big hairy arm around my shoulder.

'That's all you can do, McBride. Give it your best shot.'

I walked down to Royal Avenue and got the

bus home. I was free now and the long summer waited. Sarah had promised me some money when the exams were over and I decided that tonight I'd call for Aly McVeigh and we'd go and see a film and maybe call into Freddie Fusco's afterwards. It would be a sort of celebration.

Dr Caldwell's car was parked in the street outside our house, but I paid it no attention. There was a lightness in my tread as I pushed open the gate and walked up the path to the front door. Through the window, I could see people moving about in the front room but I assumed they were some of Isaac's pals, called to see him. The door was opened by Father Gabriel. Inside the house I could see Aunt Minnie and Uncle Paddy and some of the neighbours. No one was talking. Sarah sat in the armchair by the fire and she had her head in her hands.

I knew then that Isaac was dead.

8

Isaac died from bronchial neoplasm and pulmonary tuberculosis. Bronchial neoplasm is lung cancer and cigarette smoking is a major contributory cause. So all that time when Sarah gave out about Isaac's smoking, she had been right, even if her efforts had been to no avail. Which of the two diseases actually killed him in the end, I have no way of knowing, but both are fatal.

He must have suffered some pain during his illness but he did so silently, for I never once heard him complain. He was the sort of man who believed that pain was unavoidable and best borne without fuss. Perhaps the prescriptions which Dr Caldwell wrote for him and which I carried religiously to the chemist on the Crumlin Road were for sedatives or pain-killing drugs. I'd like to think they were and that Isaac didn't suffer much.

The death certificate is a brief formal document which captures little of his life. It lists the date and place of death, name and surname, sex, condition, age, rank or profession, cause of death. The informant is given as Patrick McCrory, brother-in-law, 25, Chatham Street, Belfast. Isaac was fifty-six years old. At that time, I thought that fifty-six was old. Now I know it isn't old at all. Isaac was a relatively young man when he died. Sometimes I wonder what might have happened if he had lived, how we might have spent the time together as we grew older, the things he might have told me. I realise now that I hardly knew him. I know nothing of his childhood apart from what I have gathered from other people's memories and these scraps of information I harvest carefully and store away.

He was born in a two-roomed house off North Queen Street in Belfast. It had no running water and an outside toilet. His father was a carter at the docks and his mother bore ten children, three of whom died in infancy. He left school at thirteen and had a succession of labouring jobs before he had the good fortune to secure the post of porter in the City Hospital.

I know the circumstances when he met Sarah, for she told me herself. He met her at a dance in St Mary's Hall. He was twenty-one and she was eighteen. I've seen pictures of him then and he was a sporting blade, his hair slicked back, chin closely shaved, wearing a spotted bow-tie. You can see the cockiness in his eyes. He was full of confidence.

They were married three years later in July 1929 on her twenty-first birthday. They lived in a succession of rooms around the city and all this time, Sarah saved her money so that when Glenard was built in 1935 she had the deposit for her own house.

They tried for children but they kept failing, a woeful litany of miscarriages and premature births, a little girl and a little boy, one after another, stillborn. Sarah grew frantic for a child. Every married woman she knew had children; her neighbours, her friends, Isaac's sisters. Why couldn't she? She prayed to Saint Jude, the patron saint of Hopeless Cases, attended novenas, lit candles, paid for Masses to be said.

Eventually, a gynaecologist in the Mater Hospital, a senior man in charge of the maternity unit, took her aside and said: 'Mrs McBride, I have to tell you that I don't think you're going to be able to have children. You can conceive, but you can't bring the child to full term.'

'Can I not have an operation?' Sarah pleaded. 'Is there nothing can be done?'

But the man shook his head. He was a kind man but he couldn't perform miracles.

'I'm sorry, Mrs McBride. Sometimes these

things just happen.'

Sarah took the tram home to Glenard and told Isaac and he said: 'Och well, Sarah. Sure it could be worse.' And they settled into their lives with the stoicism that was typical of their class and time. Isaac went to work each day, brought his wages home on a Saturday afternoon, got dressed up and went for a drink. Sarah kept the house, cooked the meals, did the shopping, washed the dishes and the clothes and hung them out to dry on the line in the yard.

I learned these things a long time after Isaac's death, bits and pieces of his life that fell out casually in other people's conversation or were quarried assiduously by me. I have many regrets, but one is that I never learnt his story from Isaac himself.

On that summer afternoon when I came home to find that he had died, Father Gabriel took me into the bedroom where Isaac lay in his crumpled pyjamas. We knelt down at the bedside and said a prayer. Father Gabriel got up from his knees and blessed himself. I did the same. He put his hand on my shoulder.

'You have to be strong,' he said. 'Your father is in Heaven. He made a good Confession and he received the Last Rites of the Church. He died in a state of grace. Now, he is at the right hand of God. You shouldn't worry.'

I stared at him.

'Do you understand?'

'Yes, father.'

'Bless you, my child.'

★ ★ ★

Sarah didn't want a wake at first. She didn't want people tramping in and out of her house, gawking at her furniture. She wanted to grieve quietly and privately. But Aunt Minnie McCrory and Uncle Paddy persuaded her that it would look odd. People might take it ill and talk about her behind her back.

So Uncle Paddy went down to O'Kane's, the undertakers, and ordered a coffin and made the funeral arrangements. He came home with a big black crepe bow which he fastened to the knocker on the front door. Two elderly women, Miss Dunlop, a retired nurse, and Mrs McAuley, a widow, were contracted to wash and dress the corpse. They arrived after five o'clock and went into Isaac's bedroom. They brought a basin of water, soap, scissors and bandages, and they closed the door. They spent an hour in there, and when they came out again, Isaac was stretched in the bed in a brown shroud. His hair was cut and his chin was shaved and his eyebrows were plucked. Cotton wool stuck in his ears and nostrils and his hands twined round a pair of Rosary beads. Maggie McAllister came in with two brass candlesticks with big white candles that she'd borrowed from Sandy Brady up the street and these were placed at both sides of the bed.

Aunt Minnie went up to Andy Molloy's shop and bought two pounds of cooked ham and a pound of sliced cheese and six loaves of bread and two fruit cakes and a pound of butter and set about making sandwiches. Uncle Paddy took me with him to Davy Bell's off-licence and bought four dozen bottles of stout and a bottle of Bushmills whiskey and a bottle of sherry and six bottles of lemonade and we carried it home to the kitchen. He borrowed glasses from John Rea, rinsed them in the sink, and left them to dry on the draining board. He surveyed the scene and rubbed his hands together. 'Is there anything we've left out?' he asked.

The people began to come in twos and threes. They said to Sarah, who sat in a black dress and cardigan beside the fireplace, 'I'm sorry for your trouble, Mrs McBride.' Then they shook hands with Uncle Paddy and me and went in to see Isaac laid out in the bed. They knelt down and said a few prayers and left a Mass card. Each card represented a Mass that would be said for the repose of Isaac's soul. Then they came out again and Uncle Paddy offered them something to drink.

Some of them had tea and a sandwich or a piece of cake. Some of them had a bottle of stout. The women mainly had sherry and the children had lemonade. The whiskey was being kept for the evening when the hard chaws would come and sit up all night till the morning came, for Uncle Paddy said it was considered disrespectful to leave the corpse alone during the wake.

At first it was neighbours who came. They came from all over the district till the bed was covered in Mass cards. Maggie McAllister came with my pal, Bobby, and two of his brothers and she brought a big pot of soup. Willie Toner came with Lizzie and the twins and Eileen. Lizzie brought more sandwiches and put her arms round Sarah: 'Och Sarah, daughter, he was a good man. Sure your heart must be broke.'

She sat down in a chair across from Sarah and started on about what a lovely man Isaac was and how they would never see a decenter cratur as long as they all lived for he would have given you the shirt off his back, so he would. Soon all the women in the room were crying and wailing and dabbing their eyes with their handkerchiefs.

Willie Toner opened a bottle of stout and said the TB was the curse of God. It was bringing many a good man to an early grave and the Government was doing nothing about it because the Government didn't care a tuppeny damn about the poor people, especially if they were Catholics.

Harry Doherty came in a nice grey suit and white shirt. He took Sarah's hand and said it was always a sad day when an old neighbour died and if there was anything he could do, she mustn't be afraid to ask.

The Mooneys came and the McCruddens and a man called Larney Bowens who fixed up bicycles and hired them out, threepence an hour and sixpence if they had brakes. Even Eddie Russell, the ragman, came. He left his handcart out in the street while he had a bowl of soup in the kitchen. Soon the house was a mass of people, blocking the door and bumping into each other and drinking stout and cups of tea and gobbling down Aunt Minnie's sandwiches. At six o'clock, Uncle Paddy and I had to go out for more provisions.

Davy Bell, in the off-licence, packed a

brown parcel with more stout and said to Uncle Paddy: 'You can put this on the slate, if you want. I know what it's like at a wake.'

But Uncle Paddy shook his head and took a five pound note out of his pocket. 'Thanks very much,' he said. 'The way things are going I might have to take you up on that.'

It went on like this all day and into the evening. At eight o'clock, half-a-dozen of Isaac's pals came into the house. They had got themselves all smartened up; best suits and clean shirts and red faces and duncher caps that came down their foreheads to their eyes. You could smell the Brilliantine off their hair. There was Swally-the-Pig, Chucky Clark, Tommy McCoy, Buttsie O'Brien and the two McDaid brothers, Francie and Artie. They were carrying crates of porter that had been donated by Logue's pub for Isaac's wake. They left the crates in the kitchen, came back into the front room and took off their caps. They formally shook hands with Sarah and said sorry for your trouble, missus, but Isaac was a good man and a decent skin and he was surely in Heaven, so he was.

Then they trooped into the bedroom and stood in a phalanx around the bed and I heard Swally-the-Pig say that he'd never seen Isaac looking better, and you wouldn't think there was a damned thing wrong with him and that bloody TB was a bastard if ever there was one and fuck it anyway. They came back into the sitting room and Uncle Paddy took the caps off some stout bottles and poured each of them a shot of Bushmills. They settled down to keep an eye on Isaac for the rest of the night.

I'd had enough. I put on my coat and went out into the night. The air smelled fresh and clean and there was a scent of perfume from the night-stock that Isaac had planted in the front garden. I called for Aly McVeigh and we went for a walk up the Crumlin Road past the Fire Station and he said, 'Are you not sad your Da is dead?'

I wanted to say, 'But he's not my father. I don't know who my father is. I don't know who my mother is either. I'm an orphan.'

Instead, I said I was sad. 'Wait a few weeks till it hits you,' he said. 'Then you'll be really sad.'

When I came back home around midnight, most people had gone to bed. Isaac's pals were sitting in a circle around the empty fire-place, drinking bottles of stout, and one of them was crooning:

Heart of my heart, I love that melody.
Heart of my heart, brings back a
    memory.

When we were kids on the corner of
  the street,
We were rough and ready guys, but
  Oh, how we could harmonise.

I closed the front door quietly, tip-toed up
the stairs and went to bed, but I couldn't
sleep for a long time.

★ ★ ★

Isaac's brother, Freddie, came home from
Birmingham dressed in a natty suit. I'd never
met him before. Like Isaac, he was a small
man, with a huge carbuncle on his nose and a
smell of drink off his breath. He had to be put
up with the McCrorys and Robert Emmet
had to share a bed with Wolfe Tone to make
room for him. He wept uncontrollably when
he saw Isaac laid out in his brown shroud and
told Sarah that no man could have wished for
a better brother. Then he blew his nose in a
big white handkerchief and headed off to
Kilpatrick's pub at the bottom of Hooker
Street and didn't come back again till after
closing time.

A man called Mr Bergin came from the
Ancient Order of Hibernians and told Sarah
that Brother McBride was a member in good
standing. As such, the widow was entitled to a

226

death grant to help defray expenses and he gave her a cheque for £100. He also brought a wreath with carnations in the shape of a harp with the legend FOR FAITH AND FATHERLAND and said he expected a full attendance at the funeral.

Another man called Jackie Fulton, came from the Ardoyne Celtic Supporters' Club and he brought a wreath too, green and white in the Celtic colours. He said the members had taken up a collection and gave Sarah £30 for the funeral.

Six of Isaac's colleagues came from the City Hospital and a man from the porter's union. A man came from the Catholic Club and another man travelled the whole way from Ballymena because he saw the death notice in the *Irish News* and knew Isaac from North Queen Street when they were growing up together years ago.

Sarah's brother, Uncle Jamesie Bradley, who was a vet in Toomebridge, came in his car. He was a heavy-built man with a red whiskey-drinker's face and a country air about him. He wore a tweed suit with a handkerchief in his breast pocket and everybody could see he was the sort of man who might have money.

He kissed Sarah and left a Mass card and said he was sorry about Isaac, but he couldn't go to the funeral because he had to attend to a cow that was about to calve any minute now and the farmer was depending on him. Sarah nodded her head and said she understood. Uncle Jamesie stood for a while looking awkward and out of place among the porter drinkers. Then he glanced at his watch and said 'God, is it that time, already?' and went out the door and into his car and we never saw him again.

It went on like that. A succession of callers and weepers, a litany of Rosaries, innumerable bottles of stout and cups of tea and ham sandwiches and slices of currant cake till the time came to take Isaac to the chapel.

Father Gabriel had been appointed to take charge. He came to the house at five o'clock with four men from O'Kane's, dressed in black suits and ties and undertaker's overcoats. He put his stole on over his soutane and said: 'My good people we are here to say our last farewells to our brother Isaac, who was a just man and lived a holy Catholic life. He was a good husband and a good father and has gone at last to his eternal reward. He is safe in the arms of Jesus. And now my good people, if you would all kneel down, I will lead you in a decade of the Rosary. The First Sorrowful Mystery. Christ's agony in the Garden.'

We all knelt down and Father Gabriel rattled out the Our Father and the Hail Marys and the Glory Be and everyone joined in the responses.

When he was finished, he stood up and motioned for Sarah and me to accompany him into the bedroom. The men from O'Kane's had lifted Isaac's body into the coffin and were standing beside the door.

Sarah put her hand on Isaac's forehead for a moment and then bent and kissed his cheek. His skin looked grey and waxy like the skin of a fish. She stood back and sobbed a little bit and then it was my turn.

I stepped forward and looked at Isaac's face. It wasn't the face I recognised, but I knew it was him. I knew what was expected of me. I could feel their eyes watching, the men from O'Kane's waiting impatiently to get their work done. I quickly leaned forward and pressed my lips to his cold skin and whispered 'Goodbye, Isaac.'

The men from O'Kane's waited for a nod from Father Gabriel. He took out a little bottle of holy water and sprinkled it into the coffin and said: 'In the name of the Father and the Son and the Holy Ghost.' Then the men took the lid from

229

behind the door and began to screw it into place.

They carried the coffin out through the front room and down the garden path to the street and the women began weeping and wailing again. There was a crowd of people waiting outside the house. Mr Bergin stepped forward and put Isaac's Hibernian sash on top of the coffin and Jackie Fulton put his Celtic scarf beside it. Then Uncle Paddy and I shouldered the coffin with Swally the Pig and Uncle Freddie behind and we started up the street for the church.

We buried Isaac in Milltown cemetery in a new plot that Sarah had bought with money saved on a weekly death policy. It was another bright day. There was a good turn-out. I saw Father Denis in the crowd and Gorilla McGrath and Uncle Tommy Bradley who managed a grocery store in east Belfast and plenty of other people I knew.

When the prayers were finished, one of the grave diggers came and offered me the spade. I didn't know what to do. I turned to Uncle Paddy and he said: 'Shovel in some earth.' I did as I was told and I heard the rattle the dirt made as it fell on the wooden coffin. I knew we were burying Isaac for good and I would never see him again.

A memory flashed into my mind; Isaac

coming into my bedroom when I was just a little boy with an egg beaten up in a cup and a big smile, saying: 'Guess what, Marty? Charlie Tully scored again.'

I turned my face away. But I didn't cry.

9

I got a summer job in Uncle Tommy Bradley's grocery store on the Newtownards Road. It mainly consisted of stacking shelves and filling bags with groceries and doing odd jobs around the shop. I got paid three pounds a week and I gave two pounds to Sarah.

Every morning during that long summer, I got up at half-six to catch the bus into town. When I got off in Royal Avenue, I had to walk for another half-hour before I got to the store. It was called The Best Value Food Store and it was situated between a large Protestant area and a small Catholic district called the Short Strand.

On my first morning, Uncle Tommy took me into the store-room and explained the situation to me.

'We get our customers from both sides here. They're all decent people, and they all spend the same money, and I want to keep it that way. I don't want you coming to work wearing religious medals, or badges or stuff like that. I don't want you making remarks about football or politics. I just want you to be nice and pleasant. Talk about the weather, talk about the traffic. Talk about any damned thing you like, but don't mention religion or politics. Understand?'

I said Yes.

'I've worked here for fifteen years and because I'm called Tommy, nobody knows what foot I kick with. You'll have to change your name. Martin's too obvious. While you're working here, you're going to be called Jack. Right?'

'Right,' I said.

'OK, Jack. Start packing those tins onto the shelves.'

I packed soup and peas and tins of spaghetti and creamed rice and boxes of cornflakes. I sorted potatoes and carrots and dumped the bad ones. I tore the leaves off cabbages and sprayed them with water to make them look fresh. I wiped the chicken shit off the eggs and polished them till they gleamed. I learned how to slice bacon and cheese and how to sprinkle flour on stale bread to jizz it up a bit. I learned how to make displays of fruit and put the best ones to the front. I delivered groceries to old ladies on a rickety bicycle. I held open doors, and carried boxes, and filled shopping bags.

I was growing tall and already stood at five-feet-nine-inches, so I got to do all the heavy lifting jobs. I hoisted sacks of potatoes and flour and boxes of baked beans. Anything that required sweat or hard labour, Uncle Tommy would shout 'Jack. You're wanted' and I'd come hopping.

There were no lunch-breaks. Uncle Tommy had a kettle in the store-room and Sarah made me sandwiches. Whenever things got slack, I would nip into the store and make a cup of tea and gobble down a mouthful of bread and cheese and then it was back to work again.

Apart from Uncle Tommy and me, there were two young women assistants; Ruby and Lily. Ruby was twenty-four and fat and she waddled when she walked. She considered everything a great trial and would go about sighing loudly and clicking her tongue to let us know she was being put upon. She spent her day sitting behind the counter chewing gum and polishing her fingernails and regaling Lily with her exploits the previous night at the Plaza ballroom.

Lily was seventeen and handsome in a plain sort of way. She came to work in a tight skirt and blouse that made her breasts stick out. She was smarter than Ruby, but careful not to show it. She would listen with a glazed look as Ruby talked about the Russian sailor she had met from the big boat down at the quay and the way he filled her with vodka till her friggen head was done in, so it was.

Lily would say: 'I wish I could meet a sailor, so I do. I think they're gorgeous with their lovely uniforms and everything. Did he give you something nice, Ruby?'

'Oh, he gave me something nice, all right.'

She would lower her head and whisper and they would both look at me and laugh and Lily would say loud enough for me to hear: 'Ohhhh, he didn't do that, did he, the dirty baste?'

'He did. He did.'

'I don't believe you, Ruby. Not *thaaaat!*'

My mind would race as I tried to figure out what exactly he had done to cause such excitement.

Because I was the youngest and the newest, I got all the dirty jobs. I was getting used to being called Jack, but Ruby didn't even condescend to address me by anything so familiar. She referred to me as 'You!'

'You! Get me a tin of beans,' or 'You! Carry these groceries for Mrs McCoubrey,' or 'You! Climb up there and get me a packet of rice.' Lily found this all very funny and would sit and grin while Ruby ordered me about the store like I was her personal servant boy.

One day Lily said to me: 'Where are you from?'

I immediately remembered Uncle Tommy's

advice so I just said 'Crumlin Road.'

Lily sniffed. The Crumlin Road was made up of Catholic and Protestant streets, so she was none the wiser.

'What part?'

'The top.'

'Oh,' she said. 'What've you got up there? Have you got a picture house?'

'We've got two.'

'What pictures do you like?'

Musicals were very popular at the time, so I told her I liked those.

'Who's your favourite?'

'Well, I like Elvis and Buddy Holly.'

'He's dead. I like Cliff Richard. Do you like him?'

'He's OK.'

'I think he's gorgeous. Those big eyelashes he's got.'

I didn't get home till after 7 p.m. and I'd be tired from all the lifting and carrying. Sarah would have a nice dinner ready and I'd get washed and change into my jeans and teeshirt and we'd sit at the table and eat.

But the house was lonely after Isaac's death. His bed was still in the room beside the kitchen and some of his personal things were there. I'd go in sometimes and pick up his shaving brush or his cartridge lighter and think of him. I missed his banter and the chat about football. Sometimes I almost heard him singing from the bathroom:

I am the wee Faloorie man, a rattling roaring Irishman.

After dinner, Sarah insisted that we say the family Rosary, the way we always did, so I would kneel down and she would go through the prayers and I'd mumble the responses, but the whole thing seemed empty without Isaac there to groan and shift and complain on the hard floor.

Sarah would get up and turn on the television and prepare to settle down for the evening. She would say: 'The family that prays together, stays together.' And I hadn't the heart to tell her it wasn't true, at least not in our case, for Isaac was the proof of that.

One Friday afternoon, Ruby said to me: 'You! Have you got a girl?'

'Not a regular girl,' I said.

'Why don't you ask her out?' She gestured with her thumb towards Lily at the other end of the store.

'Would she go with me?'

'You have to ask her to find out.' She rolled her eyes and moved her chewing gum from one side of her mouth to the other. 'I think she fancies you. She likes men with hairy chests, so she does.'

And she put her hand inside my shirt and tugged the few thin hairs around my nipple and laughed.

The first time I managed to get Lily alone, I asked her. She twisted her lip as if she couldn't be bothered.

'I'm washing my hair tonight.'

'Well, what about tomorrow night?'

'I'm baby-sitting for our Sadie.'

'I could come with you. We could listen to records or something.'

She considered for a moment.

'All right,' she said with a toss of her head. 'I'll see you outside the Pop at half-eight. But you better be on time, for I'll not hang around waiting for you.'

The Pop was the Popular cinema on the Newtownards Road. I spent a long time getting ready. I was starting to shave now so I lathered my face with shaving cream and carefully cut away the bristles on my chin. I searched my face for any offending blackheads and squeezed them out. I brushed my teeth and blew my breath on the back of my hand to make sure it smelled all right. Then I shook out some after-shave lotion and splashed it round my face until my skin stung. I studied myself in the mirror. I had dark hair, brown eyes, and I was tall. I couldn't have looked more unlike Isaac or Sarah's brother, Uncle Tommy.

A thought came into my head, something I hadn't considered for a while. Who was my real father? What did he look like? Did I get my features from him? I shook the thought away. But later, as I rode the bus into town, the thought returned. Who were they, my real parents, the people who had brought me into the world? Were they still alive? Where did they live? Did they ever think of me?

Lily was waiting outside the cinema, wearing a short skirt, nylon stockings, a white blouse and jacket and carrying a handbag. She had put on lipstick.

'Where's your Sadie live?' I asked.

'Wentworth Street. C'mon. We're going to be late.'

We hurried past long streets of terraced houses squeezed in the dark shadow of the shipyard cranes, King Billy on his white charger staring from the gable walls. NO SURRENDER. I tried to look nonchalant as we pressed deeper into Protestant territory.

I found myself tongue-tied for conversation, now that I was alone with Lily and away from the shop.

'I brought some records,' I said and showed her the handful of Buddy Holly albums.

'Mervyn's got a load of records. He's got

everything. He's got a great job in the shipyard. He's got Cliff Richard.'

'Who's Mervyn?'

'He's our Sadie's man.'

'Where do you live, Lily?' I asked.

'Chester Street.'

'Where's that?'

'It's round the corner from our Sadie's.'

'Right,' I said.

We came to her sister's place. It was a house like the ones in the old part of Ardoyne, before Glenard was built. There was a front room and a scullery and a toilet out in the yard. Upstairs were two bedrooms. There was a settee and a couple of chairs and a pram beside the fireplace. The smell of damp was everywhere.

Sadie and Mervyn were waiting. Sadie was a small, nervy blonde about twenty. She wore a tight skirt and sweater. Mervyn was a Teddy boy with a long jacket that reached to his knees, drainpipe trousers and sideburns that came down to his chin. He had his hair oiled and swept back like Elvis Presley.

''Bout ye,' he said and offered me a cigarette, but I said I didn't smoke.

'You must be Jackie.' Sadie said. 'You work in the shop. Our Lily's told us all about you.'

She looked me over.

'You're a bit of a smasher.'

'Aw c'mon, Sadie,' Mervyn said. 'We're going to be late.'

'Listen to him,' Sadie said. 'All he thinks about is gettin a feed of drink into him.'

Mervyn growled.

Sadie put her coat on.

'We're only nipping down to the Lion's Head. We won't be long. Wee Roxanne's been fed and she's fast asleep. Yiz can make yourselves a cup of tea if you want, but don't be getting up to anything bold.'

She hit Lily with her elbow and Mervyn said: 'For Christ's sake, Sadie, if you don't hurry up, the bloody pub'll be closed.'

When they were gone, Lily and I sat for a while, not saying very much. In the end I said: 'Sadie's a bit young to be married.'

'He got her up the pole,' Lily said.

'Oh.'

'They're only married a year.'

'And what age is the baby?'

'Ten months.'

'Right.'

There was a new record player on a shelf near the window, so I put on one of my Buddy Holly albums.

'Would you like to dance, Lily?'

She shrugged and stood up and I took her in my arms. Her body felt soft and warm. We moved around the floor to the sound of

Buddy Holly singing 'That'll be the Day.'

'You can kiss me, if you like,' Lily said and turned her face to me.

Her lips parted and I felt her hot tongue dart into my mouth. I moved my hands down her back till they rested on her hips and pulled her closer. She didn't resist. We danced like this for a while. I could smell her perfume. I pressed myself harder against her and worked my hands to the back of her blouse and unhooked her bra. Her breasts tumbled out, pale and shining.

I thought of all those nights when I had dreamed of something like this, all those fevered conversations with Fergus Brennan in the school yard. Now it was really happening. I felt Lily manoeuvring me towards the settee, her hands working at the zip on my jeans and her fingers inside my underpants.

'You got a frenchie?' she whispered.

'No.'

'Well, it's lucky I've got one.'

She skilfully applied the condom. She pulled up her skirt and I caught a glimpse of the pink flesh above the rim of her stockings as she climbed on top of me. I thought: This is a mortal sin. This fulfils all the conditions; grave matter, full knowledge, free will. This will damn my immortal soul.

The record shifted. Buddy Holly hiccoughed: *'Oh huh, huh, huh, huh. The crazy things that you say and do. Make me want to be with youuuuu.'*

I closed my eyes and felt Lily's breath hot against my ear, her ass pumping and her voice soft and tiny like the cooing of a pigeon as she went: 'Oh, oh, oh, oh.' Beside the window, Buddy Holly sang: *'Rave on, crazy feeling. You know it's got me reeling. I'm so glad, you're revealing your love for me.'*

★ ★ ★

I saw Lily regularly after that and she taught me everything I needed to know about sex, things that weren't in the encyclopaedia in the Central Library and even things that Fergus Brennan hadn't heard of. We had sex in Sadie's house on the nights we baby-sat for Sadie and Mervyn; we had sex up dark, damp entries against mouldering brick walls; we had sex in the open air, in the long grass in Belvoir park beside the banks of the Lagan.

Each time we did it, I went shamefaced to the priest in Confession and listened to a lecture about the sins of the flesh and entering girls' bodies and all that stuff, and said I wouldn't do it again. But every time Lily laid her head on my shoulder, my good resolutions dissolved.

In the end, I stopped going to Confession altogether.

One evening, Lily said to me: 'You know I'd love to get married, like our Sadie.'

My heart stopped.

'You're too young, Lily.'

'No, I'm not. There's a girl up our street and she's only sixteen.'

Then she said: 'You're a Micky, aren't you?'

I knew what a Micky was. It was the same as a Taig or a Fenian, a term of derision for Catholics.

'Yes,' I said.

'I knew it,' Lily said. 'It doesn't matter to me. It's all the same God. But I suppose people would kick up, wouldn't they?'

'They would, Lily.'

'I knew that,' she said.

★ ★ ★

The job in the store came to a sudden end. Ruby was growing increasingly morose and doing even less work and I began to wonder why Uncle Tommy was hiring her at all. He was going about all day in a bad temper. Lily, meanwhile, said little to me but every so often when our eyes met, she would smile knowingly as if we shared an important secret.

I had even more work to do. As well as packing shelves and humping sacks, I was now called on to serve customers. Ruby took umbrage at this, regarding it as a slight that a mere messenger boy should serve behind the counter. As a result, she didn't even bother to address me as 'You!' any longer and just stopped talking to me altogether.

The atmosphere in the store grew poisonous. Ruby would sit at her perch and glare threateningly at me. She would find all sorts of demeaning jobs for me to do. I tried to stay out of trouble, but it wasn't possible. She would point at things she wanted me to do and communicate in sign language.

One hot afternoon in the middle of August, Uncle Tommy said he was going down to the store-room for a cup of tea and to keep an eye on things for him. It had been busy all morning and at lunchtime there was the usual rush of people wanting bread rolls and pastries. I found myself alone in the shop. I didn't know where the two girls were. Sometimes when things got slack, they went out the back for a smoke, for Uncle Tommy said the inspectors took a dim view of people smoking in a store that sold food and could come down hard on him.

He was gone about twenty minutes when a lorry drew up outside with a delivery of detergent. I helped the driver unload it and when we had finished, he presented me with an invoice to sign.

'Hang on a minute,' I said, and took the invoice down to the store-room to Uncle Tommy.

I pushed open the door and saw Ruby up on a pile of boxes with her legs wrapped around Uncle Tommy's waist and her white knickers drooping from her ankle. She looked at me and screamed. Uncle Tommy turned and his face was red. I heard him mutter: 'Holy shit', as he tried to pull up his trousers. I closed the door and went quickly back into the shop. One thought kept racing through my mind. 'Is there nobody in the world that isn't screwing somebody?'

The following morning, I turned up for work as usual. Uncle Tommy said he wanted a word with me. He didn't mention the previous day and neither did I. He took me to the end of the store and said that Ruby was telling everybody that I was a Catholic from Ardoyne, and I knew his policy on this matter. He couldn't afford to give offence, and reluctantly he would have to let me go. He gave me a week's wages even though I'd only worked two days and as I was leaving, he told me to tell Sarah he was asking about her. I never saw Lily again.

★ ★ ★

I spent the last few weeks of the school holidays hanging around with Kevin Trainor and Aly McVeigh. Now that I'd tasted the fruits of the flesh with Lily, and was damned anyway as a sinner, I wanted more. We used to get slicked up in the evenings, in our jeans and sports jackets and go on the prowl for Protestant girls up around the Ballysillan playing fields. We had this notion that Protestant girls were more casual about sex because they didn't have to tell it to the priest in Confession, But if they were, they weren't giving any of it to us.

In the last week of August, the exam results arrived in an official brown envelope. Sarah gave it to me unopened. She already knew what it contained for it had the Ministry of Education crest on the bottom left hand corner. I sat down at the breakfast table and nervously tore it open.

The results were better than I expected. I got three A grades, in English, Latin and History and a B grade in Physics. The rest were Cs and Ds. I failed Chemistry, but that didn't matter. The results meant that I was eligible for another two years at St Mary's, when I would take the Senior Certificate and hopefully get a decent job.

I gave the letter to Sarah and watched a smile spread across her face.

'You did well,' she said. 'Your father would be proud of you, Lord have mercy on him.'

She opened her purse and put a five pound note into my hand. I quickly gave it back.

'I can't take that. You need it for the house.'

But she pressed it on me.

'It's Isaac's. He gave it to me before he died. He said you were to get yourself something to celebrate. He knew you'd do well. He always had faith in you, Martin.'

I felt a lump rise in my throat. Her words brought up another subject that had been bothering me all summer.

'Can we afford for me to go to school for another two years? You've only got the Widow's pension.'

Sarah made a *tsk tsk* sound with her tongue. 'Don't be talking like your head's cut. We've got plenty. There's many a cratur's got less. Just you run on there, and don't be wasting that money on anything stupid.'

★ ★ ★

248

I went back to school in September. We had to choose which stream to go into, Science or Languages, because now we were going to concentrate on a core group of subjects for the Senior. I choose Languages which meant I was studying English, Maths, French, History and Latin.

We got a whole new bunch of teachers and the regime changed because we were older and supposed to be more mature. Things were more relaxed. We were allowed to come to school in your own clothes but there was a ban on wearing jeans.

One evening as we were hanging out at Freddie Fusco's, Kevin Trainor said to me: 'What's the story with all this studying anyway?'

Kevin had just left school and was working in a pub down at Smithfield, training to be a barman.

'It's so's I get a good job.'

'What sort of job?'

'I'm not sure. Maybe I could be a reporter or something.'

'You've no chance,' Kevin said. 'Them jobs are all nailed down.'

'Well, maybe I'll get into the Civil Service.'

'They won't let you do that. They keep all the good jobs for themselves.'

'If I get my Senior, they can't stop me.'

Kevin gave me a pitying smile.

'They'll find ways of stopping you. You wait and see.'

★   ★   ★

I studied hard for I was determined not to let Sarah and Isaac down. As the dark winter nights drew in, I would retreat to my bedroom with my books while downstairs, Sarah watched her gameshows and soap operas on television.

Since Isaac's death, the television had become more important to Sarah. She never went out much before, but now she became a hermit. She hardly went out at all, except to go to Mass and then to the shops for groceries. She would check the television listings in the paper and mark the shows she wanted to watch. Once the programmes started, the set stayed on till she went to bed.

Brother O'Callaghan was our Form Master which meant he was in charge of the class and if we had any problems we were to go to him. He also taught us English. He was about fifty, a small, energetic man with receding blond hair. He came from a place called Lahinch in County Clare and he was mad about Irish music. He used to bring a concertina in a leather case and he would say:

'Just a wee blast on the box, boys, to get us going.' And he would play a couple of lively reels or a slow air and his toes would tap time with the music.

One day he said: 'Any boy in the class got a bar of a song?'

People looked at him as if he was mad. We had never seen anything like it before. But he persisted.

'C'mon, boys. Belfast's full of songs. What about all those songs the women used to sing in the mills? What about '98 and Henry Joy?'

Fergus Brennan poked me in the ribs.

'Please Sir, McBride can sing.'

'I can't, Sir.'

'You can indeed, McBride. Up here.'

Brother O'Callaghan led me to the top of the class.

'Now, boy. Sing.'

I looked at Fergus Brennan with murder in my eyes, but he just grinned back. I took a deep breath and began:

I am the wee Faloorie man, a rattling,
   roaring Irishman . . .

Brother O'Callaghan sat with his arms folded till I was finished. Then he put his hands together and clapped and the class hesitantly followed.

'That's a fine song, McBride. Where did you learn that?'

'My father, Sir.'

'Your father, indeed. And he probably learned it from his father. That's what we call the tradition. That's how the songs survive. They get handed down. Boys, never be ashamed of the tradition. Keep it alive. Hand it on. Make sure the music lives.'

He turned to me and said: 'McBride. No homework tonight.'

Out in the school yard, Fergus Brennan jostled me.

'You've got a right wee Faloorie man in your trousers, McBride.'

I caught him by the collar.

'You say that again and you'll be eating your dinner through a tube.'

★ ★ ★

I enjoyed English, mainly because it involved reading and also because Brother O'Callaghan was a very good teacher. He had a passion for English Literature. He taught us Byron and Shelley, Keats, Wordsworth and John Donne. He taught us Shakespeare and William Butler Yeats.

He didn't get us to learn off long stanzas of poetry, the way we had done before. Instead he would say: 'Boys, look at the way Yeats uses language. Look at the way he chooses words. Look at the way he puts them together, one word following another, just in its right place. That didn't happen by accident. A poet is a craftsman. A poet is an artist.'

He taught us how to study a poem, to dissect and analyse it. He taught us about rhythm and metre and imagery. He showed us the various technical devices that a poet uses. Then he read us 'Easter 1916' and the class fell silent as his soft, country voice repeated the words.

I have met them at close of day
Coming with vivid faces
From counter or desk among grey
Eighteenth-century houses.

Brother O'Callaghan encouraged us to read widely. He mentioned writers I had never heard of; John Steinbeck, G. K. Chesterton, Herman Melville, Graham Greene, Thomas Hardy. I wrote them down in my jotter and later I got them out of the library.

★ ★ ★

At home, it was plain that Sarah was struggling to make ends meet. I was eating twice as much as she was and growing out of clothes as fast as she could buy them.

She would make a pot of stew on Monday with mince meat and carrots and try to make it last till Wednesday. She stopped buying butter and got margarine instead. She would buy day-old bread which she got for half-price and make toast with it. She got rid of the window cleaner and tried to wash the windows herself. I decided to get some sort of a part-time job.

I went to Andy Molloy and told him I had experience working in a store. He was sympathetic but said he had a fella already. Neverthless, he took my name and said he'd contact me if anything came up. I tried all the stores in the district with the same result. Nobody had any vacancies. Able-bodied young lads were leaving school at fifteen, prepared to work for buttons just to get a start.

One day, Tommy McCarney told me there was a man over the brickyard who was paying a shilling a stone for waste paper. I got an orange box and four wheels from an old pram and made myself a cart and hauled it round the streets of Ardoyne after school, knocking on doors and asking people if they had any old papers they wanted rid of. I got an *Irish News* here and a *Belfast Telegraph* somewhere else, but it was slow. I decided to branch out of the district altogether and try the Protestant streets beyond Alliance Avenue.

The people up there seemed to read more newspapers. On a Monday, I'd get copies of the Sunday papers like *The People*, *The Empire News*, and the *News of the World* which had pictures of girls in bathing suits inside and stories about divorce proceedings and rape cases. I would carry the papers home in my cart, tie them with cord, and ferry them across the brickyard. Here, in a pokey scrapyard, a sullen man in overalls would weigh them on a scales, and peel off a couple of greasy ten-shilling notes.

Sarah was horrified when she learned what I was doing. She said as sure as God, it was going to lower us all in the eyes of the neighbours and have people talking about us. But I ignored her and insisted she take the money.

One day while I was knocking on doors in Velsheda Park, an elderly woman asked me into her house. She told me her son had just left to get married and would I clear out his room. I went up to have a look.

The room was filled with treasure. I stared

255

at the piles of old comics and annuals and dozens of scrap-books of boxers cut from papers and magazines.

'You want me to take all this?' I said in amazement.

She must have misunderstood, for she said quickly: 'I'll pay you, of course. Would three pounds be enough?'

I couldn't believe it.

'Sure,' I said. 'I'll take it for three pounds.'

I piled my cart high with comics and scrap-books and wheeled them home to Brompton Park. It took me five journeys. Then I settled down to sort them out. The comics were mainly American ones and highly prized; Superman and Batman and DC Marvel. They would easily fetch a shilling each.

The annuals would go for two shillings. The scrapbooks were even more valuable and I calculated I could get half a crown for them. I spread the word around the district and soon there was a stream of fellas coming to our front door wanting to buy.

I sold the lot in three days. Together with the money the woman had paid me to take the stuff away, I had made eighteen pounds. I gave fifteen to Sarah and kept three for myself.

As the winter wore on, it became more

difficult to keep up the waste-paper round. Work at school was getting more intense. We would get essays to do that required research and reading and that took time. I used to get up early in the morning to get the school-work done because I'd be out late at night with my cart trundling round people's doors.

Sometimes I would have trouble keeping my eyes open in class. I was also wearing my clothes out and Sarah was busy darning socks and patching holes in my trousers. I began to feel ashamed. In the end, I left off the trousers altogether and took to wearing jeans because they lasted longer and looked better.

One day, Brother O'Callaghan said he wanted to see me after school. He began by asking me if I had learned any new songs.

'No, Sir,' I said.

'Oh, c'mon, McBride. Your father is obviously a cultured man. Why don't you ask him to teach you some more?'

'My father's dead, Sir.'

Brother O'Callaghan lowered his eyes.

'I'm sorry, McBride. I didn't know that.'

'It's all right, Sir.'

'When did your father die?'

'Last year, Sir.'

'And have you any family?'

'Just me and my mother.'

'And does your mother work? Has she any income?'

'She has the Widow's pension, Sir.'

Brother O'Callaghan drew a hand across his chin. I could see he was thinking. Then he said: 'McBride, the reason I asked you here was to talk about your appearance. You're wearing jeans. You know that's not allowed?'

'Yes, Sir.'

'Personally, I couldn't care less what you wear as long as you're decent.'

'Yes, Sir.'

'But you see, the problem is. If you get away with wearing jeans, they'll all be at it and then where will we be?'

I didn't reply. Brother O'Callaghan went on.

'I notice some days you're half asleep in the class. What time do you get to bed at night?'

'It depends, Sir.'

'You have to get a good night's rest. Otherwise your head will be muddled in the morning and you won't be able to think straight. And you need a clear head if you're going to learn anything.'

He sat for a few minutes with his jaws clamped tight. Then he suddenly stood up.

'Let me think about this,' he said.

A couple of days later when the class had broken up, he spoke to me again. He took an envelope out of his pocket. He said: 'McBride, this is a delicate matter. We have a fund here at the school for boys whose families are in financial difficulty. I want you take this envelope home to your mother.'

He handed me the envelope. Then he opened his desk and took out a plastic bag. Inside was a record. He gave it to me. I looked at the label. It said: David Hammond. Street Songs of Belfast.

'That's a present,' he said. 'By a fine singer. It's got The Wee Faloorie Man on it and plenty more. Listen to it. I think you'll enjoy it.'

'Thank you, Sir,' I said, and went home to Sarah.

She took the envelope with an air of curiosity and tore it open. Inside was a cheque for £80. Sarah rounded on me.

'Where did you get this?'

I explained what Brother O'Callaghan had said about the fund for families in difficulty.

Her face grew dark.

'You'll take it back in the morning.'

'But, I can't take it back. He's only trying to help us.'

'You'll take it back. I never took charity in my life, nor all before me. You'll take that money back, or so help me, I'll take it back myself.'

The following Saturday, Sarah took me down the town and bought me a new pair of trousers and a shirt and pullover and new shoes. She let me pick them myself. I wondered where the money was coming from.

I found out soon enough. On Monday afternoon, as I was preparing to go out with my cart, a removal van draw up outside the door. Two men got out and came up the path. Sarah let them in and they went straight to the television set and disconnected it and took it away.

I looked at her in disbelief.

'Why?' I said.

But Sarah just tossed her head.

'I only got it for Isaac. It's just a load of ould nonsense. We'll be better off without it.'

10

Shortly after Christmas, Sarah began to complain of nerve pains. Aunt Minnie McCrory came to see her and told her Sanatogen tonic wine was a great thing for building up the nerves, so Sarah sent me down to the off-licence to get a bottle. She had never been a drinker, but every night before she went to bed, she would pour herself a glass of Sanatogen and sip it while she listened to the Hospital Sweepstakes programme on Radio Eireann. She said she could feel it doing her good.

I got a job working on Saturdays in Andy Molloy's shop. It was the same sort of work I had done in Uncle Tommy's, donkey work mainly, but I also got to serve behind the counter. He paid me a pound and if it was a busy day, thirty shillings. Sarah pleaded with me to give up the waste-paper round. She was terrified that with the good weather coming in, I'd run into somebody we knew and we'd be disgraced. I agreed to cut it back to Mondays and Tuesdays when people would be getting rid of more papers after the weekend.

Between working in the shop and collecting waste-paper, Sarah and I were able to manage. I suggested we get the television back again. We could get one on hire-purchase, five pounds down and ten shillings a week, but she wouldn't hear tell of it.

'I've never had tick men running to my door and I'm not going to start now,' she said. In the end I persuaded her to rent one. It cost us four shillings a week and came with a guaranteed repair service.

★ ★ ★

I was still lusting after girls. One evening, Fergus Brennan persuaded me to go with him to the Plaza ballroom in Chichester Street. They had a session on Wednesday nights where you could dance to rock'n'roll records. He said the women who went there were randy as hell and only dying for it.

We got dressed up and had a couple of Carlsberg Specials in the Washington Bar to give us a bit of courage. Brennan explained his strategy.

'Never go for the good-looking ones. They're always stuck up. The first thing they want to know is, have you got a job. And most of them are wearing iron knickers. You'd need a blow-torch to get at them. You're better off going for a plain one. Butter her up. Tell her she looks like Marilyn Monroe. It doesn't matter anyway, for you'll never see her again.'

It cost us a half crown to get in. The dance-hall had spangled lights and mirrors and a stage with this guy dressed like Elvis Presley playing records on a turn-table. There were all these skinny girls in tight skirts and pony-tails dancing with each other on the floor, and Teddy boys prowling the place, waiting to smash your face in if you asked their women up to dance. I didn't like the look of it at all.

I decided to take a seat and get my bearings. Brennan wet his finger tips and ran them along his eyebrows and put a peppermint in his mouth and said he was away to check the talent. Cliff Richard was singing 'Living Doll' from a loudspeaker somewhere on the ceiling and then Eddie Cochrane came on and sang 'Three Steps to Heaven'.

I saw several women I wouldn't have minded dancing with, but the last thing I wanted was a dig in the head off some heavy from the Markets. Just as I was about to give up and go home, Brennan came weaving through the crowd with two women in tow. He brought them to where I was sitting and introduced them.

'This here is Veronica and she's a hairdresser. This is Valerie and she works in Woolworths. This is my pal Tony. He works with me in the bank.'

I blinked but Brennan just smiled innocently. I looked at the two women. The one called Veronica was tall and fat and reminded me of Ruby from the Best Value Food Store. She was clinging to Brennan's arm and seemed a bit unsteady on her feet.

Valerie was smaller, with dark hair cut in a fringe. She wore a white tank-top and clip-on earrings. She swayed slightly, then hiccoughed and put her hand to her mouth.

'Jasis, I'm full. I had ten Babychams round in McGarrity's and my friggen head's done in, so it is.'

She plumped down beside me and tried to focus.

'Have ye got a feg?'

I told her I didn't smoke.

She laid her head on my shoulder and I looked around nervously in case one of the Teddy boys might claim her.

She squeezed closer.

'I'd dance with ye Tony, only I'm scared I'd fall over.'

I saw Brennan glance at his watch and straighten his tie.

'I tell you what. Why don't we walk the

ladies home? The fresh air will do us good. All this cigarette smoke in here.'

'I'm not going up no entries,' Veronica said quickly. 'I know what yous are after.'

Brennan sniffed.

'It's good manners to wait till you're asked.'

'Listen to yer man,' Veronica said and everybody laughed. 'You'd think he'd got a poker up his arse.'

The women went off to get their coats. Brennan rubbed his hands together and did a little jig.

'What'd I tell you, Mackers? Didn't I say we'd score?'

'But they're drunk,' I said.

He looked at me as if I was mad.

'That's the whole point. Drink stokes up their smouldering sensuality. It turns them into piranhas of passion. Everybody knows that. Jeez, I can't wait for it.'

Veronica and Valerie were back. They had put on more make-up and their faces gleamed under the bright lights. They said they lived in Cromac Street, which was about ten minutes away. Veronica took Brennan's arm and Valerie took mine and we started out into the dark night.

Brennan and Veronica walked ahead and Valerie leaned on me.

'What d'ye do in the bank?' she asked.

'Wellll, it's sort of em . . . complicated. We count money and look after people's accounts and stuff like that.'

'Is it a hard job?'

'Well . . . It's, em . . . it's responsible. How d'you like Woolworths?'

She tossed her head.

'Tell you the truth, I hate the friggen place. I'm standin on my feet all day and it's giving me varicose veins in my legs. I think I'll have to sign on the Broo.'

We walked along making small talk, till we came to the Royal Courts of Justice. I saw Brennan steer Veronica into an alleyway and I followed suit. Valerie brushed a lock of hair away and put her mouth up to be kissed.

I put my arms around her and nibbled her ear and tried to remember all the things that used to get Lily going. Valerie stood still as a stone as I began to unbutton her coat and grope for her breasts.

'You're a friggen fast worker,' she said and pushed my hands away.

'But I love you, Valerie.'

I struggled with her bra straps while my tongue pushed past her teeth and into her mouth. I heard her moan and push herself closer while further up the alley, I could hear grunts and groans from Veronica and Brennan.

'Do ye really love me?' Valerie muttered.

'Of course I do.'

'Ye all say that. Ye're only after the one thing.'

She seemed to be wearing layers of underclothes, brassieres and slips and vests. My cold hands finally found her breasts. They were small and firm. I felt my penis harden as Valerie's fingers fumbled in my crotch.

'Ohhhhhh . . . ' she went.

I took it as encouragement. I kept my lips clamped firmly on her mouth as I tried to negotiate my way towards her drawers.

'Jesus, I'm stocious,' Valerie muttered between clenched teeth.

'Don't worry about it.'

'Ohhhhh . . . ' she went again.

Up the alley, I could hear this boom-de-boom sound starting up from somebody's backdoor as Brennan bounced Veronica against it.

I struggled through straps and belts and elastic till at last my hand touched smooth flesh. I was beginning to perspire with the effort.

'Ohhhhh,'

'It's all right, Valerie. I love you.'

'Ohhhhh.'

'You look like Marilyn Monroe, Valerie. Honest.'

My heart was pounding now as I tried to manoeuvre her into position.

'Ohhhhh.'

Valerie suddenly jerked her head away and a dribble of saliva ran down her chin.

'Shite,' she said.

I realised with horror that these weren't cries of passion. Valerie was going to be sick. I pulled away, but it was too late. She coughed and went whooosh and the first spray caught me full in the face and splattered the front of my shirt.

'What a waste of money,' Valerie said, when she was done. 'Ten friggen Babychams up against the wall.' She wiped her mouth with the back of her hand, while further up the alley, I could hear the backdoor going Boom-de-boom-de-boom-de-boom.

★ ★ ★

One night I was wakened by the sound of someone crying. I sat up in bed and realised it was coming from Sarah's room. I got up and went to her door and knocked on it.

'Are you all right.'

I heard a muffled sound coming from the room, so I pushed open the door. Sarah was lying in a corner of the bed, the statue of St Joseph with Jesus in his arms, ghostly in the pale light.

'It's the nerves,' she said. 'They're at me bad.'

'Can I get you something?'

'Pour me a glass of Sanatogen.'

I went down to the kitchen and found the bottle and poured out a measure and held it to her lips while she drank.

'I'll be all right,' Sarah said. 'You go to bed and get your sleep. You have to be up early for school.'

I went back to my room, but I couldn't sleep. I lay awake and thought about Isaac.

★ ★ ★

The following morning she stayed in bed but she got up when I came home and made my dinner. Then she went back to bed again. I went up to see her. The room had a dank, slept-in smell, so I opened the window to let in fresh air. I looked at her. Her hair was matted with sweat and looked like yellow straw on the pillow. Her face was sunk and there were dark, purple rings beneath her eyes. I realised that she had gotten old and I hadn't noticed.

'How're you feeling?'

'A bit better. It'll pass.'

'Was it this bad before?'

'Sometimes. But it always passes. You know what I'd like, Martin? Kali Water. I find it a great comfort.'

I went up to Andy Molloy's and bought a bottle of Kali Water. I was worried now. When I came back, I said: 'Maybe I should ring Dr Caldwell.'

Sarah reached out and gripped my arm.

'No,' she said. 'No doctors.'

'But he might be able to give you something for it.'

'It'll pass. It always does.'

I tried to study, but I kept thinking about Sarah lying next door in pain, refusing to let a doctor come because she believed doctors only brought trouble. In the end, I took my jacket from the hanger and went out. I walked up Brompton Park till I came to the Crumlin Road. There was a public phone at the corner of Twadell Avenue. I took the coins from my pocket and went into the booth and rang Dr Caldwell.

He came the following morning. Sarah was annoyed with me because she felt I had betrayed her. I told her that I hadn't used the Toner's phone, so nobody would know. Dr Caldwell began by asking how long she'd been unwell. Then he took her temperature and felt her pulse.

'Tell me exactly where you feel the pain, Mrs McBride?'

'My chest.'

He probed her with his stethescope, put his head to her chest and listened. In the end, he took the stethescope off and stood up.

'I can't find anything wrong with you.'

'It's just my nerves, Doctor. It comes and goes.'

Dr Caldwell nodded.

'Neverthless, the pain shouldn't be there. I'm going to give you something for it.'

He scribbled out a prescription. Then he paused.

'There's something else. I think you should go and have some tests done. I'm going to make an appointment for you.'

Sarah began to get agitated but Dr Caldwell patted her hand.

'There's nothing to worry about, Mrs McBride. If there's something wrong with you, the tests will show it up and then we'll be able to treat it. It's all for the best.'

★ ★ ★

The following week, she went into the Mater Hospital. She packed a bag with soap and towels and books and magazines. It reminded

271

me of the time Isaac went into Musgrave Park. I wanted to go with her, but Aunt Minnie said No, she would go because I shouldn't be missing school.

I went to see her on Sunday and she was sitting up in bed and looked much better, but she was fretting to come home. She asked me how everything was and if I was able to look after myself and was I making sure to get enough to eat. She was anxious for news, so I told her everything I knew.

'The neighbours are asking about you,' I said.

'Dear, dear,' she said.

'Willie Toner said to be remembered and John Rea and Maggie McAllister.'

'I always had good neighbours, Martin. Good neighbours are a blessing.'

'Andy Molloy gave me a pound of rashers and a dozen eggs, and he sent you this.'

I gave her the box of chocolates that Andy Molloy had sent for her. Sarah was delighted.

'Och, he shouldn't be doing that. And how is school?'

'All right.'

'I hope you're studying hard. Don't be letting your father down. He always said you'd get a good job some day.'

'I won't let him down,' I said.

Dr Caldwell said the tests would only take

a few days and then Sarah would be home again. But they sent her to another place for more tests, so in the end she was in hospital for nearly three weeks.

The day she came home, I took off school and went round the house cleaning and making sure everything was neat and tidy. Mr McCarney, who was always pottering about the garden, came to the front door with a big bunch of foxgloves and sweet rocket and I put them in a vase in her bedroom.

She came home in an ambulance and went straight to bed. In the following days, the various neighbours came to see her and Father Jeremiah from the Monastery. I'd hear them in the bedroom saying: 'Och dear, Mrs McBride, but you're quare and well mended, the day.'

She began to come down stairs after a while to sit and watch television, but she could only sit for an hour or two and then she had to go back to bed again. I called the rental shop and they sent out some men and they fixed up the television in her room.

She kept saying she was getting better and it was only a matter of time. The pains were gone now and with the help of God, she'd be up and about rightly. The District Nurse came once a week to give her injections. Dr Caldwell came too. He'd sit and chat with her, then write out a prescription and I'd take it to the chemist's.

One day, after the District Nurse had gone, I noticed an empty box she had left behind on the window-sill. I took the box and examined it. The words Morphine Sulphate were written on the label.

★   ★   ★

From the time she came home from hospital, I never once heard Sarah cry in the night. The neighbours were very good. They organised a roster and took turns cooking and cleaning the house. The only money they would take was for food they bought, and even that was very little for they contributed much of their own.

Sarah's appetite had almost disappeared and she seemed to subsist on cups of tea and slices of toast. Sometimes, when the neighbours had cooked something particularly tasty, I would coax her to eat, but she never managed more than a few spoonfuls. Aunt Minnie would scold her. She'd say: 'For God's sake, Sarah. How'd you expect to build yourself up if you won't take your nourishment?' And she'd go 'Tsk, tsk, tsk.'

Sarah would eat a bit just to please her, but she had no interest in food. She kept the bottle of Sanatogen wine on her bedside table with a glass and the Kali Water which came in a syphon.

In the evenings, I would go in and sit with her and read. She liked a good story, something with romance and intrigue. I read her Somerset Maugham's *Of Human Bondage* and Daphne Du Maurier's *Rebecca*. A novel called *To Kill a Mockingbird* was making a stir at that time, so I ordered it from the library and read that to her as well.

In those summer evenings, as the light began to fade and the street sounds died away, we would sit together and I'd ask her about her childhood growing up in Ardoyne when it was still a village. She remembered the terrible days of the Troubles of 1922, the gun-battles and pogroms, the midnight knock of the murder gangs, innocent Catholics dragged from their beds in their night-clothes and taken up the fields to be shot.

She told me about her sister, Nora, who died of consumption when she was only fifteen. She told me about the times when the mills were going night and day and there was employment for everyone and how the mill-girls would go to work barefoot in the rain.

She talked about meeting Isaac and how handsome he was and always jolly and full of fun. How he took her to Bangor on the train and they had fish suppers and mushy peas in the Café Continental and she had her fortune told by Madame Florentine in a windy booth near the Pickie Pool.

She talked about the Blitz, when the Luftwaffe bombed Belfast and the people had to flee their homes leaving everything behind, Catholics and Protestants huddling together in ditches above Ballysillan, and the sky bright as day from the fires that raged throughout the city. And the following morning the radio saying that 1,200 people were dead and whole streets levelled to the ground. I learnt a lot of things I didn't know in those conversations with Sarah, but one topic was never mentioned and that was my adoption. I never raised it and neither did she.

One day as Dr Caldwell was leaving, I asked to speak to him and we went into the front room.

'Tell me honestly,' I began. 'Is she going to get better?'

Dr Caldwell puffed out his cheeks and then he looked at the floor. I noticed that his hair had grown silver and there were heavy bags of flesh below his chin.

'Who's to tell? We must never give up hope.'

I knew then that she was dying.

★ ★ ★

Aly McVeigh told me that Charlie Delaney, the newsagent, was looking for someone to deliver papers. I went to see him and he gave me the job. Most of the deliveries were to the middle-class houses up the Crumlin Road. I had to get up at 6.30 a.m. so that people got their papers before they went to work. I'd set the alarm and make a cup of tea and bring it in to Sarah.

It was beautiful at that time of the morning, the sun hanging like fire above Cavehill and the streets of Ardoyne empty and still. I'd be at the shop for 7 a.m. and Charlie Delaney would have my canvas bag stuffed with copies of The Newsletter and The Daily Telegraph and The Times and I'd set off to deliver them.

I remember the gardens of the big houses above Everton school, how they shone in the morning light and the heavy scent of the flowers. There would be trees gleaming green and gold in the sun, frail-hearted roses, gladioli and lupin, lawns trimmed and neat as a carpet.

Some of the houses had guard dogs, angry Alsatians that came barking as I approached. But after a while they got to know me. They'd raise an ear when they heard me coming and then shake themselves and go back to sleep.

I now had three jobs, and little spare time, but I always made time for reading. One day I saw a notice for a short-story competition in a magazine. I cut out the application form and left it beside my bed and forgot about it, but a few days later I came across it again. The prize was £20 and a year's free subscription. The winning entry would be published in the magazine. I thought: Why not? And sat down at my desk and began to write.

I wrote about a doomed love affair, a young man in love with a girl who disdains him, and how she comes to regret it when it is too late and he is married to someone else. I must have had Eileen Toner in mind. I made several drafts, correcting and improving as I went. I tried to inject suspense and surprise, to create atmosphere, to get inside the heads of my characters so that the reader would empathise with their plight.

When I was happy with the story, I wrote it out as neatly as I could with a pen and a new nib, put it in an envelope along with the entry form, and posted it to an address in London.

* ★ ★

I seemed to be in a frenzy of activity that summer, as if I wanted to keep myself busy so that I would have no time to think about what was happening to Sarah. But I couldn't escape it and at night when I got into bed I would hear the slow rise and fall of her breathing in the room next door.

I often lay awake for a long time thinking about the unspoken business that lay between us. Before she died, I wanted her to be plain with me, to tell me the one thing I wanted to hear from her: That I had been adopted. I wanted her to tell me how it had happened. I wanted to know who my real parents were and where they lived now. But the information had to come from her. She had to tell me herself. Some deep wound inside my head made it impossible for me to frame the words to ask.

Sarah got a bit better towards the end of August. She got up out of bed and came downstairs. I lit the fire for her and she sat watching the street. I had tried to keep Isaac's garden tidy but it had been a losing battle. I lacked his talent and patience and time and the garden had slowly reverted to nature.

Sarah didn't seem to mind. It was a patch of greenery and there was still a few flowers pushing up bravely among the weeds. She seemed content. She would sit at the window with the radio playing in the background and watch the people passing by.

There seemed to be more people on the streets now, for the mills were beginning to close and people were idle. New production methods made the old factories redundant and one by one they shut their doors. The hooters fell quiet and Flax Street, which once had been a bustle of activity, had become like a morgue; a long road of tall, silent, empty buildings from which the life had ebbed away.

The decline of the mills coincided with Sarah's decline. I went back to school at the beginning of September and came home one day to find she had taken to her bed again. She began to lose weight rapidly and to drift in and out of consciousness.

The District Nurse would come every morning to administer her morphine injection. Father Jeremiah would call and give her Communion. The neighbours would come in with food and sit with her. Aunt Minnie and Uncle Paddy would call. As she sank lower, the activity around the house increased and I realised there wasn't long to go.

I can't remember the last coherent

conversation I had with her; several encounters seem to merge into one. But I know that she kept impressing on me the need to study hard at school and to keep up my religious observance. Towards the end, Sarah became obsessed with my immortal soul.

And then, one afternoon, I heard voices raised in her bedroom. Aunt Minnie and Uncle Paddy were in there with her. I got up and went closer to listen. I could hear Aunt Minnie saying: 'You have to tell him, Sarah. He has to know.'

'Och, Sarah. It would be so easy,' Uncle Paddy said. 'We'll be here with you. Sure, why don't you tell him? It's only a couple of words.'

I strained for Sarah's response, but there was none. I didn't want her to die, but I knew that things happened that no one could control. And suddenly I knew too that if she told me, she wouldn't go to her grave with this burden on her mind and I wouldn't have to live with the doubts. I forced myself to open the door and go into her room, but she was asleep.

'Sarah. I'm here.'

Her eyes flickered but there was no sound.

'Sarah. It's me. Martin. Talk to me.'

Uncle Paddy and Aunt Minnie looked at me and no one said a word.

★ ★ ★

A few days later I came home to find an envelope with a London postmark. I knew what it was immediately. I tore it open and a cheque for £20 fell out. There was a letter from the editor of the magazine, congratulating me on winning First Prize in the short story competition, and announcing that my entry would be published in the next edition. I held the cheque up to the light and examined the firm handwriting. Pay the bearer and my name in block capitals. The sum of twenty pounds sterling. I had never won anything in my life.

I was excited. I went up to Sarah's room to tell her. Her eyes were closed but I knew she could hear me.

'I won a prize. Twenty pounds. For writing a story. Isn't that great news?'

Sarah made no response. Her chest rose and fell with her breathing. I spoke the words again but it was like speaking to a child. I sat down beside her bed and took her hand. I could feel my heart breaking with the pain. I thought: 'Tell me. For God's sake, tell me. I know already but I want to hear it from you.'

Sarah didn't speak. I felt a terrible sadness build up inside me but no tears came. I leaned across the bed and kissed her cheek.

Two days later, Sarah was dead.

Book Three

Book Three

11

A lot of people died that autumn. Granny McVeigh went in her sleep. She was ninety-two and her father had survived the Great Famine. Willie Toner had a heart attack sitting in front of his television. Spa Doherty's Uncle Fonsie was knocked down and killed by a car while drunk. A child, one of the McAlorums, died from pneumonia. There was a constant stream of black hearses driving through the gates of Holy Cross Church during those dark days as the light began to fade and winter drew in.

Sarah died from spheroidal cell carcinoma of left breast and metastases to spine and liver. That's what it says on her death certificate. It means cancer and it was all through her body. She was fifty-four.

We buried her in the same plot with Isaac in Milltown Cemetery. There was a good turn-out of old neighbours and friends, Father Jeremiah in his billowing vestments leading the prayers at the end, talking about a life well-lived, an illness bravely borne.

It was a grey day and it began to rain as the service was breaking up, so that the little hills above Ballymurphy became covered in mist. I rode back to Ardoyne in the undertaker's car with Uncle Paddy, the windscreen wipers flapping furiously against the rain. I was weary after the death and the funeral, the streams of mourners, people shaking my hand and telling me how sorry they were.

When we got to the Crumlin Road, Uncle Paddy said: 'Why don't you and me go and have a wee drink? There's some things I want to talk to you about.'

We went to the Wheatfield Bar at the corner of Leopold Street because I couldn't face Isaac's old pals in Logue's. We sat at a table near the big windows and Uncle Paddy ordered the drinks. When they came, he sucked the froth off his pint and said: 'Jesus, Marty. I don't know where to start.'

He said he supposed I'd be staying on in the house.

I said I would if it could be arranged.

'Oh, we'll arrange it alright. Dare the one try and stop us. Sure Sarah and Isaac must have bought that house ten times over with all the rent they've paid.'

He asked me what I was planning to do.

'I don't know. Finish school and look for a job, I suppose.'

'You know your Aunt Minnie and me are always here if you need anything?'

286

'Yes.'

'You're to come and see us if you have any problems or anything we can help you with. Do you hear me now?'

I said I did.

Uncle Paddy toyed with his glass. I could see he was uneasy.

'I don't know how to tell you this,' he said gently. 'But it's something you've got a right to know.'

I knew what he was going to say. I had been waiting to hear it for years.

'Sarah and Isaac weren't your real parents. You were adopted when you were a baby.'

'I know.'

'Well I'll be damned,' Uncle Paddy said. 'Here's me racking my brains trying to figure out how to tell you and you knew all the time. How did you find out?'

'I overheard a conversation.'

'And you kept it to yourself?'

'Yes.'

'Well, boys a boys. You know what it is, Marty? If you ask me, nothing good ever comes from secrets. Your mother's name was Stella. She was a lovely girl.'

And so it was Paddy who finally told me. We sat in the corner of the pub while the rain beat against the window and the story came tumbling out. Stella was only a slip of a girl up from the country. The war was raging. There was loads of work. The mills and the factories were running day and night, making parachutes and uniforms and munitions for the war.

Stella met a soldier and the next thing she was pregnant. She didn't know what to do. My father went off to France and Stella was on her own. She was out of her mind with worry. She couldn't go back home with a baby and here she was in a strange city where she hardly knew anybody.

After I was born, somebody put her in touch with a priest in Holy Cross Monastery. He thought of Sarah who was dying for a child and couldn't have one. So one day, the priest arrived on Sarah's doorstep and told her about this poor girl he knew and the wee baby boy she had and how she couldn't keep him and would Sarah and Isaac like to adopt him? And Sarah's heart leapt with joy.

I was all excited now as the details poured out.

'What age was I?'

'Five months.'

'And Stella kept me all that time?'

'Don't ask me how she did it, Marty. There was no welfare in them days. If you had a baby, that was your lookout. I suppose in the end she'd no option but to give you up. But you know, for months afterwards she kept calling at Sarah's house to see you and bring you wee presents and things.

'In the end, Sarah had to tell her not to call any more. You were getting too big. I remember that day, Stella walking up the street to get the tram and every couple of yards she would stop and look back. I think it must have broke her heart to leave you.'

I felt a lump rise in my throat.

'Where is she now?

'God knows. I never saw her again.'

'Do you know where she came from?'

'Down the country somewhere.'

'Do you know her surname?'

'No.'

'Would my birth certificate tell me?'

'It might.'

I sat for a while and my mind flooded with all the unresolved questions I had asked myself from the first time I knew. Did I have brothers and sisters? Did I have aunts and uncles? Did I have cousins?

'What did she look like?'

'Oh, Marty. She was a smasher. She was the best-looking woman I ever saw. Apart from your Aunt Minnie, of course.'

'Was she dark, like me?'

'She was, Marty.'

'And what about my father?'

'Your father was never mentioned.'

'Surely, somebody must know who he was.'

Uncle Paddy put down his beer and laid his cold hand on mine.

'Marty. Let me give you some advice. These things are best left alone.'

'But I have a right to know about them. You said so yourself.'

Paddy just shook his head.

'They should have told you. I pleaded with them. Minnie pleaded with them. All this could have been spared if only you'd been told.'

'And why wasn't I?'

'It was Sarah. Isaac wanted to do it before he died, but Sarah wouldn't let him.'

'Why not?'

'God knows. I think she had this notion in her head that you wouldn't love them if you knew. And she couldn't bear the thought of that.'

★ ★ ★

I went home and over the next few days I cleaned out Sarah's wardrobes and dressers. I gathered all her old clothes and put them in a big plastic bag. She had kept some of Isaac's clothes and I took these as well. I brought the whole lot round to Charlie Pigeon's house and gave them to his mother for the market.

At the back of her wardrobe, I found Sarah's handbag and inside were all her papers. There was a bank book with a few pounds in it and a couple of death policies and when all these were cashed, I had enough to pay the undertaker's bills. Uncle Paddy took me down to the estate manager's office and got the house transferred to my name. With the money that was left over and the money I earned from my jobs, I was able to manage.

I found old photographs; one with me and Isaac in baggy swimming togs at the Herring Pond in Portstewart. Another showed me in short pants, somewhere in downtown Belfast. I was walking between Sarah and Isaac and we were all holding hands. You could see the look of bewilderment on my face as the street photographer pressed the button down.

There was a photograph of Isaac and Uncle Paddy at a party. Isaac had a bottle of stout in his hand, his chest puffed out and his mouth open as if he was singing. There was a postcard from Uncle Paddy on shore leave in Gibraltar. The postmark read 2/5/1948. Uncle Paddy had written: 'They have monkeys here and I swear to God, they're so smart they could buy and sell you.'

On top of the wardrobe, I found a full set

of cutlery, slightly mildewed but still in its tissue wrapping. It was a wedding present someone had given her, put away for a special occasion that never came. I found invitations carefully replaced in their envelopes, old memorial cards of friends long dead, a menu from a wedding breakfast they had attended in the Grand Central Hotel in June 1936, bits and pieces of their lives.

At last, in a fading manilla envelope, I found my birth certificate. I sat on the bed and read the facts of my birth: Name and Surname: Martin McBride. Sex: Male. Date of Birth: February 29th, 1945. Place of Birth: Belfast Urban District 9. There was nothing on the certificate about Stella or my father.

★ ★ ★

I went back to school. I found it strange at first. People kept coming up to me in the yard, telling me how sorry they were about my mother dying and me being an orphan now. When I came home in the evenings, the house would be empty and cold. There was a stillness that I never knew before. Things would be where I had left them. If I put the kettle on the cooker or a dish in the sink, they would still be there, untouched. If I left a light switched on, it would still be burning when I came back.

For a while, Aunt Minnie or one of the neighbours would come to the house to ask if I needed anything; washing done, or groceries collected. They would drop in with bits of dinner on a plate covered with a cloth and tell me it was going to be thrown out and it was a terrible waste and would I not have it. But gradually they dropped away, as if they sensed that I wanted to be alone and I had the house to myself.

I would set Sarah's alarm to get me up in the morning, when I would make a cup of tea and deliver the newspapers. I would come home, have breakfast and go to school. On Friday evenings, I went up to Andy Molloy's shop and got enough groceries to keep me for a week.

I learnt to survive on stews that lasted for days, on scrambled eggs or beans on toast. I wasn't much good at cooking and anyway, I didn't have time. A lot of nights I just got a bag of chips from Freddie Fusco's and ate them out of the wrapper.

I stopped seeing people. After school I did my waste-paper round. Then I'd eat, do my homework, read and go to bed. The days began to fade into each other. Sometimes I'd go for weeks without talking to neighbours or friends.

Sundays were the worst. I gave up going to Mass. I had already stopped going to Confession, so giving up Mass wasn't so hard, even if it was another mortal sin. So that nobody would notice, I left home at ten to eleven. But instead of going into the church, I continued up the Crumlin Road past the Fire Station and walked as far as Ligoniel.

I kept thinking of Isaac on those walks; the times when I was small and we would sit and look down on the city and he'd point out the streets to me and the slender stacks of the mills with the smoke curling like blue thread from the dark chimneys.

I would pass the cottage where the old lady had lived who kept the goats. But the walls were collapsed now and huge weeds sprouted where the honeysuckle and roses used to grow. Every time I passed the cottage, I thought of him and the warm, firm clasp of his hand and the smell of tobacco off his clothes. I cursed the fact that he was dead, that Sarah was dead and that I was now alone in the world.

After a while, I couldn't bring myself to go there anymore. So instead, I caught the bus down the Woodvale Road and walked around the city centre. The shops would be closed, the pubs and cinemas locked, the cafés shut. I would walk the deserted streets, looking into the windows of the big stores on Royal Avenue or listening to the street preachers with their sandwich boards urging me to turn my back on sin and return to God. Eventually I'd get tired and get on a bus and go home to Ardoyne.

In November, there were icicles hanging from the gutters and the mill dam behind the house froze over. The top of the Black Mountain was capped with snow. It was going to be a hard winter. The mornings were dark as night. I would get up at 6.30 a.m. and my breath would be hanging like steam in the air as I made my way up the street to Charlie Delaney's shop.

I would pull on my bag of papers and start my deliveries, but the big houses on the Crumlin Road looked different in winter. They were dark and forbidding, the lawns heavy with frost, the trees spreading their branches like gaunt fingers against the early morning light.

I would hurry home and eat a quick breakfast of cornflakes and toast. I'd eat it standing up, then rush off to school, glad of the warmth of the classroom, and often I would have to struggle to stay awake. My life became a dull round of work and school.

I thought of Stella all the time. I couldn't

get her out of my head. I kept going over the conversation I had with Uncle Paddy. I wondered what she looked like, where she had come from, what she did. I began to dream about her. I pictured a tall, dark elegant woman, like the women I'd see in the glossy magazines in Charlie Delaney's shop.

I tried to imagine the life we had together after I was born. She was poor and she couldn't work but still she had kept me for five months. Where did we live? How did she manage? I kept thinking of Stella walking up Brompton Park after she had seen me for the last time and the way she kept looking back. She must have loved me. I clung to that thought. Stella hadn't abandoned me after all. It wasn't her fault. She had no choice.

An idea had formed in my mind that Stella was waiting somewhere for me. I thought of all the questions I would ask her. I knew if I could find Stella, there would be no more doubts.

One evening, as Christmas drew near, I sat down at the kitchen table and made some calculations. I decided that I could manage without the newspaper job, so I went to see Charlie Delaney and told him I was leaving. The following day, I went up to Holy Cross Church and asked to see the rector.

* ★ ★ ★

His name was Father Thomas. He was a shy man with a stoop and dandruff on the black shoulders of his soutane. He brought me into the parlour and offered me tea.

'My name is Martin McBride and I think you might be able to help me.'

'Sure I know you well, Martin. What can I do for you?'

I told him about being adopted and what Uncle Paddy had said about the priest who put Stella in touch with Sarah.

'That would be Father Ambrose.'

'Do you know where he is now?'

'The poor man is dead these ten years. He was transferred to Dublin in 1950. And then he had a stroke.'

I said I was sorry to hear that.

'Would there be any records?'

Father Thomas shook his head.

'That's not the way things were done in those days. It was all very casual. A priest would hear of a girl in trouble and he'd arrange for the child to be given a good home. It wasn't formal, like now.'

'I want to trace my mother,' I said.

Father Thomas pursed his lips and I could see he was thinking hard.

'You know, Martin, that might not be a good thing.'

'Why?'

'Because your mother might have got married. She might have other children. Maybe she hasn't told them about you. Maybe she's put you out of her mind. If you suddenly turn up again, it could cause problems.'

'No,' I said quickly. 'She thinks about me all the time.'

'How do you know?'

'Because she kept me for five months when I was a baby. She didn't want to give me away but she had no choice.'

'It's a long time ago. People change.'

'She's waiting for me. I know she wants to see me.'

'And you're determined to find her?'

'Yes.'

Father Thomas said: 'All right. What does your birth certificate say?'

I told him that it only gave my name and date of birth.

'There must be a fuller record of your birth. It would have been entered on the Register of Births. It's the law. It would certainly contain your mother's name. Once you have that, then you'll have something to go on.'

'But my birth wouldn't be registered as McBride, father.'

'No. It would be registered under your mother's name.'

'But that's the whole point. I don't know my mother's name.'

Father Thomas looked at me with a sad face.

'God help you, Martin. I think you've got a problem.'

★　★　★

I caught a bus into town. It began to rain and I watched the drops forming little streams along the window pane. By the time I reached the Registrar of Births, my clothes were already soaked.

It was a big old building near the City Hall. I was shown into a waiting room and then a young woman called my name. I was taken to another room with a desk and three chairs. There was a man in a striped suit sitting behind the desk, writing in a file. He didn't look up when I came in but just kept on writing. The young woman sat beside him and waited.

Eventually the man put down his pen and looked me over. There was steam rising from my damp clothes and my hair was plastered

on my head with the rain. I saw him wrinkle
his nose.

'Name?'

'Martin McBride.'

'Date of birth?'

I told him and he wrote it down.

'So, what can we do for you?'

I said I was adopted and wanted to find my
mother.

'When were you adopted?'

'1945.'

'That was a long year,' the man said. 'What
month?'

I told him I didn't know.

The man let out a sigh.

'Do you know how many children were
born in 1945?'

'No.'

'Thousands. Was the adoption ever registered?'

'I don't know.'

'Do you know anything?'

'I know my mother's name was Stella.'

'Stella who?'

'I don't know.'

'Do you know your father's name?'

'No.'

The man put down the pen.

'This is ridiculous. Do you realise what was
happening when you were born?'

'The War was on.'

'That's right. The town was full of floozies. They came from all arts and parts. They were jumping into bed with every Tom, Dick and Harry for a pair of nylon stockings.'

I felt my face burn and saw the woman look away.

'There were more illegitimate births in Belfast in 1945 than in all the years since. Your mother could be anyone. Finding her would be like finding a needle in a haystack.'

I felt helpless. I looked down and saw the rain from my shoes making puddles on the floor.

'If I had a copy of my full birth certificate it would tell me who my mother was.'

'Listen to him. He wants a copy of his full birth certificate. Maybe you'd like to tell us where we can start looking for it?'

'You have my date of birth. You have my mother's first name.'

'Stella? How do you know it's real?'

'It's what people told me. People who knew her.'

'Well maybe *they* can tell you who she was. I can't. Anyway, you're not entitled to your full birth certificate. Even if we could find it.' He turned to his file.

'Not entitled?'

'No.'

'Why not?'

'Because it's the law.'

I was overwhelmed by the injustice of it all. How was I ever going to find Stella if nobody would tell me her name?

'That's not fair. I have a right to know who my mother is.'

The man began to smile.

'Look. You were adopted. Your mother gave you away. She severed all connection with you. The law says you have no right to information.'

'Please help me. I'm desperate. I've nowhere else to go.'

The man looked at me once more and then he bent his head and started writing again.

I stood up. I fought back the tears. I walked out of the room and into the hall. When I reached the street, I heard someone calling my name. I turned and saw the woman from the Registrar's office come running after me.

'I'm sorry,' she said. 'Mr Armitage has been like a bear all morning. If you give me your address, I'll try to help you.'

I told her and she said: 'I'm not promising. It's going to mean hours of work sifting through the records. But if I find anything I'll write to you and let you know.'

★　★　★

Christmas drew in and people began to take an interest in me again. Aunt Minnie asked me round to their house for my Christmas dinner and Aly McVeigh invited me to a party on Christmas night. One evening I heard a knock at the front door and John Rea was standing on the step with a brown paper bag. He thrust it into my hands.

'I was just passing by and I thought I'd stop and say Hello.'

I opened the bag. Inside was a dozen bottles of stout.

'Come in, John,' I said, and we sat down beside the fire in the front room and I took the caps off the bottles.

John Rea stretched his legs.

'Jeez, Marty. How time flies. It seems like only yesterday you were a wee nipper and you and Isaac were pulling the big Christmas tree down the street from Stewarts'.'

I said it did.

'Your mother was very proud of her Christmas tree. She had the best tree in the district. And she always put an angel on top instead of a star because she said it wasn't a peep show and people should remember they were celebrating the birth of Christ, the Prince of Peace. Do you remember that?'

I said I did.

'Do you remember when I used to take you

to the station for your summer holidays? Isaac was a great man for a good tip. I'll say one thing for Isaac. He was a decent skin. I don't think there was one mean bone in his whole body.'

We finished the stout and opened two more and sat talking about old times till the fire burned out and the bottles were gone and John Rea went home.

★   ★   ★

At school, we had exams in the run-up to the holidays. When they were over, Brother O'Callaghan took me aside.

'You're doing well, Martin. Your grades are very good.'

'Thank you, Sir.'

'Have you thought about a career yet? What you'd like to do with your life?'

I told him I'd like to be a journalist.

'You'd be good at it. At least you can spell. That's more than can be said for some of them.'

He laughed and then his face grew serious.

'Can I ask you, Martin? How are you coping with your recent troubles?'

'All right, Sir.'

'I don't mean to intrude, but you've had more to bear than most. It must be hard for you. And you've performed better than some boys who've had far better opportunities. Sometimes it would make you wonder what God is up to at all.'

'Yes, Sir.'

'Are you still interested in the music?'

I told him I was and he brightened up.

'Never forget the music. It will turn out to be a good friend to you in the end.'

He opened a drawer and took out a package.

'Here,' he said. 'It's just a wee Christmas present. I hope you like it.'

I took the wrapping off. It was another record, by a group I'd never heard of before. There was a strange drawing on the cover in red ink and underneath the legend: *The Chieftains*.

★ ★ ★

Christmas Day came. I got up at nine o'clock and put on my best clothes and went to Mass. I hadn't been to church for months and it was like returning home. It was warm and bright and the choir sang carols I remembered from when I was a little boy. Afterwards, I called on the McAllisters and sat drinking beer and watching television with Bobby till it was time to go round to

Chatham Street to Aunt Minnie McCrory.

Their house was filled with the smell of cooking turkey. Aunt Minnie met me at the door in a pinafore like the one that Sarah used to wear. Uncle Paddy brought me into the parlour and said: 'It's been a long ould winter, Marty. Will you take a wee tincture to keep out the cold?'

He drew a bottle of whiskey from under the sofa.

I said I would pass and Uncle Paddy said; 'Well, I'm just going to have the one, for it's good for my arthritis.'

'Arthritis my arse,' Aunt Minnie called from the kitchen. 'You wouldn't know arthritis if it jumped up and bit you. You get drunk this holy day and I swear to God, I'll brain you.'

Uncle Paddy winked at me and retorted: 'I love you too, Sweetheart.'

We had a big dinner with brussel sprouts and gravy. Uncle Paddy had the giblets. Betsy Grey turned up her nose and said she didn't know how anybody could eat stuff like that. Uncle Paddy said the giblets were the best part of the bird and that's where all the goodness was. Betsy Gray said maybe it was but they still smelt like cat's piss.

Uncle Paddy got tipsy and toasted our absent friends. He said there was Wolfe Tone working away in the outback of Australia making his fortune in the goldmines and getting ready to come home and open his own pub. But what sort of Christmas dinner was he having? And Patrick Pearse who was married now and had his own wee place over in Divis Flats. And, of course, poor Sarah and Isaac, God rest their souls.

'For God's sake, don't be getting maudlin on us,' Aunt Minnie said. 'Put that bloody whiskey bottle away.'

'Minnie,' said Uncle Paddy, 'do you remember the time Isaac was going over to London and he got on the wrong train and ended up in Glasgow?'

We all laughed.

'And he wondered why everybody was talking like they came from Ballymena?'

Uncle Paddy took another drink of whiskey and shook his head.

'There's one thing nobody can take away from you, Marty. You came from decent people.'

Soon it was time to go to McVeigh's party. I walked up the empty street with the frost glistening on the rooftops and a big yellow moon hanging in the sky. I felt light-headed after all the beer I'd been drinking and when I came to McVeigh's house I could see the light streaming out and hear the noise inside and somebody singing 'San Francisco'.

I'm having a good Christmas, I thought. Who needs a family, anyway?

I went into the crowded room and there was Aly with a glass in his hand, and Mr McVeigh with a red cap like Santa Claus and all these people laughing and enjoying themselves. Immediately my heart filled with remorse and I felt the old familiar sadness return.

12

I went back to school in January, but my heart wasn't in it. I was coming up for seventeen with no sign of a job. I was fed up knocking on doors for wastepaper and hauling bags of spuds round Andy Molloy's shop. I wanted a real job with real money.

Kevin and Aly both had jobs. Kevin was pulling pints in Clancy's bar in Smithfield, training to be a barman. Aly was working with his father as a builder's labourer. I'd see the two of them coming home in the evening covered in cement dust like real working men and I'd feel jealous. Kevin and Aly had money. They could buy themselves new clothes. They could take a girl out and go for fish suppers and Cokes in Freddie Fusco's and put money in the juke-box to play records any time they wanted. I was struggling to make ends meet and restless to be earning money.

I would take my Senior Certificate exam in June. If I wanted to go on to university, I would have to study for another year, and if I got accepted, I would have to spend a further three years before I got a degree. It seemed like an awful long time to keep struggling the way I was, in the hope of getting a decent job at the end of it all. I began to toy with the possibility of getting out.

One day Brother O'Callaghan said he wanted to talk to me. He began by asking if I'd had a chance to listen to The Chieftains' record. I told him I had.

'And, did you like it?'

'Yes.'

'Isn't your man, Paddy Moloney, a gas ticket all the same? You know, he can nearly make those pipes talk.'

He told me about a man called Sean O'Riada who had revolutionised Irish music.

'I have some of his records too. I could lend them to you.'

'I'd like that, Sir.'

Then he said: 'You're not happy, are you?'

'No.'

'I could tell. Do you want to talk about it?'

I told him I was sick of studying and scraping to make ends meet. I told him I wanted to have money in my pocket and be independent.

When I had finished, he said: 'Would you not stay till the summer at least and sit for your Senior?'

'What use would that be?'

'Well, if you get a decent result, it would get you into the Civil Service. You'd have a job for life. A nice comfortable job, working in an office, out of the rain. And a pension to look forward to at the end of it all. That wouldn't be bad now, for a boy from Ardoyne.'

I thought of myself sitting behind a desk all day signing bits of paper.

'I don't want to be a civil servant.'

'You still want to be a journalist?'

'Yes.'

'All right. Give me a few days and I'll talk to you again.'

He came back at the end of the week and said there was a man he wanted me to go and see. His name was Fergus Pyle and he was the Northern Editor of a Dublin paper called *The Irish Times*.

'Tell him you can sing,' Brother O'Callaghan stressed. 'He's a great man for the tradition.'

I went to see Fergus Pyle. I put on my Sunday suit and a clean shirt and tie. I got my hair cut and polished my shoes and clipped my finger nails to make myself presentable. I had to hold my breath to stop myself from shaking.

Fergus Pyle was a heavy-built man with bright eyes and untidy hair and he spoke with a Free State accent. He began by asking me why I wanted to be a journalist.

'I can write and I'm interested in current affairs.'

I told him about the short story competition I had won, and gave him a clipping.

He said: 'If you were interviewing the Prime Minister and he was called urgently from the room, what would you do?'

'I'd wait till he came back.'

'No you wouldn't. You'd read the letters on his desk. See what the hell he was up to. A famous American, called H. L. Mencken, once said that news is what they want to hide and all the rest is advertising. Have you got shorthand and typing?'

'No, but I'm willing to learn.'

'Do you know Belfast well?'

'Yes.'

'If I sent you up the Shankill Road, would you go?'

'Sure, I go up there on my way home from school every day.'

'But if there was a riot on, would you go?'

I hesitated.

'That's what a reporter has to do. Report. Get in the thick of things. Tell the reader what happened.'

'Then I'd go.'

Fergus Pyle put his hands behind his head.

He was wearing red braces to hold up his trousers.

'Journalism is a very disruptive business. You never know when you'll be called out. You work Saturdays and Sundays and evenings. You never have any home life. You never get any peace. Some people think it's a glamorous job, hobnobbing with the rich and famous. But the rich and famous can be the most boring people on earth. You shouldn't get into this business unless you're prepared for that.'

'I am prepared for it.'

'Then it's the most satisfying job I know.'

He sat up straight.

'I'll take you on as a copy sorter. You'll be largely running messages, doing jobs for me. We won't be able to pay you much.'

'That doesn't matter.'

Fergus Pyle shook his head sadly.

'Never say that money doesn't matter. We'll pay you eight pounds a week. And you'll get some expenses on top.'

I thought I was hearing things. Eight pounds was a fortune.

'Will I get to write?'

'That depends on you.'

He gathered some papers together.

'You can start on Monday. Ten o'clock.'

I thanked him and stood up.

313

'Brother O'Callaghan says you can sing?'
'A wee bit.'
'That'll make a change around here. Do
you know 'The Flower of Magherallyo'?'
I closed my eyes and stuck out my chest
the way Isaac used to do.

*'Twas on a Summer's morning and all
the flowers*
were bloomingo.
*Fair Nature was adorning and the wee
birds all*
were singingo.
*I met my love near Banbridge town, my
darling*
blue-eyed Sallyo.
*She is the Pride of the County Down
and the*
Flower of Magherallyo.

The Irish Times office was two rooms over a
grain warehouse down near the Albert Clock.
There was a permanent smell of flour about
the place and pigeons on the roof. There was
a main office, with a secretary called Janet,
and a smaller room which Fergus Pyle used
as his office.
'Fergus didn't tell me anything about you. I
suppose you'd better sit and wait for him,'
said Janet.

I took a seat and at five to eleven he came storming in the door with his hair askew and his tie on crooked. He took a list of phone calls from Janet, collected his post and went into his office. Ten minutes later he reappeared in his shirt sleeves.

'I want you to run round to the station. There's a parcel on the eleven o'clock train from Dublin. You'll have to sign for it, so you'll need identification. I don't suppose you've got a driving licence?'

I said I didn't.

He went into his office again and came back with a card and gave it to Janet.

'Type his name on that. Martin McBride.'

He gave it to me. It said PRESS in large letters on the front and underneath THE IRISH TIMES.

'There's a space for your photograph. You can get one taken in the photo booth in the station. And don't lose it. It's valuable.'

And off I went.

That was my first journalistic assignment, picking up a parcel off the train. I hurried through the streets of Belfast with the words of H.L. Mencken ringing in my head. I proudly presented the card that identified me as an editorial employee of *The Irish Times*. I folded it away in my wallet and several times that day, I took it out and looked at it, as if it

315

was a magic passport to my life as a reporter. I kept thinking of the old black and white movies I had seen; Spencer Tracy with a card marked PRESS in his hatband. That was me. I was somebody important and that card would open doors.

I loved every minute of it. Besides running messages, I would monitor the wire services from Reuters and PA, which came clattering into the office every day in a deluge of paper. I also kept the newspaper files up to date, and organised a library service which meant reading the national and local papers, cutting out articles, and filing them away for reference. At 5 p.m. Janet left, and I manned the phones, taking messages from the police and fire brigade, other journalists and the public. When I could, I sat behind an old Remington typewriter and practised my typing.

There was a man called Frank Nelson who came in the afternoons to operate the machines and transmit Fergus's typed reports down the wire to the main office in Dublin.

I was always busy. Some nights I didn't get away till nine or ten o'clock. But I didn't mind. I loved the atmosphere of the newspaper office, even if this was only a one-man provincial operation. I loved being at the centre of things, hearing tidbits of news and information, taking phone calls from politicians and dignitaries.

One afternoon, Fergus Pyle came out of his office and said to me: 'What are you doing tonight?'

I said I had nothing planned.

'Would you like to come to a meeting of the Corporation?'

I said I would.

'Right. We go at half past six.'

I was excited. As we hurried along Royal Avenue to the City Hall, he explained.

'I want you to take notes. And when you go home this evening, I want you to type up a six-hundred-word report.'

'For the paper?' I asked nervously.

Fergus smiled.

'No. I'll be filing the report for the paper. I just want to see what you can do.'

We went to the seats reserved for the press. There was about a dozen reporters there, and they all seemed to know Fergus. He introduced me to the people sitting closest, and we all shook hands. At seven o'clock, the meeting began.

Tape recorders weren't allowed, and everybody had to scribble like mad to take down what was said. I watched as Fergus's pencil flew along the page. At a quarter to nine, he looked at his watch, snapped his

317

notebook shut and said: 'That's it. Time for the first edition.'

Down we went to the foyer, and he dropped some coins into a phone. I heard him call up Copy and then he was dictating at a furious rate down the line. I went home to Brompton Park, made myself a boiled egg and sat down to write my report.

The following morning, Fergus called me into his office and asked to see what I had written. He put on his glasses and took out a blue pencil. I waited anxiously for his reaction.

'Councillor Gerry Fitt delivered an interesting speech last night at the monthly meeting of Belfast Corporation.'

He pushed his glasses up his forehead.

'Who said it was interesting?'

'I did.'

'But the readers mightn't think it was interesting. They might think it was the greatest load of old cobblers.'

'The readers weren't there.'

'Exactly. And your job is to give them a straight report. Just tell them what Gerry Fitt said. Don't editorialise. Let them make up their own minds.'

He took the pencil and scored out the word interesting.

'What was so interesting about it anyway?'

318

'He said the Corporation Housing Department was discriminating against Catholics.'

'Why don't you say that?'

'I do. It's in the fourth paragraph.'

Fergus shook his head.

'Readers are busy people. They mightn't have time to read to the fourth paragraph. If you think that's the most important thing, it should be right up there in the first paragraph.'

He took the pencil and scored out the first three paragraphs.

'How long did it take you to write this?'

'Three hours.'

'Far too long. This isn't a school essay. You have to edit and cut. Exclude everything that isn't relevant. Next time you go to a Corporation meeting, read the order paper carefully. You should be able to tell from the order of business what the news is, before it happens.'

He gave me back my report, scored through with pencil, redundant adjectives removed, spellings corrected, sentences tightened up. I went out to my desk feeling foolish, took a copy of that day's paper and read his own report, filed last night in ten minutes on the end of a phone line.

The sub-editor had written FITT ACCUSES BELFAST HOUSING DEPARTMENT. The report began: 'Councillor Gerry Fitt last night accused Belfast Corporation of discrimination in the allocation of houses to Catholics.'

The report was a concise, accurate summary of the previous night's meeting. I could see at once what Fergus had been talking about. I was learning to be a reporter.

★ ★ ★

On Saturday afternoons, if I wasn't working, I liked to go to Pat's Bar to listen to the music. Pat's was an old-fashioned pub down at the docks. People used to say it was the second last pub before you got to England. Next door was Barney's Bar and that was the last.

There was a long counter and a couple of back rooms and a rough wooden floor and the toilet was out in the yard. On a rainy night you got soaked when you went for a pee. But it had the best traditional music in Belfast and if you sang a song they gave you a chit that got you a free pint of Guinness.

One Saturday afternoon, a young woman stood up. She was very good-looking. She pushed her fair hair away from her face, put her hand over her ear and began to sing:

The rain beats at my yellow locks, the
   dew wets me still,
The babe is cold in my arms love, Lord
   Gregory let me in.
Do you remember, Lord Gregory, that
   night in Cappoquin?
You stole away my maidenhead, and
   sore against my will.
So, I'll leave now, these windows, and
   likewise this hall.
And it's deep in the sea, I will find my
   downfall . . .

I felt the hairs rise on the back of my neck. She had a beautiful, clear voice and it silenced the room. It was a song I had never heard before about a poor girl who gets into trouble and is abandoned by her rich lover. It made me think of Stella.

I asked someone who she was and he said 'Maura Magee.'

I met her later at the bar and we got talking. She was a student at Queen's University, she told me, and was studying English. I asked her if she'd like to come to a Dubliners' concert with me and she said Yes and we started going out together.

Maura was very interested in traditional music and we would spend our time together going to folk clubs and sessions. She lent me books and in the long summer evenings, we'd go for walks along the Lagan embankment and talk about Thomas Hardy and Wilfred Owen and W.B. Yeats.

One night, she brought me to a poetry reading at the university. The poet was a tall, thin man with glasses and everybody sat quiet as mice and listened to him read. Afterwards we all drank sherry out of tiny glasses.

I would feel proud when I walked out with Maura on my arm and when I introduced her to my friends I saw them all gawking with envy. Kevin Trainor took me aside and said: 'Is she out of her tree, or what?'

'How do you mean?'

'Why does a cracker like her want to go out with an eejit like you?'

I knew he was jealous and I took it as a compliment.

★ ★ ★

Fergus Pyle said: 'The Editor in Dublin is called Douglas Gageby and he's a man of passionate interests. If you want to get on in this organisation, you pay particular attention to the following subjects. Politics, rivers, trees, Cavehill, megalithic tombs, Armour of Ballymoney, Wolfe Tone, the Irish army and trout. Any of those subjects crop up, you make good and sure it's well covered. But particularly politics. Mr Gageby is *very* interested in politics.'

In West Belfast, there was trouble brewing. The republicans had put an Irish flag in the window of their office and Ian Paisley was warning if the RUC didn't take it down, he'd march up the Falls Road and take it down himself. There was an election on and Fergus was run off his feet. Candidates were sending in press statements and making speeches and holding rallies and Mr Gageby in Dublin was demanding that every line get covered.

Fergus had to go to an election meeting at Stormont, so he said to me: 'Why don't you go up there and keep an eye on things? If there's any trouble, file a couple of paragraphs.'

I took my notebook and went up to Divis Street. When I arrived, there were crowds already gathering and the people were in angry mood. There was a line of RUC men in heavy riot gear trying to hold them back. I pushed through the crowd and met Aly McVeigh. He had a big grin on his face.

'What are you doing here?' I asked.

'Same as yourself. I'm here for the craic.'

'I'm working,' I said. 'And this doesn't look like craic to me. This looks like trouble.'

'Damn right,' he said. 'If those bastards

think they're going to take that flag down, they've got another think coming.'

He pulled back his coat and showed me a milk bottle of green liquid with a piece of cloth sticking out the top.

Before I could ask him any more, the RUC began to push the crowd back. A growl went up and people started shouting abuse. I could see that the policemen were nervous. They drew their batons and began beating them on their riot shields and it made an awful din.

Somebody threw a brick and it bounced off an RUC man's helmet. Somebody else threw a stone. The crowd starting shoving and pushing and the police fell back. I saw an inspector with a blackthorn stick form the police into ranks. He gave an order and they began striking out right and left with their batons. The crowd scattered. People pushed each other aside as they tried to get away. I ran to the safety of a shop doorway and suddenly I saw Aly standing in the middle of the road.

He took the bottle from his coat, lit the cloth with a cigarette lighter and threw it at the police. It smashed at their feet in a pool of yellow flame. A cheer went up from the crowd. The police stopped beating people and looked at one another. Another bottle came flying through the air and made a whooshing sound as it broke. Petrol splashed the policemen's tunics and they started flapping with their batons to put out the flames. More youths come out of the side streets with bottles. The police hesitated for a moment, then they turned and ran.

I couldn't believe my eyes. The inspector tried to rally his men but they just pushed past him as they tried to escape. Bricks and bottles fell on them like rain. He stood, bewildered. Then he too turned tail and ran.

I had never seen the police lose control like this. They struggled down Divis Street in their heavy riot gear, got inside their barracks, and locked the doors. People pelted the windows with bottles and stones and starting shouting: 'Come out, you Black and Tans.'

Gangs of youths rolled rubber tyres to the front of the barracks and set them alight. It looked like they were going to burn the place down. The air was thick with black smoke and the sound of breaking glass. Somewhere in the background, I could hear the clang-clang of a fire engine.

I looked around for Aly, but he was gone, so I hurried back to the office and told Fergus what I had seen. He was as excited as I was. He got onto Dublin and ordered space as I sat down at the old Remington and began to type.

'Colour,' Fergus kept shouting. 'Give it plenty of colour. Describe the crowd, describe the police, describe the petrol bombs. Just write what you saw.'

I typed as fast as I could. Fergus tore the sheets from the typewriter as I wrote, marked them up with his blue pencil and handed them to Frank Nelson to transmit.

When I was finished, the sweat was dripping from my hands.

Fergus said: 'You'll be pleased to hear it's going on Page One in a big splash. Mr Gageby is delighted. You deserve a drink.'

We went round to the Duke of York. The bar was filled with reporters and everybody was talking about what had happened. Fergus got me a pint. I stood at the crowded bar and felt a strange sensation, like my blood was racing and I would never go to sleep.

Later, I lay in bed and closed my eyes. I saw the road and the petrol bombs smashing and the RUC running away. I saw the crowd trying to burn down the police station. I knew that something important had happened and things would never be the same again.

13

One evening I came home to find a letter waiting for me in the hall. I took it into the kitchen, sat down and opened it. Inside was a single sheet of paper, photo-copied from a ledger.

It had my date of birth in one column and my Christian name in another. Place of birth was given as 31 Stranmillis Court, Belfast. The columns for father's name and dwelling-place were blank. Informant's name was given as Avril Baxter, 31 Stranmillis Court. Present at the birth.

My eye jumped to the one piece of information I most wanted. In the column for name and surname of Mother, I read the following: Margaret Stella Maguire, barmaid, 28 Iveagh Place, Belfast.

The woman in the Registrar's office had scribbled a note in the margin. It read: This is the best I can do. Do you think it might be her?

I made a cup of tea and sat down and read the paper again. I felt like I had come to the end of a long journey. I had found my mother. Margaret Stella Maguire. And I had her address. Now It would only be a matter of contacting her and we would see each other again. I couldn't wait.

I told Fergus and he said: 'The best thing is to write to her. If you turn up on her doorstep out of the blue, it might give her a terrible fright. Just write her a short note and explain the circumstances. Tell her you'd like to meet her.'

That evening, I sat at the kitchen table and composed my letter to Stella. I told her that Sarah and Isaac were dead now and I was well and had a good job working as a reporter for *The Irish Times*. I told her I would like to meet her again and talk to her whenever it was convenient.

I wrote a second letter to the woman in the Registrar's office, thanking her for finding my birth certificate and the following morning, I posted them in the letter box outside Charlie Delaney's shop.

A couple of weeks went by and there was no reply. I told myself that Stella could be busy or she could be away. When she got back she would surely write to me. But when a month had passed and still no response, I began to wonder if she was going to write to me at all. I remembered what Father Thomas had said. That Stella might have got married and had a family of her own. Maybe she had put me right out of her mind and didn't want to see me again.

Then one morning, I heard the postman at the front door. I rushed down the stairs and tore open the letter that lay in the hall. My own letter was inside and with it a note written in biro in childish handwriting.

Dear Sir,

I am returning your letter to you as the person you are looking for no longer lives at this address. I'm sorry, but she hasn't lived here for the past nineteen years.

Yours sincerely,

Tess O'Neill.

I went back to work and kept as busy as I could so that I wouldn't be disappointed. Mr Gageby had asked Fergus to write a daily column so I got to take on a lot of his old reporting jobs. But I couldn't get Stella out of my mind. I thought about her all the time and wondered how I could find her.

One evening I went looking for the place where I was born: 31 Stranmillis Court. It was a grim building with big boarded-up windows and the slates falling off the roof. There was a shop nearby and I went in and talked to the man behind the counter. He said the building used to be a maternity home for unmarried girls but it had been closed these fifteen years. For weeks, I went back there and stared up at the boarded windows. It was sad, thinking about Stella inside that terrible place, waiting for me to be born.

I racked my brains trying to find ways to trace her. I thought of putting an ad in the personal columns of the *Belfast Telegraph*. I thought of contacting the Social Services or the Labour Exchange to see if they had any records of her. In the end, I decided I would have to go and talk to Tess O'Neill.

I took a bus up the Falls Road and went looking for Iveagh Place. It was a row of tiny terraced houses in the shadow of a derelict mill. No. 28 had net curtains and a potted plant in the window. I knocked on the door and it was opened by a big-bosomed woman in a cardigan with patches on the sleeve. I told her my business.

She stared at me. For a moment, I thought she was going to send me away. Then she advanced out to the step, threw her arms wide, and hugged me.

'My God,' she said. 'I can't believe it. Stella's wee boy come back at last.'

★　★　★

She brought me into the kitchen and sat me down at the table. All the while, I could see her peeking at me as she fussed with the kettle for tea.

She said: 'You know what? You look exactly like her. Tall and handsome. I always told Stella you'd grow up to be a film star some day.'

My face went red. 'So you knew me when I was a baby?'

'Of course I did. Sure didn't you live here till poor Stella had to go and give you away. You were so small she kept you in a drawer upstairs in the wee room.'

I was excited. 'Why were we living here, anyway?'

'Because Stella had nowhere else. The poor cratur hadn't got a button. I could hardly put her out on the street, now could I? Especially since she had a wee baby to look after.'

'But how did you know her in the first place?'

'We worked together. In the American Eagle.'

We sat in the little kitchen, with the two china dogs on the mantelpiece beside the clock and the picture of Jesus pointing at his bleeding heart. We drank our tea and Tess O'Neill told me how they met.

Stella had just arrived up from the country

and she had nowhere to live, so Tess let her stay with her. They worked together in the American Eagle, a club for US servicemen in Royal Avenue. They were barmaids, but the Yanks called them Hostesses because it sounded better and had a bit of class.

'I was glad of the rent. And Stella was hardly ever here. She was out every night enjoying herself. The Yanks were real gentlemen. They would light your cigarette for you and ask you up to dance. There were parties and dinners and trips in their motor-cars. Your mother was very good-looking. The men used to go mad over her.

'Anyway, that went on for a while and the next thing poor Stella was in the puddin club. I came home one afternoon and she was sitting by the window and she said there was no doubt about it. She had been to see the doctor and she was three months gone.

'She didn't know where to turn. The cratur hadn't a bob and she couldn't go home to her parents for they would have disowned her. So when the time came, she went into this place for pregnant girls and had you there.'

'Stranmillis Court?'

'That's right. And an awful bloody place it was too. It looked more like a borstal than a nursing home. They treated those poor girls like dirt. Had them scrubbing floors and washing laundry. Most of the ould ones who ran it were dried-up ould sticks. I think they were jealous of the girls for at least they'd had a man. When she came out, I let her stay on here for a while, but it was plain she couldn't hold onto you. In the end she'd no choice but to give you up.

'Somebody told her about this priest up in Ardoyne and she went to see him. He arranged for you to be adopted. It near broke Stella's heart. I used to hear her lying up there in bed, crying her eyes out. I don't think she was ever the better of it.'

I felt my throat go dry.

'What about my father? Couldn't he do something?'

Tess O'Neill frowned.

'Martin. Don't ask about him.'

'Why not? Did Stella not tell you who he was?'

'She didn't talk about him. He took a powder. And any time I mentioned him, she changed the subject.'

'I was told he went to France.'

'Maybe he did. Main thing was, he wasn't around when she needed him.'

'What did she look like?'

'She was lovely. Tall and dark. And she had this beautiful hair down to her shoulders. She looked just like a picture.'

'What age was she?'

'Oh, she was very young. Too young for her own good. She wouldn't have been more than eighteen or nineteen.'

'Have you got a photograph of her?'

'Do you know, Martin. I used to have one. But it must have got lost. I haven't seen it for years.'

'Do you know where she went?'

'I haven't a clue. She would go up to Ardoyne to see you every Sunday and then the people who adopted you told her not to come back any more. They said she was unsettling you, calling all the time. She took it very bad. It wasn't long after she packed her bag and left.'

'Do me a favour,' I said. 'Let me see the room where we stayed.'

Tess O'Neill took me up the stairs. I looked at the tiny room with the single bed and the cracked mirror on the dressing table. My mind filled with images of Stella, struggling to look after us in this room with no money and only Tess O'Neill to help her.

'I'm trying to find her. Do you know anybody might know where she is?'

'There's her sister.'

'She has a sister?'

'Oh yes. Stella had a sister down in Enniskillen. She said she was a teacher.'

'Do you know her name?'

'I think it was Kathleen.'

'Do you have her address?'

Tess O'Neill shook her head.

'I'm sorry, Martin. I'd love to help you.'

And then she brightened up.

'What am I talking about? Sure, she must be in the telephone book.'

★ ★ ★

The following evening when Fergus and Janet had left the office, I went through the directory. There were dozens of Maguires in Enniskillen. There were three called Kathleen. I rang them all in turn.

The first two said No, it wasn't them. But the third one said: 'I think the woman you're looking for got married and she's called Mrs Fagan. She's a schoolteacher all right and she lives out the Belcoo Road.'

I went back to the directory and got the number. When I rang, a woman answered.

'Have you got a sister called Stella?' I asked.

'Yes.'

'I'm ringing on behalf of some people who knew her in Belfast during the War. They're trying to contact her.'

'Stella's in America,' the woman said.

'She's been there these sixteen years.'

I tried to keep my voice steady, for I was very excited.

'Have you got her telephone number?'

'Who's looking for her?'

I told her the first name that came into my head.

'Tess O'Neill. She used to stay with her.'

'Oh, Tess. Sure I remember her. How is she keeping?'

I said she was keeping fine.

'Stella's living in New Jersey. A town called Freehold. If you ring her now, you'll get her, for I was talking to her only half an hour ago.'

She gave me Stella's address and phone number and I wrote them down.

'Thank you very much,' I said.

'Don't mention it,' said Kathleen Maguire. 'Sure, Tess was very kind to Stella and she never forgot her.'

★ ★ ★

I looked at my watch. It was nearly ten o'clock. That meant it was five o'clock in New Jersey. I lifted the phone again and dialled Stella's number.

It seemed to ring for ages. I felt my hand shake as I held the phone and then I heard a woman's voice.

'Stella Garvan speaking. Who's calling?'

My heart was beating like a hammer.

'I'm ringing from Belfast.'

There was a slight pause.

'What can I do for you?'

'Some people are trying to contact you. People who used to know you.'

'What's their name?'

'McBride.'

This was the moment. If Stella didn't want any contact, she would put down the phone.

But instead she said: 'I used to know people called McBride.'

'They were called Sarah and Isaac. They lived in Brompton Park in Ardoyne.'

'That's right. How are they?'

'They're dead,' I said. I felt the tears well up. 'Do you remember a priest called Father Ambrose? He lived in Holy Cross Monastery?'

Stella had gone quiet.

'I do.'

'You had a wee boy called Martin?'

'That's right.'

'You gave him up for adoption?'

'Yes.'

'You gave him to the McBrides?'

I heard Stella start to sob on the phone.

'Yes.'

'Do you know who this is speaking to you now?'

I will never forget Stella's reply.
'Of course, I do. It's you, Martin.'

★ ★ ★

I could hear Stella sniffling and crying on the phone. She said: 'God help me, Martin. This is an awful shock. I'll have to sit down and have a cigarette.'

I told her I was feeling shocked myself. She asked me how I was and I told her I was doing well and had a good job, so she didn't have to worry about that.

'And poor Mr and Mrs McBride are dead?'

I said Yes, they both died of cancer.

'So now you're all alone?'

I told her I still had Uncle Paddy and Aunt Minnie and my pals, Aly and Kevin. And there was Fergus and the people at work. And I told her about Maura.

'Is she a nice girl, Martin?'

'She's a lovely girl and I'm very fond of her.'

I asked her if I had any brothers or sisters. She said No.

I was sad. I would have loved to have brothers and sisters. I was sad for Stella too because it meant she gave away the only child she had. She must have been very lonely.

'But you got married? I know because

338

you've changed your name.'

'I married a man called Joe Garvan, but it didn't work out. We're split up now.'

I said I was sorry to hear that.

'How did you get my number?'

I told her about Tess O'Neill and how she put me in touch with her sister, Kathleen.

'You didn't tell her who you were?' Stella asked.

'Oh, no.'

'That's good. How is Tess?'

'She's fine.'

'She was very decent to us. I always meant to write to her and I just never got around to it. If you're talking to her again, tell her I was asking about her.'

I said I would.

We talked for a long time. I had so many questions to ask her and no sooner had she answered them, than I thought of another. She told me that coming to America was the best thing that ever happened to her. It was a land of opportunity, she said, and anybody could get on if they were prepared to roll up their sleeves and do a bit of work. But she still missed Ireland because the people were different and knew how to enjoy themselves.

'Did you ever think of me?' she asked.

'All the time.'

'I'm glad you found me, Martin. I always

knew you'd turn up again. There wasn't a day went past that I didn't think of you. I have a picture of you taken on your christening and I keep it beside my bed.'

When at last I put down the phone, I felt drained. I locked up the office and went round to the Duke of York and bought a large whiskey to calm myself. I thought over and over, I have found my mother at last and she loves me.

★ ★ ★

We started writing because I couldn't use the phone while Fergus and Janet were in the office. Stella told me how she ended up in America. When she left Belfast, she went to Dublin and got a job in a big department store in O'Connell Street. She stayed there for a couple of years until one of her sisters back in Enniskillen decided she was going to emigrate to the U.S. and Stella said she'd go with her. They had an uncle in Albany, New York who had done well and he was going to sponsor them.

She stayed for a while in Albany before moving to New York City, meeting Joe Garvan. Together they went to live in New Jersey. But the marriage didn't work out, so now she was living on her own. Her sister,

Bridgie, was married and was living close. She had four children, so I had cousins.

Stella painted a wonderful picture of life in America. She was working in a legal office and her boss was a man called Mr Morrison. He was very good to her. She had her own house and her own car and a good job. She was always going to dinner parties. The sun was always shining. Everybody was enjoying themselves and making buckets of money. It was a great life. It was the America I knew from all the films I'd seen.

She sent me photographs. Some of them were taken in Dublin but most were in America. She looked just like people had described her; dark and handsome, like a Spanish lady. I would take them out and study them, trying to find any resemblance. I showed them to Maura and she said Yes, there was no doubt. We had the same nose and cheekbones. She had proud eyes and I had them too.

Sometimes I would ring her when I was alone in the office but mostly it was letters. She told me about the first months of my life and how she had tried to keep me. She said she even thought of taking me to England where nobody would know us and starting all over. They had places where you could leave a baby while you went out to work. But it was

341

impossible. The odds were too great. She made it sound like we were together against the world.

She wanted to know if I was a good Catholic boy and went to Mass and the sacraments. She was just like Sarah before she died. So I told her I went to Mass and Communion every Sunday. It wasn't the truth but I wanted her to feel good. I didn't want her feeling guilty about something she couldn't help. I even sent her a photo of me in my new suit taken on my Confirmation Day to go with the one she already had beside her bed.

The letters went back and forth for months. Each one filled in more details. And then I asked about my father and if she could tell me who he was. Nobody had seen him. Nobody had any stories about him. It made him all the more mysterious.

Stella's next letter didn't mention him till the last paragraph and then it was just tossed in like an afterthought. She said his name was Bill O'Dwyer and he was an officer in the US Army and came from Chicago.

The news got me all excited. I began to think that maybe I could find him too. So I wrote back to Stella and asked her what he looked like and if she would tell me how they met. I asked if she had any idea where he might be and if there was some way I could contact him; maybe a social security number or an army number or even an address.

She became evasive. Bill O'Dwyer was the past, she said, and she didn't want to talk about it. She didn't want to open up old wounds. He had his life and we had ours, that was the way it was. She had put him right out of her mind and it would be best if I did the same.

But I wasn't satisfied. I thought about Bill O'Dwyer the way I used to think about Stella. I pictured him in his smart officer's uniform, lighting a cigarette for Stella and asking her up to dance, the way Tess O'Neill said the soldiers did in the American Eagle. I thought if I could track him down, we could get to know each other. And maybe he was married and had children, so I could have brothers and sisters after all. I rang Stella again.

She was full of chat. She said she was going to a cook-out in her neighbour's backyard and she was getting a salad ready. The weather was scorching and everybody was drooping with the heat.

I started to ask about Bill O'Dwyer but she cut me short.

'How'd you like to come over here and stay with me for a while?'

'What?'

'I've been thinking about it. We should really meet, Martin. I'd love to see you. And it won't cost you a penny. I'll send you the money for the airfare. You'll love it here. It'll be a great vacation for you.'

I couldn't believe what I was hearing. 'That would be brilliant.'

'OK,' Stella said. 'I'll fix it up.'

14

Uncle Paddy said: 'If you ask me, it isn't a good idea. You should let sleeping dogs lie. You're twenty years of age and you've managed well enough so far without ever clapping eyes on her.'

'But, she's my mother.'

'Well, if she is, she had precious little to do with the rearing of you.'

'You're the one told me about her in the first place, remember? After Sarah's funeral. You're the one told me how she gave me away to Father Ambrose.'

'Well, I didn't mean for you to go gallivanting over to America after her.'

Aunt Minnie said: 'Tsk. Tsk. Don't mind him, Marty. He's been at the whiskey bottle again. Sure, it will be lovely to see her after all these years.'

'If you ask me,' Uncle Paddy said, 'you'll stay where you are and let her run on there.'

I felt like telling him that nobody had asked him anything and I was going to America whether he liked it or not. But I just kept my mouth shut and finished the tea that Aunt Minnie had made and said Cheerio and walked up Chatham Street and out to the Crumlin Road.

Maura thought it was wonderful news and very romantic.

'After all these years, she kept your picture beside her bed. You know, she's had a tough life, Martin. Giving you away and not having any more children. And then her marriage breaking up like that. That would be hard on any woman. I think it's very sad.'

I said she sounded all right on the phone apart from the first time I called. She had a good job and a nice house and a good life over there in New Jersey.

'But all the time she was thinking about you and wondering if you would ever return. It's like a fairytale. And the way she tried to hold onto you till she was forced to give you away. How could you ever forget something like that? I think she was very brave. I think you should be proud to have a mother like that.'

I said I was.

'I'll bet you'll have a great time. She'll spoil you, Martin. I know I would if I was in her shoes.'

I had to buy new clothes. Maura came with me and helped me to chose. It was important that I should be presentable she said. First impressions were lasting and the Yanks were very peculiar about the way people dressed.

I bought a nice new lightweight suit because Stella had warned that the weather was very hot. I bought slacks and shoes and runners and six shirts. I spent more money on clothes that day than I ever had in my life. When we were finished, we had to carry it all home in four shopping bags.

I told Fergus I was going to America to see my mother and needed some holidays. He said that was great news and I could have two weeks at the end of July once the Orange parades were out of the way. He said when I was in New York, I should keep an eye out because there would be good material for a couple of articles and it would be extra money for me. He said I should make sure to keep a notebook and pen with me at all times.

I couldn't wait to go. My mind was filled with all these images I had seen, skyscrapers and yellow taxis and neon lights. America was a golden place, the land of opportunity. And the Irish always got a special welcome because they were hard workers. They built the railways and the Brooklyn Bridge and ran the police force for generations.

The cheque arrived from Stella for the airfare and with it came a long letter filled with directions about getting from the airport into Manhattan and then catching the New

347

Jersey Transit bus from the Port Authority.

'I'll be waiting for you at the depot,' Stella wrote. 'I'm counting the days till you come.'

I had to tell Kevin and Aly. We went for a drink in Madden's bar in Smithfield and I made up a story. I didn't want to tell them the truth about being adopted and every-thing, it would take too long to explain. So I told them that Isaac had a sister over there and she had invited me to stay with her for a few weeks.

'I didn't know you had relations in America,' Kevin said. 'You never mentioned her before.'

'I haven't seen her since I was a baby.'

I told them she lived near New York and we'd be in and out of the city all the time, riding the subway and eating hamburgers and hot dogs and drinking Budweiser beer.

'I'll probably go to the top of the Statue of Liberty. And the Empire State Building. And I might go to a ball game in Yankee Stadium.'

'Some people have all the luck,' Aly said enviously. 'And those American girls. They say they would suck you in and blow you out in bubbles.'

I reminded him that I was going steady with Maura.

'That's all mallarkey. You're not married to her, are you? And those American women don't care. They're just out for a good time. Take any chances you get. That's my advice.'

★ ★ ★

The day came. I had my suitcase packed and ready, the old case we used to take with us on our holidays to Portstewart. I had thought about getting a new one, but rather than spend the money, I decided to keep the one I had.

Maura came with me to the airport and a drizzle started as we walked up the street to catch the bus. I stopped at the top of Brompton Park and looked down at the little houses of Glenard as if I was seeing them for the last time. I thought of all the times I had growing up here, all the people I had known. I looked at the houses once more before I turned to go. They seemed to cling together for support, and their huddled rooftops were shining black in the rain.

★ ★ ★

I got to the Port Authority terminal in Manhattan as the afternoon rush was beginning. I was tired after the long journey and I was hungry and my new nylon shirt was sticking to my back with the heat. The terminal was packed with people and they all seemed to be in a hurry. But I didn't care. I was in America at last. And I was going to meet my mother.

I got on the bus and squeezed into a seat near the back. I pressed my face to the window as we emerged from the Lincoln Tunnel and the New York skyline suddenly burst into view. The city was bathed in sunlight. I could see the tower blocks and the steeples and the flashing billboards. I could see the Hudson River with the sun shining on the water. I kept my nose pressed to the glass till the bus bore us away into New Jersey and the city was just a speck on the horizon.

We arrived in Freehold shortly after five o'clock. I heard the driver call out the destination and the squeal of brakes as the bus pulled into the yard. I felt my chest tighten with excitement. I stood up, took my case from the overhead rack, and joined the line of people waiting to get off.

I knew Stella the second I saw her. She was standing beside the booking office out of the sun. She was older than the photographs but she was still beautiful. She came running towards me and put her arms around me and hugged me close.

'Oh, Martin,' she said. 'I can't believe it. You're back at last.'

'It's great to see you, Stella.'

She held me and then she stared into my face and examined me. I felt my heart pounding in my breast.

'You look exactly as I pictured you. You've got the Maguire features. Oh, I'm so happy.'

She kissed me and I thought she was going to cry. The bus started up again and people got into their cars and drove away and soon we were the only people left in the depot. Stella took out a handkerchief and dabbed her eyes.

'How was the trip?'

'Fine.'

'You must be tired. I'll take you home and you can have a shower. Then we'll go out and have a nice dinner and you can tell me all about yourself.'

She reached for my suitcase. Suddenly it looked so shabby and I regretted that I hadn't bought a new one after all. I took it from her and carried it to a shiny Buick parked beside the footpath.

We drove through the streets of Freehold. Stella talked the whole time, the way she did on the phone, so I scarcely got a chance to speak.

'Mr Morrison's given me a week off. So we've got plenty of time. How was the flight?'

I told her about the traffic and the heat in

351

New York and she said: 'Manhattan's terrible. I never go in there anymore.'

We came to her house. I couldn't believe the size of it. It was just like the ones I used to admire when I delivered papers for Charlie Delaney on the Crumlin Road. It had its own lawn at the front and another one at the back. It had a sun deck and a garage and trees and bushes blazing with colour.

'Stella, it's beautiful,' I said.

'You like it?'

'It's the nicest house I ever saw.'

She seemed pleased.

'Joe built it.'

'Who's Joe?' I said.

'The guy I was married to. When we came here, this was just a shack. Joe stripped it down and extended it. He laid the lawns and gardens. I'll say one thing for Joe, he wasn't afraid of hard work.'

She took me into the house. It was cool inside after the heat. She showed me the sitting room and the kitchen. It was the biggest kitchen I had ever seen. It had a refrigerator, a dishwasher, and a big cooker with an oven and an extractor fan for taking away the cooking smells.

'Stella, you live in this big house all on your own?'

'It's not so big,' she shrugged. 'And I like my privacy.'

She showed me to my bedroom. It had a double bed with a blue coverlet and a wardrobe for storing my clothes. I stripped off and got under the shower. Then I changed into a fresh shirt and went down to Stella again and gave her the bottle of duty free I had bought at the airport.

'Irish whiskey? I haven't had that for a long time.'

She put it in a cupboard with other bottles.

'Do you take a drink, Martin?'

I said I drank beer.

'We'll have a toast.'

She got a can out of the fridge and poured herself a vodka and tonic. She clinked her glass against mine.

'This is the happiest day of my life. Now that we've found each other, we'll never part again.'

I took a drink of the cold beer and thought how wonderful everything was. It was just like the fairytale Maura had said it was.

Out the back, the sun was going down behind the trees and a squirrel was digging a hole in the lawn.

★   ★   ★

We went to dinner in a swanky Italian restaurant with little lamps on the tables and opera music on a hissing gramophone. I had never been in a restaurant like this before and I felt nervous. But Stella was at ease. She bossed the waiters and ordered the wine.

'You're supposed to be twenty-one to drink in this state. But you look old enough. We'll have a bottle of Chianti. What do you think?' she said.

I said Sure. It sounded good to me.

It came in a little straw basket and Stella poured. It tasted sweet and burnt my throat as I drank it down.

'The waiters seem to know you,' I said.

'I should hope so. I've spent a fortune in here. I used to come a lot with Joe. Joe loved Italian cooking.'

'What did he work at?'

'He had a landscape business.'

'Is there much money in that?'

'Round here there is. Everybody wants their place to look better than the guy next door.'

I asked her what happened to Joe.

'Let's say we didn't see eye to eye. Joe drank. But the trouble was, he didn't know when to stop. He was up to two bottles a day before I threw him out.'

'Two bottles of beer?'

Stella laughed.

'Two bottles of Old Crow. Poor guy was a lush. He needed a tumbler of whiskey to get started in the morning. He was going round in a daze all day long. You just can't live with somebody like that.'

'Stella, how did you get divorced if you're a Catholic?'

She gave me a strange look and said: 'Martin. Things are different in America.'

★ ★ ★

It was a lovely meal. She talked about her job and Mr Morrison and the Ladies Club she attended and her busy social life around Freehold. She told me about arriving in America and that the first thing her Uncle James did was give her a one hundred dollar bill to buy candy.

'Can you imagine how much candy you could buy for one hundred dollars? Uncle James was loaded. He was boss of a steelworks up in Albany. When he arrived here, he just had the shirt on his back. America is a great country, Martin. You can do anything in America if you're prepared to work.'

I listened to Stella talk. She seemed so elegant and sure of herself. I thought of the time she had nothing and we lived with Tess O'Neill in the tiny house in Iveagh Place. I thought how different things would have been if she had brought me with her to America and the life we could have had.

It came time to go. Stella paid the bill and gave the waiter a five-dollar tip. He was delighted and held her coat for her while she put it on.

When we got home, she said we should have a night-cap. We sat on the porch at the back of the house. There was a scent of flowers and a big yellow moon riding the empty sky.

'Martin,' she said, 'there's something I have to tell you. You know I had to give you up?'

'Yes.'

'It's important that you understand that. I tried to keep you but I couldn't.'

'Stella. You don't have to explain. I know you had no choice.'

'Good. That puts my mind at ease.'

★ ★ ★

When I woke the next morning, the sun was shining and the birds were singing. I was happy as a lark. This was my first morning in America and I had two whole weeks to look forward to. I glanced at the little clock beside my bed and it said 9.15 a.m. I got washed and went down to the kitchen. Stella had the radio on and Roy Orbison was singing 'In Dreams'. She had prepared an enormous breakfast. She piled my plate high with goodies: sausages and little strips of bacon and the nicest eggs I had ever tasted. She had things I had never seen before: bagels and waffles and stuff called yoghurt that she said was made from milk. A pot of coffee was perking away on the stove.

'Stella. I'll never eat all this,' I said.

'Martin. You're a growing boy and you need your food.'

So I tucked in and ate as much I could, just to keep her happy.

When we were finished, Stella put the dishes in the dishwasher, pressed a button, and the dishwasher began to whirl.

'There's only you,' I said. 'What do you need a dishwasher for?'

'Nobody in America washes dishes, Martin.'

We sat on the porch and drank our coffee and Stella smoked a cigarette. She had on a blouse and slacks but they were too tight for her and I could see little folds of flesh peeping out above the waistband.

'Tell me about this job you've got,' she asked.

So I told her about Janet, Fergus and Mr Gageby, about how I covered Corporation meetings and interviewed people and wrote articles.

'It sounds like an interesting kind of job. Do you like it?'

I said I loved every minute of it. I loved meeting people and bringing the news to the readers and I told her what H. L. Mencken had said.

'You've done well, Martin. I'm proud of you.'

'I've just been lucky.'

'No, it's more than luck. It's down to hard work.'

'You're the one who's worked hard, Stella. You arrived here with nothing and look at the lovely house you've got and the great life.'

She smiled and I could see she was pleased.

'Well, sometimes you make your own luck.'

★   ★   ★

We got in her car and drove to the beach. Stella called it the shore. I noticed that her Irish accent had got overlaid with American expressions.

'While you're staying with me, we have to establish some ground rules. OK?' she said.

I said that was all right, thinking she meant where I was to put the used towels and dirty clothes and where to leave the coffee cups when I had finished.

'I don't want you answering the phone. If I'm not in the house and the phone rings, just let it ring.'

'But it might be important.'

'It doesn't matter. I'm fussy about the phone. Another thing. Anyone asks who you are, tell them you're a friend visiting from Ireland.'

I stared at her, stunned.

'You mean nobody knows about me?'

'No. Why should they?'

'Not even your sister Bridgie?'

'Especially Bridgie. This is something between us. There's no need to tell people our business. OK?'

'But they might guess. They're not stupid. I suddenly turn up out of the blue and people will want to know who I am. If people look closely, they'll see we've got the same features.'

'They can see what they want.'

'Stella. You're not ashamed of me, are you?'

She laughed and pinched my cheek.

'Oh, Martin. Don't be such a fool. It's got nothing to do with shame. I'm proud of you. But it's our secret. You and me. People talk too much. They love to gossip. Why should we give them something to talk about?'

★ ★ ★

We came to the beach. It was a big, long beach like the one at Portstewart except the water was warm and there was a lifeguard sitting in a little perch where he could see out over the ocean. I swam in the warm water and Stella sat under an umbrella and read a book. I thought: This is the life. If Aly and Kevin could see me now, they'd be jealous as hell. About two o'clock, a cool breeze began to blow in from the sea so I got dressed and we went off to have lunch.

I wasn't hungry, but Stella insisted that we go to another expensive place where they had waiters in white jackets and long-stemmed roses on the stiff linen tablecloths.

'Stella. You don't have to spend money on me. I'd be just as happy eating at a diner.'

But she shushed me quiet. It was her money, she said, and how she spent it was her concern, for it wasn't every day she had her only son to stay with her. It made me feel good so I ordered a steak. But when it came, it was so big that it covered the whole plate and I could only eat half of it and I felt it was a terrible waste.

I asked her to tell me about her life when she lived in Ireland. She said she came from a small farm in Ballinaleck in County Fermanagh. There were five children; three girls and two boys and life was very hard. One boy, Peter, died of a brain haemorrhage when he was only sixteen.

'It was a small farm and the land was very bad. My poor father was just about able to scrape a living out of it so you can imagine we didn't have much. Then the War came and there was plenty of work in Belfast. The first chance I got, I was away. I was just turned eighteen.

'They were crying out for people to work in the factories, but I thought it would be dirty work and I wanted something better, so I took a job in the American Eagle. That's where I met Tess O'Neill and she let me stay with her.

'They were very good to us and the work was flexible and you got good tips. The Americans were fantastic. We had a great time. It was parties every night of the week. You know, during the War, people lived differently. We squeezed every bit of enjoyment we could because we didn't know when we were going to die. Then I got pregnant with you. And you know the rest.'

She took out a handkerchief to blow her nose and I could see she was sad. So I reached across the table and held her hand.

'You shouldn't have any regrets, Stella. You did your best. Tess O'Neill told me all about it.'

'I just wish I could have kept you.'

'Tell me about my father,' I said.

Stella stiffened and pulled her hand away.

'I don't want to talk about him.'

'I'm curious, Stella.'

'He's dead. Why don't you forget about him.'

'Dead? You never told me he was dead.'

'Yes, I did. In one of my letters.'

'No,' I said. 'If you'd told me that, I would have remembered.'

'Well, he is dead. He was killed at the end of the War. Out in Europe somewhere.'

'Where?'

'How would I know? Germany or Italy or one of those places. Wherever the fighting was.'

'Tell me about him.'

'I told you already. His name was Bill O'Dwyer. He was an officer in the U.S. Army. He got me pregnant. And before I could tell him, he went off to Europe and got himself killed.'

'Were you in love with him?'

'Of course I was. We were at a Christmas party.'

'It couldn't have been Christmas, Stella.'

She looked confused.

'You're right. It must have been Independence Day or one of those goddammed American holidays. It was a very worrying time, Martin. I can't remember everything.'

'I want to trace him,' I said. 'Maybe he's not dead at all.'

'He *is* dead. Just leave well enough alone.'

'The U.S. Army keeps records.'

Stella suddenly looked frightened.

'Why don't we talk about this some other time?'

'Stella. When I was trying to find you people kept putting obstacles in my way. And now you're doing the same.'

'We've got plenty of time, Martin. We'll talk about it again.'

★   ★   ★

One day Mr Morrison called. He left his car in the drive. He was about forty. He wore a well-cut suit and shirt. He had grey hair and a confident lawyer's face.

He came into the house and took my hand in a strong grip. I could smell his aftershave.

'Having a good vacation?' he asked.

363

I said I was.

'Stella showing you around?'

I told him where we had been and what we had done.

'That's Stella. She just loves to entertain people. You like it here?'

I said I did.

'And how are things in Ireland, right now?'

I told him things in Ireland were OK. He nodded politely, then seemed to run out of conversation.

'Can I have a word?' he asked Stella. They went off to the front room and I could hear them whispering. Later when she was showing him to the door, I saw him hold her waist and kiss her.

★ ★ ★

Bridgie came to visit. She was older than Stella and didn't look like her sister. She was a small, bird-like figure, full of energy. She couldn't settle. She kept hopping around. She brought an apple cake she had baked herself and we sat in the kitchen and had coffee. Bridgie asked me how I was enjoying America. I said I was having a wonderful time.

'There's plenty of good things in America, but you know what I miss? I miss the good wholesome Irish food.'

I thought the food here was marvellous, I said. Especially the eggs, I'd never tasted eggs like them.

Bridgie sat forward in her chair.

'You think so?'

'Yes. I think the eggs are delicious.'

She turned to Stella.

'You hear that? He thinks the eggs here are better than the eggs back in the old country. How do you account for that? Wouldn't you think the hens in Ireland had a better life, running around the farmyard and eating whatever took their fancy? And the good fresh air? And the lovely green grass that you get nowhere else in the world?'

I didn't know how to account for it, I said, but that was my impression.

'How is your mother keeping?' Bridgie asked.

'My mother?'

'Tess O'Neill?'

I thought I was hearing things. I looked quickly at Stella but she looked away.

'She's keeping fine,' I said finally.

'She must be delighted for you, getting a nice holiday like this. Stella and Tess were great friends when she worked in Belfast. Make sure to tell her I was asking for her.'

I said I would.

'We talk a lot about the old country. It's all so long ago. But you never forget the past. The past never goes away.'

Bridgie poured more coffee and I could feel her eyes on me. After a while, I moved out to the porch and left them alone to talk, but when I looked up from the book I was reading, I would catch her studying me.

★ ★ ★

When she was gone, I confronted Stella.

'Why did you make up that stuff about Tess O'Neill?'

'I had to explain you, Martin.'

'But you didn't have to tell lies about me.'

'It wasn't a real lie.'

'Why don't you just tell them the truth? Why don't you tell them I'm your son?'

Stella made a soothing noise.

'There, there. Don't get upset. If I told them the truth, they wouldn't be able to handle it. Sometimes it's better for everyone if you tell a little lie.'

'It's not better for me. You told me you were proud of me, but when Bridgie comes, you deny me.'

'No,' she said. 'It's not like that.'

'I don't think less of you because of the

366

way I was born. It's nothing to be ashamed of.'

'I'm not ashamed of you.'

'Then why don't you acknowledge me? If I had known you were going to behave like this, I wouldn't have come.'

I stormed out of the house and down the lawn as far as the trees, waiting for my anger to die. I could hear a lawnmower humming in a garden further up the block. I sat on the grass and the realisation came to me, I was trapped. There was nowhere for me to go.

After a while I saw Stella come out of the house. She brought me a cold beer.

'Don't be upset,' she said and ran her fingers through my hair. 'I love you Martin. It's just that people wouldn't understand.'

★ ★ ★

One day, she took me to the shopping mall on the outskirts of the town. We had to go on the freeway to get there. It was filled with fancy restaurants and stores selling anything from television sets to furniture to sports equipment.

We went into the shops and I looked at all the goods piled as high as the ceiling. I thought, how rich the Americans are that they can afford all this stuff.

Suddenly Stella said: 'I want to buy you something.'

'Please, Stella. Don't spend your money.'

'But I like spending money on you. It gives me pleasure.'

'You've done enough for me. Please.'

She looked at my bare wrist.

'I'll buy you a watch. Then you'll think of me when you check the time.'

'Stella. You don't have to do this.'

'It'll be a birthday present. It was your birthday last March and I meant to get you something.'

I stared into her face to see if she was joking.

'It wasn't March.'

'What are you talking about? March 29th.'

'No,' I said. 'It was February 29th.'

'You're sure?'

'Stella,' I said, 'I know my own birthday.'

She shrugged.

'I'm hopeless with dates. Sometimes I don't even know when it's Christmas. Anyway, it's still a birthday present.'

She took me to a jeweller's and insisted on paying twenty dollars for a watch that I didn't want. Afterwards we went to an ice-cream parlour and had flapjacks and syrup.

But all the way home, I kept thinking: 'How could she not know my birthday? This is the woman who thought about me every day. How could she not remember the day I was born?'

★ ★ ★

The weather got hotter and I grew bored with Freehold. There was nothing to do. I wanted to see the bright lights of New York, but every time I mentioned it Stella made some excuse.

'New York is such a hassle. You saw what Manhattan was like, everybody's rushing around like blue-ass flies and the traffic's so loud you can't even hear yourself think.'

'But I want to see it. I've come all this way. I want to be able to tell people when I get home.'

'There's nothing to see, Martin. Believe me. I lived there four years. Anybody with any sense is trying to get out of the place.'

'I could go on my own,' I suggested. 'You don't have to come.'

And Stella would say: 'If you want to go that bad, I'll take you next week. We'll go on a Sunday when things are quieter.'

One by one, the neighbours came to call. Stella introduced me as a friend from Ireland. I was getting used to her lies and I went along with them, even though they hurt me every time. I just wished she would be honest and admit who I was. I just wanted her to acknowledge me.

Even though it was a big house, there was no privacy. No matter where I went, I could never be alone. If I sat in the front room to read a book, Stella would find me. She was always hovering, asking me if I was all right and if there was anything I needed. In the end, she drove me out of the house altogether and I would walk the streets of Freehold and sit in the public library where I could get some peace.

Stella's days had a pattern. She was an early riser. She would get up at 6 a.m. She said it was the best part of the day and shouldn't be wasted. She would do her household jobs before the sun got too hot and then she would have the rest of the time to spend with me.

I tried to stay in bed, listening to the birds in the trees outside my bedroom, but the sound of Stella running the Hoover or mowing the lawn would force me to get up. She insisted on cooking a big breakfast, getting bagels and muffins from the bakery, piling my plate with bacon and eggs.

Sometimes she'd take me for drives in the car to the surrounding towns, but they were all much the same, only the names differed. The highlight of Stella's day was the cocktail hour. It was at five o'clock and she really looked forward to it. As the sun began to go down behind the trees, she would get out her shaker and her book of recipes.

'What'll it be today? Why don't we try Pina Coladas?'

She would mix the drinks and we'd sit on the sun deck and Stella would say: 'I heard on the radio. Bobby Kennedy might run for the White House. I think he deserves it after what those bastards did to his brother. They say it was the Cubans, but personally, I think it was the WASPs.'

I asked her what a WASP was and Stella said they were like the Orangemen back in Ireland. They hated Catholics and didn't want to see them get on. When Jack Kennedy became President, they were sick to their stomachs and that's why they had him done in.

We'd sit and drink and watch the squirrels running across the lawn. At six o'clock, we'd eat again.

She was a good cook but she overfed me. She gave me vegetables that I hadn't seen before, squash and corn and sweet potatoes. I would force myself to eat, just to keep her happy, but there was always food left over, steaks and chicken breasts. Stella would wrap these carefully in tinfoil and put them away in the fridge for another time.

'Waste not, want not,' she would say.

It was a phrase that Sarah used to have. Even though Stella had settled in the land of opportunity, she hadn't managed to shake the dust of Ireland entirely from her feet.

★   ★   ★

One evening Stella had Mr Morrison over to dinner. He brought her a bouquet of roses and she put them into a glass vase and placed it on the sideboard. She made Manhattans and we drank them on the porch, listening to the crickets sing in the grass.

Mr Morrison didn't have much to say. Stella tried to keep the conversation flowing, getting him to talk about the legal office and the casework but Mr Morrison wasn't interested in me. He asked several times about Ireland but I don't think he knew where it was. I think he was confusing it with Scotland. Mr Morrison was only interested in Stella.

Another night I asked her again about my father. The more Stella tried to avoid it, the more determined I became. This time, I tried a subtle argument.

'Maybe he's waiting to hear from me, the same way you were.'

'No,' Stella said. 'He isn't.'

'How can you be sure?'

'Because he's dead. Why are you going on about him?'

'Where did you meet him?'

'At the American Eagle. He asked me to dance. That's how it all began. He was the best-looking man in the room. And such nice manners. You've got to remember I was only eighteen.'

'What part of Chicago was he from?'

'How would I know? All those places sounded the same to me.'

'And his name was Bill O'Dwyer?'

'That's right.'

'Why didn't you put it on my birth certificate?'

Stella looked surprised.

'Didn't I?'

'No.'

'Well, it was a confusing time. I was all mixed up.'

'Do you know what rank he was?'

I had taken out an envelope and was beginning to take notes.

Stella stood up suddenly.

'Hey, what is this? A Federal investigation? C'mon, give me a break.'

⋆　⋆　⋆

At the end of the week, she went back to work and I was left alone in the house. I had peace at last. A stillness would descend when the front door closed and I heard her car drive away.

Stella had a big television set in the sitting room and it got about a dozen channels. I would drink coffee and watch the news programmes. But there was nothing about Europe, they were all about local politics. I would switch over and watch the sports shows and when I got tired of television, I would read or lie out on the sun deck and listen to the radio.

But even the weather got monotonous and I longed for rain or cloud or wind, anything to break the tedium of the long, hot days. I began to look forward to going home.

I began to prowl the house, in my boredom. It started innocently enough. There was a cellar under the kitchen and one day I went down there. It was like Aladdin's cave. There were bundles of old magazines and shelves of tools and tins of nails and screws, which I supposed must have belonged to Joe Garvan.

There was a big wooden chest and I prised it open. It was full of old clothes and knick-knacks and papers belonging to Stella's parents. I sat for hours in the cool cellar going through the treasures in that chest.

I found a family photograph album which Stella kept in a drawer in the dining room. There were pictures of Stella as a little girl in Fermanagh; pictures of her as a teenager in a thin dress with her black hair tumbling down her shoulders. There were wedding pictures; Stella in a long white dress and veil and Joe Garvan holding her hand as the knife pressed into the wedding cake. He was a smart-looking guy in black coat and tails and a spray in his button hole. And then I did something which I've regretted ever since. I went into Stella's bedroom.

It was the room beside mine. I remember how careful I was, making sure not to disturb anything, listening for warning sounds. There was a heavy smell of scent in the room and a wardrobe full of dresses and suits and rows of shoes. There was a sideboard with bottles and jars and a box for her jewellery.

My eye was drawn instinctively towards the bed. There was a little table with an alarm clock and a radio and a photograph. It was the one I had sent of me in my Confirmation suit. I looked around the room again to make sure, but there was no mistake. It was the only photograph there.

★ ★ ★

I waited until Stella came home and we'd had our cocktail and finished dinner and then I said: 'Stella. Let me see the picture you have of me on my christening day. I'd like to see what I looked like when I was a baby.'

She got up from the table and I heard her climb the stairs. She came down a short time later and said: 'You know what? I can't find it.'

I tried to stay calm, but my anger was building.

'You said you always kept it beside your bed.'

'So I did. But, it's not there now. I must have moved it. I'll find it again.'

'Did you ever have it, Stella?'

She stared at me.

'What do you mean by that remark?'

'You made that up, didn't you? There never was such a picture.'

She began to protest but I interrupted.

'You're living a lie. You want me here with you, but you deny my birth. You try to pretend that it never happened. You won't acknowledge me in front of people. You won't talk about my father. Don't you think I have a right to know who my father is? Don't you think I have a right to be recognised and not passed off as some friend from Ireland? What are you ashamed of, Stella?'

This time I had shaken her, but my anger was in full flood.

'All that's in the past. Why rake it up again?'

'Because I have rights. And you're not fooling anyone. They all know who I am. I can tell by the way they look at me. Everybody knows I'm your son. Even Bridgie knows.'

She was weeping now. I had wounded her. I stood up from the table and walked out to the back of the house. It was getting dark and the stars were coming out. I sat in Stella's rocking chair and listened to the sound of the crickets in the woods.

The following morning, I took the bus into New York. But even though I had looked forward to it for weeks, it was a disappointment. I bought a street map and some postcards and sat on a park bench where I wrote to Maura, Kevin, Aly and Aunt Minnie. I told them I was having a wonderful time but it was all lies. I didn't want them to know the truth.

I walked the hot, dusty streets of Manhattan as far as Battery Park and all the time I was thinking what a terrible mistake I had made by coming here. Uncle Paddy had been right. I should have left well enough alone.

Stella is a stranger, I thought. The only thing we have in common is that she gave birth to me. She wants me here, but she's not prepared to admit who I am and I can't accept that.

I walked back through Wall Street and Chinatown and Little Italy. I passed Madison Square Garden and Radio City Music Hall, but I didn't even stop to look. Any attraction they might have had for me was gone. When I got tired I stopped at a deli for a pastry and coffee, and then I took the subway to the Port Authority and caught the bus for Freehold.

★ ★ ★

On my last night, I took Stella to dinner. I had put money aside to give her a treat. Since our row she had become wary of me, and she didn't object.

I took her to a steak house. It wasn't expensive. We drank beer and I said: 'Stella, I'm sorry we fought. I'm sorry if I hurt you.'

She reached out and held my hand.

'You know I have that goddamned picture somewhere. I'll bet the minute you go, I'll find it again.'

'It's not just the picture, Stella. It's the fact that you won't acknowledge who I am. You made a mistake when you were young. You shouldn't punish yourself for the rest of your life.'

She sat, meekly toying with her steak, while I talked. I thought how the roles had been reversed in a few short weeks. Now it was Stella who was in awe of me.

We finished our meal and went home. Stella said we should have one last drink and poured vodka and tonics and we sat for a while watching television. She was subdued. It was as if we had exhausted all conversation and there was nothing left to say.

Eventually she kissed me goodnight and went to bed. I sat for a while nursing my drink. I was glad to be going home. I was glad to be escaping Stella's house. It was wrong to have come here. Maybe it was wrong to have sought out Stella at all.

Finally, I turned off the lights and climbed the stairs. I could hear a low moaning sound from Stella's bedroom, like an animal in pain. I put my ear to the door and she was weeping. I thought of that conversation with Tess O'Neill. How Stella used to cry herself to sleep after she had given me away to Father Ambrose.

15

There are no happy endings in life, unlike Sarah's stories. There are always disappointments. Things fall short of expectation. People let you down. I left Freehold vowing never to return. Stella drove me to the bus depot and waited till the bus bore me away to New York. I waved from the window as she stood in the depot yard with her handkerchief in her hand, dabbing at her eyes. I felt sorry for her. She was a lonely woman and she had no children to comfort her as she grew old.

I returned to Belfast and went back to work. Everyone wanted to know how my trip had been and I made up stories to hide the truth. Stella sent me letters but I refused to answer them. She rang me at the office but I wouldn't take her calls. She sent me a card at Christmas and when I saw the postmark, I put it in the rubbish unopened. Gradually the correspondence stopped. I had hardened my heart to her.

I never found my father. For a long time I was obsessed with him, just as I had been obsessed with Stella. I used to picture him in a smart uniform, the way Stella described him when they first met, a cap perched at a rakish angle above his handsome face and officer's bars on his shoulder.

Sometimes I think of him still. I imagine him smoking a cigarette: Camels or Lucky Strikes, some American brand, a band playing Glenn Miller music, maybe a glass of bourbon in his hand. I see him smiling as he asks Stella for a dance. He would have been polite. That's important. When I think of my father, I want him to be perfect.

I wasted a lot of time and money trying to trace Bill O'Dwyer. I wrote to the US Defence Department and the army veterans' associations. I even hired a woman in Washington who spent months trawling through car registrations and voting registers without success. In the end, I accepted that my father would forever remain a mystery to me.

Maura and I were married in June 1970 and Aly was my Best Man. We had our wedding reception in Pat's Bar and singers and musicians came from all over. A man who played the hammer dulcimer travelled from Glenarm in County Antrim. A group of fiddlers came from Toomebridge. I invited Brother O'Callaghan and he turned up with his concertina, looking like he had died and gone to Heaven. Pat Brennan made corned beef sandwiches and I gave him one hundred pounds for beer. The party went on all day. It became so crowded in the little pub that in the end, they locked the doors and if you wanted to get in, you had to rap on the window.

I have fond memories of that day; Aly awkward in a hired suit, making the Best Man's speech as Kevin Trainor heckled from the bar. Maura in her wedding dress singing 'Maids When You're Young Never Wed an Old Man' and everybody rocking with laughter. Uncle Paddy, tipsy on whiskey, singing 'I Dreamt I Dwelt in Marble Halls' while Aunt Minnie told him he was making a holy show of us and would he For God's Sake shut up or we'd be disgraced forever. A man who didn't know me very well asked where my parents were and I told him they were dead.

'Both?' he said, surprised.

'Yes,' I said. 'They're dead. Father and mother both.'

He shook his head.

'That's very sad. You're far too young.'

Fergus drove us to the airport and we flew to Majorca for our honeymoon. Shortly after we got back, he brought me into his office and closed the door.

'Mr Gageby is reorganising this place. He

thinks we've been here too long. Maybe he's right.'

'What does that mean?'

'It means I'm going to Brussels to open a new office. You're going to Dublin. They'll pay removal costs and a rent allowance till you get on your feet.'

'Well,' I said, 'if we're parting company, I want to thank you for everything you taught me. If it wasn't for you, I would never have become a reporter.'

He ran a hand through his unruly hair and I could see he was embarrassed.

'Come on,' he said. 'I'll buy you a pint in the Duke.'

I was glad to go. By now, The Troubles had engulfed Ardoyne. Parts of the Crumlin Road and Hooker Street had been burnt down in the riots of August 1969. The Wheatfield Bar was gone and Logue's pub, where Isaac spent so many Saturday nights, was just a blackened shell.

Soldiers with English accents would stop me on the street and search my pockets and ask me to identify myself. Maura and I would lie in bed at night and listen to the gun battles raging for hours between the IRA and the British Army at the bottom of Alliance Avenue. In the morning, we would find spent cartridge shells in the road.

We moved to Dublin where I worked at the main office of *The Irish Times*. We found a house in Howth, a fishing village on the outskirts of the city, and in December 1973, our first child was born. We settled down and got on with our lives.

Years passed. I rarely thought of Stella. I had lost all contact with her. I was too busy with my family and my job. And then one day in August 1985, I got a phone call in the office from her sister, Kathleen. She said that Stella had suffered a stroke and was gravely ill. She wanted to see me again.

I didn't want to go. I had put Stella out of my life. To see her again would only waken sad memories. But I talked to Maura and she said: 'You should go. She's an old woman now. You should go and make her happy.'

So I flew to New York and got the shuttle to Freehold. It was hot and the trees were turning brown and they shone like gold in the evening light. Mr Morrison met me at the depot. I realised that I had never learned his first name, so I asked him and he told me it was Jack.

He said Stella and he were married now.

'How is she?'

'Poorly. She's paralysed on her right side. The prognosis isn't good.'

I said I was sorry to hear that.

'Ever since she had the stroke she's been asking for you. She asks for you every day. That time you visited. She said you had an argument. She never got over that.'

We came to the house. It looked run down since the last time I'd been here, almost twenty years before. Paint was peeling off the window frames and the lawn was overgrown.

Jack took me into the house.

'I've put her bed in the front room so she doesn't have to use the stairs.'

He brought me to the room and left me at the door.

The curtains were drawn and only a thin light filtered into the room. Stella was propped up on pillows in the bed. I hardly recognised her. She had aged terribly. Her hair was grey now and her skin was brown and cracked like an old leaf. One side of her face was caved in where the stroke had affected her.

'Martin,' she said, 'thank God you're back.'

She held out her hand. I took it and sat beside her. I could see the tears starting to roll down her face. I told her about Maura and the children and the job. I told her I had a good life. She held onto my hand as if she didn't want to let me go.

'I'm sorry we fought,' she said.

'Stella. Don't talk about it. It's past now. I've forgotten it.'

'No. It's important. There are things I want to tell you. You asked about your father. I told you lies because I was too ashamed. There never was a Bill O'Dwyer. I made him up. I don't know who your father is.'

I felt a knot tighten in my chest.

'Stella, I already guessed.'

'I thought if I told you the truth, you would think I was a tramp. But it wasn't like that. We were at a party and I got drunk. It was all parties at that time. I ended up in bed with this good-looking soldier. I can't even remember his name.

'I couldn't tell anybody. I couldn't tell my family. It would have broken my mother's heart. I'm sorry, Martin. I had to keep it all a secret.'

I looked at her poor, twisted face and felt this incredible pain for her.

'Stella. Don't talk about it. It doesn't matter.'

'It does matter. And I'm not finished.'

She called for Jack and he came slowly into the room and stood beside the door.

'Jack. I want to introduce you. This is my son, Martin.'

We looked at each other and he nodded.

'I'm pleased to meet you, Martin.'

I felt my heart swell with emotion. I felt like a burden of years had been lifted from me. I leaned across the bed and put my arms round Stella and kissed her damp cheek.

I stayed with her for three days. We sat and talked in the quiet room with the curtains drawn and in the evenings I walked the streets of Freehold, or sat with Jack and drank whiskey on the back porch.

The day I was leaving, Stella said: 'You'll come again soon? And bring the kids. I'd love to see my grandchildren.'

I said Yes, I would certainly do that, but in my heart I knew it would never happen.

Six weeks later, Stella died from another massive stroke. They brought her back to Ireland to be buried in Ballinaleck churchyard with her mother and father. It was a grey overcast October day. I stood with Jack while they shovelled the earth on Stella's coffin and afterwards we all went to the local hotel for a meal. All her family accepted me. Nobody asked me who I was. It was what I had suspected all along; that everyone knew Stella's secret. Everyone knew I was her son.

I still think of her. I think of what might have happened if things had been different. She would have been a good mother. But it was not to be. I know now that my mother was Sarah. My father was Isaac. When I dream of childhood, which is more frequent as I get older, it is of Sarah and Isaac I dream. And in my dreams, Isaac is always singing.

THE END